THE
NIGHTLAND
EXPRESS

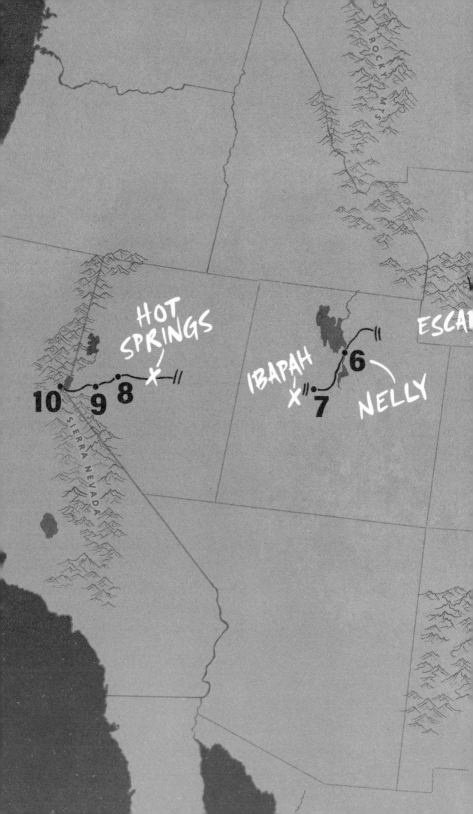

RAMIE
PEAK

LARAMIE MOUNTAINS

4

SHRIKE

PLATTE RIVER

SNOW

3 **2** **1**

MOCK

RANDALL

THE NIGHTLAND EXPRESS

1. St. Joe's
2. French Bottoms Station
3. Cottington Station
4. Ft. Laramie
5. Devil's Gate
6. Salt Lake City
7. Fish Springs
8. Carson River Station
9. Carson City
10. California Border

THE
NIGHTLAND EXPRESS

J.M. LEE

EREWHON BOOKS

THE NIGHTLAND EXPRESS
Copyright © 2022 by J.M. Lee

First published in North America, Canada, and Other Territories by Erewhon Books, LLC, in 2022

Erewhon Books
2 W. 29th Street, Suite 3S
New York, NY 10001
www.erewhonbooks.com

Erewhon books are available at special discounts when purchased in bulk for premiums and sales promotions as well as for fund-raising or educational use. For details, send an email to info@erewhonbooks.com.

Library of Congress Control Number: 2020942478

ISBN 978-1-64566-003-3 (hardcover)
ISBN 978-1-64566-011-8 (ebook)

Cover art by Jeff Langevin
Cover design by Dana Li
Pony Express recruitment poster by Dana Li
Map by Kelley Brady

Printed in the United States of America

First Edition: October 2022
10 9 8 7 6 5 4 3 2 1

For all who walk in two worlds,
from one double-good to another.

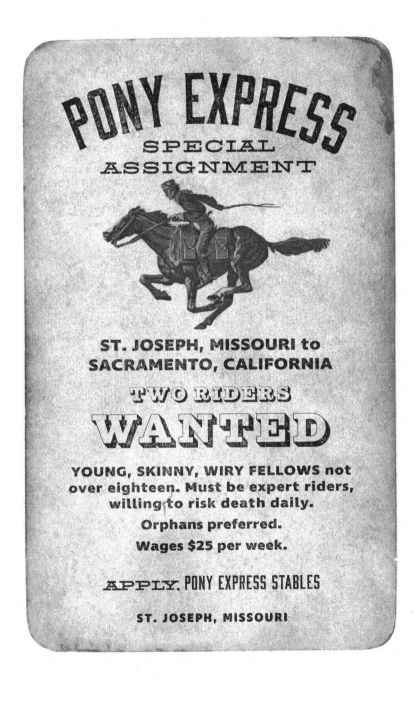

CHAPTER I
BEN

September 3, 1860

The razor stung, but Ben didn't flinch.

He bit his tongue, forced himself to stay still and watch Penny's hands in the mirror as they flicked the straightedge across his scalp. Shaving away the last sign of what he shared with her until all that remained in his reflection was his father, staring back.

When she was done she wiped his head with a wet cloth and rested her hands on his shoulders.

"I don't want to go," he said. He couldn't see her face in the mirror, just her hands and, behind them both, the open door of their one-room shack. The morning was young, green and white broken by the cobalt blue of the bottle-tree in the yard.

"I know," came her reply from above. "But you must. Before they return from the funeral."

The thought awoke a hot, familiar, trembling feeling. Anxious and afraid, coiled deep inside him. It twitched and writhed.

"Come with me." He'd asked so many times. Pleaded. Maybe this time, she would change her mind.

"You'll get twice as far without me," she replied. The same reply as always. "I can only run in moonlight. But you can walk in daylight, too. That is your magic, Ben. Your power. Use it. Get as far away from here as you can. Don't you worry about me."

"I'll find a place where we can be," he said. "I'll come back to you, and we'll go there together . . . I promise."

As an answer, she pulled him against her, stroked his head and hummed. Her voice soothed the wriggling shape inside him. He resisted at first. He was a man now, sixteen. But no matter how he aged, she would always be older.

He gave up and closed his eyes, letting her enfold him in her warmth and song for what he feared would be the final time. All the world went away and he let it.

CHAPTER II
JESSE

September 24, 1860

Jessamine stared at the copper braid coiled in the bottom of the washbasin. It reminded her of the dead fawn their dog had found under the apple tree behind the farm, all tiny and still wet from birth. Stuck-to with blossoms and leaves, hanging limp out of the hound's mouth. They'd left a candle to burn out over the little grave.

For the Faeries to find, Alice had said.

Jessamine set down the shears and ran her hand along the back of her neck, where the hem of her hair was jagged and thick. She wondered if she should put her braid in the ground, too.

Alice was in the front yard chopping wood, a chore she insisted on doing even at eight months pregnant. Her bangs, a browner shade of red than Jessamine's, were matted with sweat. She looked up when the top step squeaked, then wrung her hands round the handle of the axe when she saw her younger sister.

"Oh Jess," she said. "Can't the trousers be enough?"

Jessamine rolled her eyes and strode past her—indignant strides were easier in trousers, after all—to chuck the braid into the brush beyond the yard.

"The meadowlarks can make a nest of it, I reckon," she said. "How do I look?"

Alice set down the axe and looked her up and down, taking in the shirt and vest, the trousers and boots. Though Jessamine was tall for her age, and lean, she'd still had to alter almost every seam. The top half had come in at the sides while the lower half shrank up from the bottom, and everything puckered in the middle where she'd tried to pull it all together with a belt. But she couldn't have felt prouder.

Alice's disappointed frown was proof that the outfit was a success. "Like a boy," she sighed.

Jessamine beamed and tipped an imaginary hat. "Well thank ya, ma'am. And how d'ya do."

"It ain't natural, Jess. Aunt Mary says so. A woman riding a horse astride like that."

"Alice . . ."

"She says if you can't bear children, that'll be the end of you!"

"Aunt Mary says if you look a leprechaun in the eye and say his name three times, he has to tell you where he keeps his lucky gold."

"It's not a joke, Jess!" Alice whispered, as if someone were listening from the woods beyond the yard. "Little folk keep their power in names. And in gold."

"Listen. You should be happy I'm going to join the Pony. Once I'm back you'll have your sister *and* your father. The bank won't take the house and we'll be warm and well fed through the winter. It's all going to be all right."

That evening they ate supper in silence, listening to the crackling in the fireplace. Jessamine only had one thing on her mind, but she didn't say anything for fear of hurting Alice's feelings. Her plan had never been a secret, and neither had Alice's disapproval. They had both seen the advertisement on the door.

Pony Express Special Assignment, it read. *Two riders wanted.*

It even said *orphans preferred,* just like the usual ones soliciting thin, wiry fellows, but the rest of the assignment details were different. The most startling difference was that these riders were to take a parcel from St. Joe's all the way to California. The Pony's full route was almost two thousand miles, made up of relay and home stations. Dozens of horses and their thin, wiry riders.

Jessamine had dreamed of it all. Escaping the growing tensions in Missouri, just her and a horse and a saddle between them. But she'd never thought there might be a chance to ride all the way to California. It seemed impossible that a single rider would be assigned the full route, with no handoffs, but she wasn't about to argue with destiny. This special assignment was the miracle she had wished for.

All the way to California.

Edward Murphy had always said migrating along the Overland Trail was as close to following the anointed path of God as any man was like to get. Laden with terrors and adventures, rewarding only the most virile with unending milk and honey in the wealth of the West.

In and out of their lives he'd been, seeking that ambrosia. Until one day he'd left for good.

Now, finally, Jessamine could go after him. She knew what she would say to him, had rehearsed it before she slept, long before she'd seen the poster and every night since. Daydreamed about her father's face slowly changing from shock that she'd come all the way to Carson City for him to remorse for what he'd done, understanding that he'd been a cowardly father, a rotten dad. Knowing that the right thing to do was to admit how awful he'd been to Jessamine. To Alice. And come home.

If she'd been born a boy, none of this would matter. Even without their father, they'd be able to convince the bank to give them longer. Negotiate some kind of payment plan. But the bank wouldn't give the time of day to two girls, one that had a bastard in her belly and the other that got the side-eye from everyone in town for her unladylike manner.

They were still human, both of them, and hard workers. But that didn't matter to no one. There was no man of the house, not even Edward Murphy. It made Jessamine so mad she wanted to spit.

Alice cleared the table while Jessamine collected the dishes, setting them on the floor for Old Dix to lick. She'd wash them clean in the basin tomorrow, but crumbs attracted mice, especially as the days grew chill. Jessamine shivered at the thought of the cold water under the late September air.

"When I bring pa back, maybe he'll have found some of that gold after all and he can buy us a proper cook-stove. We might as well be living in a cave at this rate."

She brought Alice a blanket, and the two of them sat by the fire. Alice rocked gently in her chair, her knitting draped over her belly. Jessamine sat cross-legged on the floor, stitching the final piece of her costume.

"Oscar's family has a cookstove," Alice murmured. "Cast iron, from Charleston. Four burners with an oven, and the iron would keep Faeries out. It said in the advertisement in the *Courier* that it will make you cry for joy."

"*Oscar*," Jessamine grumbled. "I'll give him something to cry about."

Alice sniffled, not because she had actually started crying but as a warning that she might if Jessamine didn't school her tone. They had informally agreed not to mention the young lawman, but his name still boiled up. Like a rash. Some good he and his four burners were doing Alice and their baby now.

Jessamine reached up and put her hands on Alice's knitting needles. The wool yarn was thick and rough.

"Alice. Listen. While I'm gone, you have to promise not to try and find him. He left you like this. He's no good. And if something were to happen to you while I'm out west, I wouldn't forgive myself. Hear? Even if you find him, he made it clear what his priorities were when he ran out on you." Alice found it impossible to lie, and they both knew it. It was one of the things that Jessamine found most endearing about her. She squeezed her sister's hand. "All I ask of you, while I run this little ol' errand, is don't go looking for that trouble named Oscar Montero."

Morning came quick, but Jessamine was ready.

While her sister slept and the white light of the morning crept through the cracks in the farmhouse's old wood walls, she stripped off her vest and shirt. She'd slept in them, like she reckoned she'd be doing on the trail. It felt good to wake dressed like this, but the look was incomplete. Missing something Jessamine had been reluctant to wear yesterday in front of Alice.

The undershirt was waiting where she'd left it folded at the foot of her bed. It was snug and hard to get on, but once she had it tugged down over her chest and most of her ribs it wasn't too bad. Back on went her shirt and vest, and she quietly crossed the room to steal a moment in the mirror.

Cut hair tousled from sleep, breasts flattened under the tight garment, the result was astonishing. She smoothed her hands over her chest and tossed her bangs, watching her reflection with a surprising spark of pride. The person staring back at her was bright-eyed and confident, androgynous and handsome. For the first time in a long time, Jessamine felt she recognized the face in the mirror.

She heard Alice stirring in bed and splashed some water on her face, ran her fingers through her hair. It was time to go.

"You'll call on the doc if anything feels strange, right?" she asked as she wrapped rolls and some cheese in a kerchief. "I asked Danny to come round once a day and check on you. And Aunt Mary is planning to be up from Kansas City in two weeks. Anything feels wrong, take Annie into town and someone'll get you what you need."

Alice pulled her shawl tight and followed Jessamine to the door. She stood on the porch while Jessamine saddled Morgan.

"But it's you I need, Jess. Why can't you just stay here? We can do all right on our own. Without pa. And without Oscar, even, if that's what you think is bettermost. We could even go live with Aunt Mary—"

"But we shouldn't have to," Jessamine said. "Edward Murphy helped bring us into this world. The least he could do is provide for us like a respectable father now that we're here."

Alice sniffled. Jessamine patted Morgan's sturdy neck and left him to meet her sister on the porch.

"Don't cry. Hey, ain't you the older one here?"

"Years on God's earth don't mean nothing in the big world, and you know that."

"Well, in my world you'll always be my big sister. Listen, I'll be back before the baby comes. Draggin' pa by his bootstraps if I have to. Okay? I promise."

Alice was crying, but she nodded. "Oh . . . I almost forgot."

Out of her shawl came a dried flower. It was delicate and flattened from one of Alice's books, its little white star-shaped blossoms paper-thin and fragile. She tucked it in Jessamine's vest pocket.

"Your namesake," she pointed out. Then she smiled. "So you don't forget where you came from."

Jessamine wrapped her sister in a hug from the side, making room for the baby and squeezing tight. "I will think about you every day."

Then, to keep any more tears from falling between them, Jessamine turned away. For a moment, as her heel pressed into the stirrup, doubt sprang through her. But when she felt the worn leather seat of Morgan's saddle, warm from the rising sun, it steadied her. With a cluck and a nudge he was off, and Jessamine was on her way to St. Joe's.

CHAPTER III

BEN

Welcome to the City of St. Joseph.

A dozen brick buildings stood against the blue autumn sky, squatting proudly over clusters of smaller structures like red hens over clutches of eggs. Penn Street cut between them, full of horses, ox-drawn wagons, and young white boys offering to do anything and everything for a penny.

"Carry your bag, mister?"

"Got a horse, mister? Need someone to brush it?"

"On your way to the California Road, mister? I got dried beans, just a half dime a quart! Gallon molasses, fifty cents!"

"Public meeting of the state of the Union!" This time it was a less-young white boy pushing a handbill into Ben's chest. He was immediately off to pin his broadside to the next man. "Defend our rights! Vote Breckinridge!"

Ben crumpled the paper and threw it in the street without reading it. He already knew what it said and what it meant. *Defend our rights.* The second half of the sentence was implied: *to own slaves.*

The call to arms, in all its versions, had flitted along the streets of every border city from Kentucky to Missouri. Many of the posters and handbills simply depicted a Black man with a cane and top hat, as if the mere image were enough to convince anyone of the cause. They flew in the wind, like flags marking territory already won. Ben wanted to burn every one of them.

But he couldn't. He had to pull through. And keep pulling through, all the way to California. That was the way to make good on his promise.

He yanked his hat down further over his brow and took the folded advertisement from his breast pocket to confirm the address of the Pony Express headquarters. *REGISTER AT THE PATEE HOUSE HQ*, the ad read. *1202 PENN STREET.* Only a few blocks away.

The Patee House took up a full block, a white-trimmed brick building with big arched windows on the ground floor and rectangular ones on every floor above. It had been a luxury hotel since it had been built in '58. Ben guessed not a one of those fancy rooms was empty, even so late in the season; St. Joe's was one of the busiest jumping-off places at the head of the California Road.

Jumping-off place. The phrase reminded Ben of the old dock back home, where on the hottest summer nights he and his friends would line up to jump off into the river.

But the currents these settlers were leaping into would take them far away from here. All the way west, if they were lucky. Family after family, a fleet of wagons, on a journey that would take most of them months, if not years, along the Overland Trail. Through Kansas and Nebraska prairie and the Rockies, through Salt Lake Valley and the unforgiving southwestern desert. All the way to Sacramento.

Thousands had made the journey, even before James Marshall struck gold in '48. And though the rush had subsided some five years ago, thousands more continued to make it. Ben couldn't imagine traveling two thousand miles with a family and all their belongings. Good thing he had neither.

The quiet office was empty except for the clerk, who glanced over his spectacles and the *Gazette* when Ben doffed his hat and entered. A painting of the Pony Express founders hung at the back wall: Russell, Majors, and Waddell. The three suited businessmen whose partnership formed the basis of the country's most beloved and patriotic enterprise.

Ben cleared his throat.

"Good morning. I'm here to register for the Pony," he said, pushing every ounce of white inflection he could muster into the words. He'd found the first impression was the most important; if he could pass in the first moment, there was never a second glance.

It was the case now. The clerk saw a white boy with hazel eyes and a tan. He nodded his chin at Ben's brow. "What happened to your hair, son?"

Ben ran a hand over the top of his head. "Caught fire," he said. "Would have burned my eyebrows off, too, if it weren't for the loving embrace of the Platte."

The clerk chuckled at the idea of the brown, slow-moving Platte River being anything but dank sludge. Ben unfolded the advertisement he'd found nailed to the fence post out front of his father's property line, placed the sheet on the desk. The clerk let his spectacles slide down his nose to read it. He seemed to forget all about Ben's shaved head and tabled the *Gazette*.

"Hm. Stationmaster Declan's special assignment, eh?" He peered up at Ben, eyelids heavy with doubt. "You sure?"

"What's not to be sure of, sir?"

The clerk took a long look at him, and Ben resisted the urge to hide his face. Maybe this was a stupid idea. If he went back to Penny now, she'd still be there. It would be bad, but at least they would be together. Maybe they could find another way.

But the clerk just shrugged and turned in his chair. He yanked open a drawer full of paperwork and slapped a simple, empty form on the counter.

"Sign here and record your next of kin. Bring the form to the station where they're doing the hiring. If you get the job, it'll serve as your employment contract. If you get thrown out of the saddle and break every bone, it'll serve as a safety waiver." As Ben read it, the clerk added, "Or let us know where to send your body."

Ben didn't hesitate. The regular ads for the Pony Express read *orphans preferred* for a reason. It was a dangerous job, and it wasn't a stretch to believe that a special assignment might be even riskier. He took the form, folded it, and slipped it in his breast pocket alongside the other piece of paper hidden there. The three sheets that documented his life: his past, his present, and—he hoped—his future.

"Sir, I've been in the saddle since I was a baby, driving cattle and sheep. I didn't come all the way here from Louisville to turn back now."

The clerk seemed neither surprised nor impressed. "Stables are down the street," he said. "And you better hurry—I think they're starting soon. Majors himself is here for the hiring."

Ben nodded, shoving his hat on his head before turning to leave. He shouldered out the door, nearly barreling over a slender white boy with dark copper hair who was on his way in.

"Watch it!" the boy snapped in a high, almost sweet voice. His glare, on the other hand, had nothing palatable about it. Ben would have liked to admire such a pretty face, but he had a one-way ticket to California to earn. So he settled for a polite tip of the hat before he jogged out into the bustle of Penn Street.

The Pony Express stables were a modest brick building in front of a grassy stable yard, practically within spitting distance of the Patee House. Past the yard were the actual stables, sheltering half a dozen hardy horses of all colors:

Morgans and thoroughbreds, some famously plucked from cavalry ranks. The beasts were the lifeblood and the namesake of the Pony Express.

He followed the cracking, uneven laughter of boys and hopped the log fence, rounding the stable and entering the yard. A group of young men, all close to his age, stood round, most of them thin and trying to be manly in shirts and trousers borrowed from fathers or older brothers. Each had the same advertisement in his hand.

Ben sized up his competition. There were eight of them—seven boys and one girl, Ben realized, dressed up like a boy with her blonde hair tucked into her hat and her body drowning in a boy's shirt and trousers. They were observed by a handful of aloof young men, who stood leaning against the fence in riding clothes and deerskin jackets. Each had a red neckerchief hanging at his collar—Pony riders. Real ones.

Ben tried not to envy those neckties too much. He didn't want the riders to notice him noticing them. He wanted to stay as invisible as possible. Before the afternoon, he told himself, he would have his own kerchief to wear round his neck. Then it could be as soon as ten days that he'd lay eyes on the green hills of California, where he'd build the house he'd dreamed of. Make a plan to find Penny and bring her there, too.

"Gather round, boys. Gather round."

It was a tall man in a black coat calling them over. He had a thick beard and the stiff posture of a longtime businessman, and Ben recognized him from the photograph in the clerk's office. It was Alexander Majors, as narrow and gaunt as Ben imagined Abraham Lincoln might be, from the stories Penny had told.

"Sad lot, ain't they?" The apple-sweet voice from earlier popped up from Ben's shoulder. The pretty boy from the Patee House stood beside him. From his clean skin and clothes, skinny arms, and soft, shining hair, Ben wondered if he'd ever worked a day in his life. To someone who hadn't, anything less fortunate must seem "sad."

"Speak for yourself," Ben said.

The boy snorted, then chuckled. He pointed at his neck, decorated with no bright scarf, and waved his own copy of the special assignment ad. "Sorry. Sad lot, ain't *we*?" he said, voice softening. Then, as an afterthought, he said, "Jesse Murphy."

"Ben Foley," Ben replied. They shook hands. Murphy's was slender, but calloused in the palm from reins and horse tack, and along the fingers, no doubt from chopping wood. Maybe Ben had been too quick to judge. "Best of luck in whatever's coming next."

Jesse's eyes twinkled. "When I win, luck'll have nothing to do with it," he said.

Ben raised a brow. Took a certain kind of boy to have confidence like that—or a certain kind of upbringing, anyway.

"Now then. As you're aware, we've a special assignment requiring two riders. The supervisor of the assignment has requested fresh blood, and he is seeking a certain manner and demeanor which will befit the unprecedented nature of the assignment."

Majors spoke in the same slow, proper Kentucky drawl as Ben's father had, and for a moment Ben felt like a child in a schoolyard, being instructed in letters and numbers. Not that he had ever attended school, of course. That had been an opportunity bestowed only on his half brother. But Randall had had no qualms about describing the experience in great detail, and as a child Ben had committed the fantasy to heart.

"Thus, any one of you is eligible, regardless of your riding experience or the status of any noteworthy referral." Majors paused to clear his throat, looking down at the ground for a breath as if repressing any personal objections to the vetting process.

"On what criteria are we to be judged?" asked one of the boys. He, like all of them, was impatient to be on with it.

"Speed, horsemanship, and understanding the rules," Majors replied. "This is the Pony Express, after all. Now then. There is a welcome sign on the eastern side of town. On the back of it is a basket, and in it are ten gold neckerchiefs. One for each of you. And there are ten horses in the stable yonder—again, one for each of you. The first two riders to bring back one of those neckerchiefs will be hired."

Ben found it uncomfortably fortuitous that a basket on the other side of town would already be filled with exactly the number of neckties as there were candidates in the yard, especially since it seemed several of them had just arrived. But he tried not to pay it too much mind.

The girl dressed like a boy whooped. "A race! Howdy! When do we start?"

Majors was unimpressed. He flicked a stray sliver of stable hay from his shoulder. "Right now, I'd imagine."

Ben turned when he heard Murphy bolt from beside him, taking off like a bullet. The other boy's movement was like a spur in Ben's side, and he leapt into a sprint for the stables, shooting a glance over his shoulder for only a second. Murphy was headed away from the stables at top speed. Where was that kid going?

Focus! It doesn't matter what he's doing!

Ben slowed as he reached the stable aisle. The horses were alert to the sounds of running men, ears perked and hooves pawing. But they weren't nervous, hand-picked and trained as they were for the Express. Ben laid eyes on a lovely blue roan mare and swung himself into her saddle. She was well trained and ready, and they charged out of the stable and onto the busy St. Joseph street.

It was not the open road race he'd hoped for. Wagons and people crisscrossed the street and meandered like fish in a river. The mare wasn't shy—on the contrary, she was prancing and eager to *run*—but there was simply no avenue through.

Ben turned at the sound of the other boys on their horses behind him. Only four had made it out of the stables so far, the others probably struggling to get in the saddle.

"Move!"

Jesse Murphy, astride a chestnut gelding with a white blaze on his nose, shouted down at a family standing about on the curb. They scattered, triggering a ripple through the body of people. As a lane cleared open, Murphy tapped his heel into his horse's side and they were water bursting through a dam, breaking free and charging down the road.

"Out of the way, please," Ben called. It got some traction with the pedestrians on his side of the road, but not enough. He groaned, watching Murphy and his gelding pulling further and further ahead. Behind him, the other boys were gaining. He couldn't fall behind.

"Damn it!" he finally erupted. "*Out of the way!*"

It worked. Seconds later he and his mare were fast after Murphy, pounding down Penn Street as people jumped out of their path. The welcome sign, jutting from a stone pedestal, loomed ahead. Murphy reached it first, leaping from the saddle and dashing toward the pedestal. Ben made it seconds later, running up behind the other boy. Over his shoulder he heard the chaos of their incoming competition.

Murphy had found the basket. In it were the neckerchiefs Majors had promised, one for each of the riders. And Murphy was shoving every last one into his vest pockets.

"What are you doing?" Ben shouted.

"Making sure I win," Murphy said. He pushed one of the ties into Ben's hand and winked. "But I guess there's two spots in the roster."

Then he dashed for his horse, up in the saddle like he'd been born there. The horse reared and they were off, racing into the eight riders that were on their way, soon to find they'd been cheated. Majors had said the test was about understanding the rules. If the rules were taken strictly, without a necktie, the other boys couldn't win.

But there was no time to debate Jesse Murphy's morality. Not if Ben wanted to win, too.

Halfway back to his mare, he skidded to a stop in the gravel. A piece of golden fabric lay crumpled on the road. It must have fallen from Murphy's coat when his horse had reared. Ben had only a moment before the others would make the spot, but in that moment all he could think of was California.

The moment passed. Ben snatched the loose neckerchief from the ground and vaulted into his mare's saddle just as the earth began to shiver under the approaching hooves of the other riders. As Ben urged the mare back into town, he heard the other boys curse.

"Where are they?"

"The neckerchiefs! He stole them!"

"After him!"

Ben's roan mare was a blur. The other boys shouted after him, but their already inferior riding was now hobbled by anger. One of the horses had enough and threw her boy. He tumbled to the street and cried out when something snapped and broke. Ben kept his attention forward. Now and again he thought he saw flashes of chestnut ahead, but it wasn't until he slowed and landed back in the stable yard that he confirmed for certain that Murphy had returned first.

And there he was, like a little dandelion seed, standing in front of Majors and a second, enormous man. Together, the three watched Ben arrive, the large man puffing on a pipe that bubbled great clouds of gray smoke over his head.

"Here, sir," Ben said, breathless. He held up the trophy Murphy had given him as proof, though in his other hand he shoved the second deeper into his pocket.

"First and second. It seems you two are the winners," Majors said. His dour tone had no inflection of either praise or disappointment. "And just in time to meet your new employer. Mr. Darcy Declan, the stationmaster at French Bottoms Station."

The man with the pipe was even larger up close. He was both tall and wide, dressed in a long black tailcoat. Under his stovepipe hat fell black curls that matched his impressive beard and mustache, and he looked out into the street with the weight of a mountain. Ben lowered his eyes out of respect, staring instead at the big man's golden vest buttons.

"Here come the stragglers!" Declan boomed in a heavy

accent that Ben couldn't place, though he reckoned it was from somewhere across the Atlantic.

The first of the other riders to arrive jumped off his horse and made straight for Ben, pushing his sleeves up past his elbows. Ben widened his stance, the coiling shape in his breast coming to life, readying every muscle in his body for a fight. But the boy didn't make it past Stationmaster Declan, who held him back with a hand that engulfed the boy's entire shoulder.

"What's wrong, son?" Declan asked with a jolly, patronizing chuckle.

"Cheat!" the boy said. "They cheated! They stole all the neckerchiefs!"

The girl joined them. She was red with rage. "They should be disqualified. Mr. Majors said this was about *understanding the rules*."

The others dissolved into a caucus of accusations. Ben kept his mouth shut, clutching the neckerchief in his hand. He saw Murphy doing the same, though the boy's eyes still had the flicker of lightning. Ben pushed down the knots writhing in his stomach. He couldn't lose this. If Murphy hadn't cheated, they might have won fair and square, and now . . .

"I see," said Declan. "And what were the rules?"

"The two that returned first with neckerchiefs would be hired!"

The stationmaster's intimidating gaze fell upon the boys that had lost, the shadow of his attention silencing them with a mighty weight. "As far as I can see it," he said with a voice heavy as pipe tobacco, "only two of you returned with one."

He turned to Ben and Murphy and waved them along. "Come along, boys. Welcome to the Express."

CHAPTER IV

JESSE

". . . And so I expect you young men to abide by these strict and good laws of life yourselves. Now then, raise your hand and swear."

Jesse's heart was still galloping. She wondered if it would ever slow.

Beside her, the boy with the shaved head—Ben Foley —held a Bible in his left hand and raised his right. Jesse did the same with the one Majors had given her. It was bulky and leather-bound, with gold lettering on the cover that read *Presented by Russell, Majors & Waddell, 1858.*

Round her neck was the golden neckerchief—not red like ones the other Pony riders wore. She wondered if the color was because of the special assignment. In the periphery of her vision, she sensed the boys who had lost slinking away like coyotes. She ignored them and repeated after Majors as he raised his right hand and read out of his own book as if they were in a courthouse.

"I do hereby swear, before the Great and Living God, that during my engagement, and while I am an employee of Russell, Majors, and Waddell, I will under no circumstances use profane language. That I will drink no intoxicating liquors. That I will not quarrel or fight with any other employee of the firm. And that in every respect I will conduct myself honestly, be faithful to my duties, and so direct all my acts as to win the confidence of my employers, so help me God."

After they'd sworn the oath, Majors had a deputy bring a fountain pen and gestured for them to open their Bibles. Inside the front cover was the same oath: "The Frontier Pledge," it was titled. Jesse drew her name without hesitation, eager for the formalities to be over. Riding Morgan to the edge of town had been the thrill she wanted from this adventure, not standing round in a stable yard swearing not to swear.

"Mr. Murphy. Mr. Foley. Congratulations on your enrollment!"

Jesse turned at the big voice that tumbled out like an avalanche. The stationmaster's accent was foreign, from the British Isles, though Jesse couldn't place it as Irish, Scottish, or Welsh. His huge hand swallowed hers when they shook. He was so large and his gaze so heavy that Jesse couldn't bring herself to look him in the eye. She felt cowardly, until she noticed that Foley was looking down, too.

"Thank you, sir," she said, trying as best she could to keep her voice deep and her back straight. "Mighty excited to get started on our special assignment."

"Very good, very good! And I, as well. Let us away to French Bottoms Station, then, where I can equip you in utility and wisdom. Meet me outside the stable in a minute. I've business to square with Mr. Majors, and then we'll be off."

The stationmaster left them, waving to Majors, who now stood under the eave of the stable house, dismissing the other riders. The men met and spoke, their words inaudible, glancing at Jesse and Foley every now and again.

"What do you make of this?" she asked.

"I don't know," Foley said. It was the first time they'd spoken as colleagues instead of competition, but his voice was as quiet and unreadable as it had been before. "All I know is we got the job. And that's all I care about."

Jesse nodded. It was a wise sentiment.

Even so, she glanced back. While Stationmaster Declan spoke, Mr. Majors stood like a post, beard jutting out of his chin. Though he seemed calm—or at least stoic—she couldn't help but notice his knuckles were white round the Bible he clutched in his hand.

"I'll meet you and Declan out front," Jesse said. "I brought my own horse."

By the time she and Morgan met the stationmaster and Foley, both were mounted, Foley on the blue roan he'd ridden during their trial. Declan was on a stunning black Shire stallion, easily twenty hands. No other horse could've borne his weight besides this one with a shining coat and white feathering at its hooves.

When he saw Jesse, he grinned broadly. "Your own horse? A beauty he is!"

"Thank you, sir. His name's Morgan."

"Morgan!" the stationmaster crowed. He turned his beast of a horse and rode out, heading northwest. "Murphy. And Foley. Oh! They are all good Irish names, are they not? Well done."

Jesse again exchanged glances with Foley, who shrugged. His roan might as well have been a pony next to the stationmaster's enormous Shire. Even Morgan, usually even-keeled, flared his nostrils and tensed his shoulders around the big horse.

It was less than half an hour to French Bottoms, across the river to the west. Jesse sometimes detoured through the field on her way back from St. Joe's, on days when she didn't want to come home right away. There was no official Pony Express station there that she knew of, but she decided not to ask questions so early in her new position.

The stationmaster whistled a cheery tune as they rode, and even his whistling was big and loud over the rushes of autumn wind that swept the land. Before long, he surprised her with a small brick station outfitted with a modest stable near the edge of the French Bottoms field, right on the Missouri River, which divided Missouri from Kansas and Nebraska Territories to the west.

"Now, my boys, I will tell you a bit about the task you are about to undertake. Mr. Majors and I agreed at the inception of the Pony Express that there might be the occasional need to transport goods that other riders may object to transporting, no questions asked. And so, *my* station is not on any Express map, nor will you see any fanfare flags a-flyin' when you race out of here just after I'm done explaining. Do either of you have any quarrel with such an assignment?"

Jesse glanced at Foley, who met her eyes with the same determination and willingness she'd seen on her own face in the mirror when she'd cut her hair.

"I'll do whatever it takes to perform the job, sir," she said.

Foley agreed. "Never needed any flags before."

The stationmaster roared with laughter. "Well done! Very good! Very good, indeed!"

They dismounted at the station. A boy was waiting for them, and when Declan waved a hand, he dashed inside. Declan patted about his waistcoat. He produced a glass vial of blue tonic, stoppered with cork, and gave it to Jesse.

"Cooling tonic, for Morgan," he said. "Administer one drop to each of his nostrils at every stop along the route. It will keep his spirits and energy up all the way to California."

Jesse frowned, holding the vial in her hand. It felt cold to the touch, and the liquid inside sparkled as if it were full of tiny diamonds.

"But . . . sir, there's no way one horse can make it all the way to California in the time required for the

Express," she said, unsure how to protest when she was so newly under the big man's employment. She'd been expecting to board Morgan until Alice or Aunt Mary could retrieve him. "Morgan can pull a cart thirty, sometimes forty miles a day, but to run him all the way to Sacramento . . . I thought I'd be riding out on one of the Express horses like Foley."

Declan chuckled.

"Oh, no, not necessary," he said. "Just wait and see. Two drops, every station. You'll find, I think, that you've underestimated Morgan's virility quite substantially. He is a mighty fine horse, finer than you know."

Jesse wasn't reassured, but she didn't argue. If they reached the first post and Morgan was overheated, the station attendant would have to give her a new horse. Then Jesse could arrange for someone to bring him back to Alice. She pocketed the tonic.

"Bill! With haste, my lad!" Declan shouted.

The boy emerged from the station with his arms full. Declan lifted two leather mochilas from him and handed one each to Jesse and Foley. She took hers and threw it over Morgan's saddle, fitting the biscuit and cantle into the holes cut and stitched for them. On both sides were pockets for mail. Morgan was handsome in the uniform, just as sharp as she hoped she was in her neckerchief.

Next, Bill gave Declan two copper lapel badges, which the stationmaster likewise handed to the riders. They were in the shape of shields, with an eagle perched atop and a rider on horseback in the middle. *PONY EXPRESS MESSENGER*, they read, and at the bottom, *NIGHTLAND ROUTE*. Jesse pinned hers to her vest and noticed how heavy it felt for such a small thing.

"Nightland?" Foley asked.

"Aye, boy. The Nightland Express, we call ourselves— as opposed to the Overland. Now, you're to be off at once. Follow the posts until you reach Cottington Station in Nebraska Territory. One hundred miles west as you follow these compasses."

Out of his pocket came two more trinkets: a compass for each of them. At first, Jesse saw nothing peculiar about hers, but on a second look she noticed the needle was pointing hard to the west. She lifted it and shook it gently, but it did not waver. Her fiddling earned her a stern look from Declan, and she hastily put it in her pocket.

He continued, "You'll have three relay stations between here and there for a minute's rest, but understand I expect you to arrive at the station by nightfall. There, you will pick up your parcel and head west until you deliver it at the California border."

"Cottington . . . The Nightland doesn't follow the Overland?" Jesse asked.

"It does not," Declan agreed. "You're to stop only at Nightland stations. The compasses will guide you. Is that a problem?"

The proper Pony followed the Overland Trail from St. Joseph clear to Salt Lake Valley, making use of the same stops and passing through Fort Kearny, Fort Laramie, and Fort Bridger, a proud tour of America. Jesse tried to remind herself that this was about Carson City and Edward Murphy, not the glory, but the disappointment still stung.

"No, sir," she mumbled.

"And me?" Foley asked.

The stationmaster shook his head, his mustache quivering. "The same," he said. "You're to go together."

"Wait—together?" Jesse exclaimed. The words on the poster flashed through her mind: *Special Assignment. Two riders wanted.* Somehow she'd assumed they'd be performing the assignment separately, perhaps one of them riding west while the other rode east. Or maybe one would take the Overland Trail while the other took the Santa Fe. All other Pony riders rode solo, after all!

But the implication was painfully obvious in retrospect.

"Pardon me, sir, but I work best alone," Jesse said.

"And I," added Foley, with the same surprise and urgency. Jesse wasn't sure whether she was glad for his agreement or resentful that he didn't want to ride with her as much as she didn't want to ride with him.

The stationmaster barely heard their protests. "The assignment called for two riders, did it not? You'll go together or not at all," he said. "That's an order."

Jesse looked Foley up and down. He seemed average for their age, if quiet; at least he knew how to handle himself on a horse. But if he posed any threat to her getting to Carson City as quickly as possible, she'd do the same to him as she'd done to the other boys to ensure her employ on this assignment: whatever it took.

"Yes, sir," she said, and Foley echoed her. Whatever he was feeling about the development, he was done showing it. Men held their feelings close—like a hand of playing cards. Jesse kept her own face stern and square. Declan stroked his beard.

"Now, the both of you, raise your hands. As riders of the Nightland Express, you will hereby swear you'll not discuss your assignment nor any other details of your employ with any riders or station attendants other than those of the Nightland. You'll not disclose anything mysterious with anyone who was not there to see it with you. And finally, no matter the hardships of the trail or your meaningful, courageous assignment, you'll not abandon one another until your duty is done."

A solemn, uncomfortable silence followed, and Jesse waited for the stationmaster to invoke God. He didn't. She wondered if Foley would abandon her, should the occasion arise. She didn't know. And she didn't care.

Foley's hazel eyes shone as if he were thinking the same thing. It was a secret between the two of them, then, an unspoken accord they could make while swearing the opposite to their employer.

"I swear it," they said in unison.

The stationmaster nodded his approval and pierced the quiet with a renewed burst of energy and volume.

"Very good! One last thing, before you're off. Bill! Compensations!"

Little Bill darted in and out of the station, like a chipmunk in the shadow of a tree. He returned holding two small satchels. When Jesse took hers, the jangling from the weighty metal inside made her mouth water.

"Overland Pony riders are paid monthly, but I pay my boys by the job. Half now and half when you return. I trust you'll find it a suitable rate for both your loyalty and your discretion."

Jesse didn't dare open the satchel in front of all and God to see, but from the bulk and weight she guessed it was enough to last her and Alice for months. Maybe years. She had never held so much money and hardly knew what to do with it.

First things first, she had to finish the job to claim the rest. She stashed the satchel in one of her mochila pockets—opposite the bulky Bible for balance—then swung herself into the saddle.

"What about guns?" Foley asked, doing the same. "I heard Express riders are armed with a Colt each, in case of bandits or Indians."

"Not my boys," the stationmaster said. "They're armed with quick wits and a tireless fortitude fueled by profound determination. That is your circumstance, is it not? You have something to prove—some greater reason rooted deep within you both? And that is stronger, fleeter, and more . . . *piercing* than any iron we could put in your palm or at your hip."

Jesse shivered. Then she rested the reins against Morgan's neck, and he turned west, white blaze pointed the same as the needle on the Nightland compass in her pocket. "Come on then, Foley. Let's move."

She didn't wait for his agreement. Morgan responded to her heels and broke into a canter down the trail toward Cottington Station.

CHAPTER V

BEN

Ben thought over the events of the morning as he and Murphy galloped through the northwest corner of Kansas Territory and headed toward the Nebraska Territory line. They rode hard through the flat prairie, all greens and golds under bright blue. It seemed unreal that he was actually, finally on the trail. On horseback, putting miles and miles between him and Louisville. Eating up the distance to California bite by bite.

As his mare kept pace behind Murphy and Morgan, the other boy said nothing save for the occasional encouraging word to his horse. The trail was not well worn, but it was visible, especially as the sun climbed. It was after sunset that would be dangerous. To the south, he could make out the slow-moving brown and gray caravan of wagons and carriages and people on foot. They traveled the Oregon Trail, the Mormon Trail, the Santa Fe Trail. The California Road. No matter which path each group would cut further west, in that moment they cut it together. Right outside St. Joe's, where all the trails began as one.

And here he was on the Nightland. What kind of name was that, anyway?

"One hundred miles before nightfall," Murphy called as they mounted a hill, some twelve miles and less than half an hour into the journey. "You know, Declan didn't say how quickly we'll need to move this mysterious package to California. Reckon he's abiding by the regular Express—ten days? Or is that something the Nightland does different, too?"

Ben frowned. Most riders had less than a hundred miles to concern themselves with, with a fresh horse every ten or so along the way. Running their leg as quick as possible was the goal. He hadn't even thought to ask about a timeline on a longer journey.

All this went through his mind, but all he said was, "Don't know."

The less he said to his partner the better. For both of them.

They crested one of the soft, rolling hills to see a cabin resting in the shallow valley ahead. Ben's mare was slick with sweat, eager to make it to the post for water and rest. When they arrived, both horses threw their heads into the trough like they might drown themselves.

No attendant waited, no horses saddled and ready to go. The porch was bare save a rocking chair and a pail for tobacco spit.

"Not the hero's welcome I was expecting," Murphy muttered, putting his hands on his hips. "Where the hell are the horses? And the attendant? Helloooo?"

Without a knock, the boy walked right into the station, so Ben followed. *Station* was a generous term—in reality, it was no more than a one-room cabin convenient to the Nightland route. On the kitchen table was a collection of coins and bills, letters and notices. Next to it all was a Colt revolver, sleek and silver. Murphy glanced at the pile, then whistled and called for the attendant.

While he did, Ben felt something looking at him. From the table, a pale eye stared at him from a face mostly covered by the other papers scattered across it. A familiar face. Fingers suddenly cold, Ben reached out and pulled the corner of the poster out just enough to see the face looking back at him, and the text printed across the top.

LOUISVILLE: Ranaway slave . . .

Ben's heart slammed against his ribs.

"There's no one here," Murphy said. "Damn!"

Ben shoved the poster back under the other pages as Murphy came to stand by his elbow. The other boy looked over the pile, and Ben hoped to God he hadn't seen what Ben had.

"You're gonna have to stop swearing, since we swore not to," Ben said. Jesse responded with another curse. "Go get the horses ready. I'll be right there."

"Right."

To Ben's relief, Murphy went out without giving the table or the gun another glance. When he was gone, Ben pulled the poster back out and looked over it fully. It had only been three weeks since he'd left. How had Randall gotten a wanted poster drawn up and sent so far west so fast? He wadded it up into a ball and shoved it into the fireplace.

His eye caught again on the gun. Resting on the table like it had been left for him to see.

Ben grimaced. If trouble was going to catch up to him no matter how fast or how far he ran, at least he'd be ready.

When he joined Murphy at the trough, his mare was looking fine, grazing as if she'd been doing it all day. Her sides heaved a little, but she wasn't frothed, and her ears and eyes were bright and alert. Ben felt her over and frowned. He knew horses; it was his role to tend the four his father owned, or it had been before he'd run. Any normal horse would be done for the day, but the roan shrugged as if she were eager to set off again.

Murphy's horse was less relaxed, though he didn't seem beat by any means. Murphy took out the tonic Stationmaster Declan had given him. When he unstoppered the vial and let Morgan smell it, the horse turned away at first. Murphy took a sniff and wrinkled his nose.

"Worse than turpentine. Blech."

"What is that stuff, anyway?" Ben asked.

Murphy shrugged. "Hell if I know. Come on, Morgy. Try it. If you don't like it, I guess we'll just have to wait here 'til the attendant shows up and gets us horses. Not my fault if Declan didn't prepare his Nightland stations. But why don't you just give it a try, hey? It's fine, I promise. I'll take care of you, old boy. You can trust me. Shhh!"

Murphy sweet-talked the Morgan horse a little more, until he was finally able to lay a jewel of the sparkling liquid in each of his nostrils. The effect was almost instant, washing over Morgan like a cold shower. All signs of fatigue vanished, and he thrust his head at Murphy, asking for more.

"Oh, so now you love it, huh?" Murphy cried, stopping the vial and pocketing it. "No more for now, you wild thing. You get exactly what the doctor prescribed."

"No horses," Ben observed. "No attendant. And Declan said you'd ride Morgan all the way to California."

Murphy stroked his horse's forehead, brows in a loose knot. Ben knew what he was thinking: what was in that tonic? The hesitation was natural, but Ben also saw some relief in the boy's shoulders. He hadn't wanted to say goodbye to his horse, and now it looked like he might not have to.

"Your mare's raring to go, too," Murphy said. "Should we press on?"

Ben wanted nothing more. He unhitched the mare and led her from the trough to see if she'd follow. She did, nickering and even giving a little dance to show she was ready.

"I reckon we should," Ben said. "First sign of trouble with the horses and we rest, though. Wouldn't do for us to get stranded between stations on our first special assignment."

"Three cheers for the Nightland Express," Murphy quipped, and they were off.

Northeastern Kansas Territory wasn't much different from northwestern Missouri, so far as Ben was concerned, but he tried to absorb the sweet, grassy plains all the same. It was the only Kansas they'd see before they crossed into Nebraska Territory. A lone farmhouse studded the prairie in the distance, but their route would take them wide round it. Sometimes, to the south, they could still see the meandering Overland. It wasn't heavily traveled this time of year, yet even in the dead of winter the waning line of wagons and carts never completely ceased.

They slowed enough to share a strip of beef jerky in the saddle. Though neither of the hardy animals seemed touched by fatigue, Ben didn't want to push their luck. When their path crossed a struggling creek, he thought his horse might try to stop for water, but she barely paused to splash through, kicking up cool droplets before mounting the opposite bank.

Once, Ben thought he saw a figure behind them, but the shadows peeking over the distant hills could just as easily be trees. He reached down and pressed his hand against a pocket of his mochila, opposite the gold and Majors' Bible. The heavy, cold weight hidden there comforted him. He hoped never to use it, but just knowing it was there made all the impossibles seem less daunting.

He glanced at Murphy. The boy's slight frame was in perfect harmony with his horse, his eyes fixed ahead with the certainty of a fox on the hunt. A fox—that was what

Jesse Murphy was. Small with sharp teeth, fast and clever. He had an edge that made Ben wary, a sharpness that could turn to cut anyone, as long as it served him best. He'd proven that during the race that morning, when he'd only offered Ben a neckerchief as an afterthought. That kind of generosity was nothing to count on.

They passed through another relay station and found it just as abandoned as the first. Again the horses drank, but again no attendant joined them as the sun dragged the day onward, so Ben and his partner hurried west.

When the third station came into view, Ben was relieved to see it had smoke rising from the chimney. He pressed his hand against his mare's shoulder; her stride was even, her breath regular. It was unnatural, after this long and at this speed.

"What kind of enchanted beast are you?" he asked. But the horse, if she was enchanted, was not bewitched enough to reply.

They slowed and dismounted, letting the horses drink. An attendant was waiting this time, though not with fresh horses. He was an old man, halfway through reading last year's *Almanac*. He greeted them with a sack of bread and two perspiring tin cups of water.

"Making good time, eh, fellas?" he asked. "Bully for you."

Ben took the cup and a big gulp. Nothing like cold water on a warm fall day. Murphy, though, had taken off round the back of the station, probably to relieve himself.

"I reckon so, even despite no one manning the station back there," Ben said. "We weren't able to change for fresh horses."

The attendant laughed. "What fresh horses? Dusky's one of Declan's. She'll be good 'til the end of the line."

He pointed, and Ben realized Dusky was the name of his mare. He hadn't thought to ask it when he'd taken her, assuming he'd be changing her for a new mount every station. That was the idea of the Pony Express, after all—fresh horses every ten miles, all the way to California. But it seemed the Nightland was different from the Pony in more ways than one.

"The Nightland mares are bred for their job," the attendant said, noticing Ben's hesitation. "Don't worry about Dusky. She'll keep running straight through California into the Pacific if you don't stop her."

Beside Dusky, Morgan finished drinking, then moved to the feed bag on the hitch post and grumbled happily to himself as he filled his belly. Ben felt uneasy at the idea of burning a horse nonstop so far and so hard. But he knew an overheated horse when he saw one, and these two looked as though they'd just been brought out of the stable.

"How far is it to Cottington, then?" he asked. The sun had long since passed the top of the sky, heading toward its own home station in the west. They'd be chasing it all the way to bed.

"'Bout thirty miles. You're on schedule."

"Yeah. So long as my partner comes back."

Ben tipped his hat to the attendant in thanks and went to find Murphy. There were a couple obvious places to piss behind the station, a crop of birch trees and some tall grass, but Murphy wasn't to be found at either. Maybe the events of the day had finally caught up to him and given him the flux.

"Murphy! Hurry it up, wherever you are."

The sound of hooves came from the east. A rider, about seventeen years to him, came over the hill, his horse hammering through the earth as he headed toward the station.

"THIEF!" he bellowed. "Stationmaster, arrest him!"

Ben's fingers went cold as ice when he recognized the boy's dirty yellow hair. The hateful stare burning from under the shadow of his hat, the same hazel eyes they both shared with their father. The rider reached for the gun at his hip—their father's LeMat—and Ben bolted toward the station.

Murphy was waiting with the horses at the hitch, giving Morgan drops of the tonic.

"What the blazes?"

Ben yanked Dusky's reins from the hitch and threw himself into her saddle. He dug his heels into her sides, and she let out a squeal and burst into a gallop as gunfire cracked behind them, blowing from the muzzle of Randall Foley's revolver.

CHAPTER VI

JESSE

"Morgan, go, go, *go!*"

Jesse scrambled onto Morgan and they exploded like a stick of dynamite after Foley, who was tearing away from the station at full tilt. The gunman fired as they broke away, but the bullet went wide, biting a chunk out of a birch a good ten feet off.

"Foley! What the hell is—? Who—?"

But her partner was too far ahead and riding too hard to hear, much less reply. Another gunshot went off and Foley veered away from the trail, so Jesse followed, ducking under the whips of sapling branches until they broke out of the tree cover. The horses were made of fire, blazing into the open country, hooves devouring the earth below them.

Before long, they had put nearly a mile between them and their pursuer. The gunman's horse was suffering, slowing and finally refusing to push on any further. When Jesse heard a wild series of frustrated shots, she knew they'd lost him. At least for now.

Foley slowed his mare to a trot, and they took shelter in a small wood of peeling white birches that followed a creek. They didn't stop until they were sure the gunman wasn't still following and that they would be hidden in the cover of the trees if he came over the hills. The black eyes of the birches watched them unblinkingly.

Jesse's thighs and calves ached from the ride. She was short of breath, too, though she didn't dare loosen the binding that squeezed her ribs. She toppled out of the saddle and stalked over to Foley, who was stooping to splash water on his face.

"What the hell was that about?" she demanded. "I signed on to this assignment knowing we'd be bending some rules, but running from a trigger-happy bad egg wasn't part of the deal! You want to tell me who that was and why he was shooting to kill?"

Foley wouldn't face her, doffing his hat and rubbing creek water over his head and neck. His shirt was soaked in sweat, and where it clung to him she could see the faint ripple of raised skin—two long scars that stretched from his shoulder to the dimple above his hip. She'd seen scars like that on the bare backs of the enslaved people who worked the plantations in Clay County, but never on a white boy.

Normally Jesse would've counted it none of her business. Wherever Foley had come from, whoever he was, didn't matter. Except that maybe it did, if where he'd come from was now chasing them both.

"That man would've killed us if not for his poor aim!" she said. She grabbed the back of Foley's shirt. "I think you owe me some answers!"

Then he pointed the gun at her.

Jesse'd never stared into the icy black eye of a barrel before. It was like a basin drain, sucking the life and mind out of her. A single thought spiraled round and round that hole: she didn't know who Ben Foley was at all.

She forced her eyes up to his face. Saw his locked lips and tense jaw, his intense, fearful hazel eyes. He'd run off without her, in an instant. As if he'd been expecting to have to run—as if he'd been on the run the whole time. What had the other man with the gun shouted?

Thief.

"What did you steal?" she asked.

"Only something he thought belonged to him," Foley said bitterly. "Myself."

The pieces came together. The scars. His shaved head. Jesse felt something relax inside her while something else tightened. He wasn't a murderer or a violator. But he was still on the run, with someone dangerous chasing him.

"I'm going ahead to Cottington," Foley continued. His voice was quiet, deliberate. "Alone. You're going back to St. Joe's. You're going to tell Declan and Majors that you changed your mind. Make up whatever story you want, but if you don't, I'm going to put a bullet in your leg and you can wait for the station attendant back there to find you and bring you back. Either way, you're not coming with me."

He kept the gun on her and held his mare. Morgan pawed the ground nervously as Foley took his reins, too. Jesse thought for a moment the horse might resist her treacherous partner, but Morgan was mild-tempered, and Foley was calm. In a moment, he would be gone, with both the horses. Even if she lived, Jesse's overland journey would be over before it had even started.

"Wait!" she said. Her voice squeaked, and she hated it. "Wait. I have to get to Carson City!"

"Then do it next week, after I'm gone."

Life crept back into Jesse's limbs at the thought of not making it to Carson City. Her need to get there outweighed her fear of Foley—whoever he was—and his gun. She couldn't go back to Alice until she'd found their father.

She scrambled forward onto her knees. She'd beg if she had to.

"No!" she said. He didn't fire. He didn't even move his finger to the trigger. "I can't wait until next week. I can't wait until tomorrow. I don't care if you're . . ."

She didn't finish the sentence, and the shadows in Foley's cheeks deepened as he grit his teeth.

"If I'm what?" he asked.

Jesse opened her mouth but couldn't bring herself to say any of the words that came to her mind. They didn't feel right, especially not to his face. Discomfort burrowed through her gut.

"You can't even say it, can you?" he asked, reading her face and knowing her mind. "Can't even say it, though you curse like a sailor. You see it every day and yet you can't even say the word."

"My family's never had slaves," Jesse shot back, proving she could even though her cheeks were burning. "I don't believe in it!"

He narrowed his eyes, drew himself up. "How happy for you and your family."

It stung like a yellowjacket, but Jesse realized she deserved it. Her face grew hot, but she fought the urge to start shouting again, tried to snuff the flames of defensiveness. Foley's eyes, the color of the moss growing on the early autumn trees, were hard. She had thought him to be stoic, but now she wondered if there was a storm of emotion under that careful expression. But he still hadn't shot her.

"I'm sorry," she said. "I guess I don't know what I'm saying."

They fell silent at the sound of footsteps in the brush. Jesse held her breath and the two of them looked through the quiet wood. It hadn't been that long, she'd thought, but it was suddenly the brink of evening. The sun was setting, and the trees were tinted with the last gold of the afternoon. In the silence, she realized even the birds had stopped singing. An airy breeze whispered through the leaves, and she swore she could hear a voice. Feel a presence.

Something tiny and white floated down beneath the trees, drifting between her and Foley like a tuft of white feather. Jesse reached out to let it land in her palm. It was cold, and it melted when it touched her skin.

It was a snowflake.

"In September . . . ?"

Noise came again from deep in the thicket, but this time it wasn't footsteps. It was the sound of trees growing cold, the brittle crackling of twigs and sticks. The icy scent of winter wafted through the trees. The creek froze in its wake, the leaves and foliage on either side frosting in brilliant white.

"*Oathbreakers.*"

The cold voice was a whisper on the wind. Out of the corner of her eye, Jesse saw Foley's gun arm drop. Together, they stared into the gloom. Something *moved* in there, a glimmer of light in the shadows. A slender figure, translucent as ice, obscured by the unnatural snow and frost. Jesse couldn't tell if it was a man or beast, had two legs or four. The only thing she could make out were the branching white structures jutting from its brow—antlers, like a stag's.

They watched it, flickering solid and then airy again, wavering on its slender legs as if disoriented. It stumbled, apparently unaware of them at first. But then it turned, and Jesse saw cold blue eyes in its ethereal face.

It had seen them.

Foley's hand found her collar, yanking her up. They scrambled into their saddles and the horses bolted out of the thicket, bursting through a flurry of cold, glittering snow. Where the flakes touched Morgan's hooves, they vanished, as if his iron shoes were fresh from the forge.

Jesse looked back when they had gained some distance, bringing Morgan to a stop and catching her breath. Foley turned, too, and together they stared back in silence. There was no sign of the snow or ice, or the phantom figure in the whispering wood. The birches stood quiet, dressed in the pale yellows and golds of autumn, flocked and noisy with blackbirds ready to fly further south. Beyond the horizon, the sun was winking goodbye, filling the sky with pink and red. The waxing moon hung in the sky.

Jesse shivered as the last of the chill faded away.

"That just happened ... didn't it?" she asked.

"Yes." Foley's stern face was empty as he searched the wood behind them for any evidence of what they had seen. "I reckon it did. Though what it was, exactly, I couldn't begin to tell you."

They were silent for a minute longer. Foley's gun disappeared into his mochila and he clucked his tongue, turning his horse back toward the trail.

"I'm going with you," she told him. "I'm letting you know so you can point your gun at me now instead of later when you turn round and are surprised to find I'm there."

Foley didn't respond straight away. He kept his hands on the reins and nudged his horse into a canter, then a gallop, his square shoulders bobbing in time with the horse's gait. Any moment she expected he might try to break away from her, but he finally called over his shoulder, "Fine."

With the help of the strange compasses and the last glimmers of sunlight, they found the trail again. Jesse had so much she wanted to say but didn't. Now that she knew his secret, she worried it would come between them and wondered what would happen if she told him hers in exchange. But that could go over poorly, she reckoned, and she didn't want him to try to leave her behind again, especially not after what they had just seen. Maybe if they didn't discuss any of it, they could forget it had ever happened.

It was fully dark by the time they rode into town. Cottington was no more than a dozen houses, a general store, a bar, and the station, and they tied the horses at its trough and stretched. Though the horses again drank with a great thirst, they otherwise showed little fatigue despite having traveled a hundred miles in a day. Morgan was eager for the tonic, his coat shivering in pleasure the moment the drops touched his nostrils.

The station was more or less how Jesse had imagined a Pony Express station would be: a small log shack that, from the windows, appeared to have a loft built above the single main room. Within were a stone fireplace, a lantern on a wood-block table, and an empty rocking chair pointed at the back door on the far end. The dreariness of the place was further punctuated by the overwhelming scent of spoilt milk and cat piss.

"Hello?" Jesse called. "We're sent by Stationmaster Declan. We're supposed to pick up a parcel."

As if in response, the clock near the door rang eight thirty. The two of them listened to the tolling in full. A cat yowled at the end.

"It's not here yet. You might as well get something to eat and rest. You'll have a long journey ahead of you."

Jesse hadn't seen the station attendant before he spoke. He was standing at the back door holding a pitcher. Without any further advice, he left. As he did, the shadows in the corners of the station moved. Six black cats emerged, eyes like yellow moons. They followed him out, leaving Jesse and Foley alone in an empty, foul room.

Jesse hated the smell, and now the attendant and his cats, so she left out the front door and spat. She still didn't know what to say about any of it, and she and Foley stood there in an awkward silence. But how long could they put it off?

"So, uh," she mumbled. "Are we gonna . . . talk about it?"

It. Even that seemed too direct a way to refer to the blue specter in the wood and the supernatural snow and ice that had emanated from its chilling, unexplainable presence.

Foley took in a long breath, held it, and then let it out all at once. It was wordless, but a reaction all the same, confirming to Jesse that he had, in fact, seen what Jesse had. It had happened. They just weren't going to talk about it.

"I could use a drink," he said, and walked off toward the saloon.

"Like in a saloon?" Jesse asked, trying not to sound unsure. "Yeah—of course. Lead the way."

She had never been in a saloon before; respectable women weren't to be found in such places, and even unrespectable women weren't allowed service unless it was through the back door. Or if they were the ones providing the service. But she'd always wanted to see the inside of one, to know what went on in those mysterious, awful-smelling places.

Then she frowned. Women weren't the only ones disallowed in bars. "But you're . . . What if someone notices . . . ?"

Foley snorted. "What do you mean?"

"I mean what if someone finds out—about you? Is it worth it?"

Foley fixed her with those hazel eyes, solid and steady. "Just because you found out today doesn't mean I haven't dealt with this my entire life," he said mildly. "You sound real late telling me it's noon when I've been awake since the sun come up."

Jesse's ears burned as he walked past, waving her to follow.

The inside of the saloon smelled of ale and whiskey, with an undercurrent of vomit and piss. It was dead quiet, with two men at the bar drinking their weight in liquor and a third passed out on the stairs, half lying in a puddle of his own sick. The rest were trappers immersed in a card game, and all looked up at Jesse and Foley when they entered.

Jesse tried not to shrink away from their gazes but was nearly left behind when Foley walked right up to the bar, confident and direct. That was all that mattered; no one gave him a second glance. Jesse didn't know his full story and figured she wouldn't until—or if—he told her. But whatever his circumstances, he seemed to know what he was doing and how to conduct himself. Jesse wished she could do the same.

Foley leaned on the bar and nodded to the tender while Jesse scooted next to him, trying to ignore that every man in the one-room had at least a foot and a hundred pounds on her. If she were found out, a young woman in a bar of drunkards, it would be awful trouble.

But what if they found out about Foley? It would be worse, and yet he walked with his head up, unflinching. Fearless.

The man closest at the bar assessed them from under his heavy black brows and thick mustache. Any minute, Jesse expected he would unpack her secret—or Foley's— but he only nodded in welcome.

Foley nodded back. "Barkeep. Another for him, and one for me. Kentucky bourbon, if you have it."

The barkeep filled the order, sliding the amber liquid in front of Foley and the other man at the bar. Having never been in a saloon, Jesse wasn't sure if Foley knew the man or had some reason for buying him a drink, but as soon as the exchange was made, the scrutiny in the place dropped to a minimum. Conversation started up again round them, and she let out a strangled breath of relief.

"You sure make all this look easy," she said under her breath.

Foley knocked back the whiskey as if he'd done it many times before. But when he set the glass down, Jesse saw his hand shake. Perhaps he wasn't so fearless after all.

She craved some liquor herself; she had a bottle hidden under her floorboards at home, left by her father years ago, and snuck sips out of it occasionally when Alice's anxieties and particularities threatened to test her patience. Superstitions put in her head by Aunt Mary. Panic when Jesse didn't dress and behave like other girls, and dread of what might become of her.

Not here. Not tonight. For the first time in her life, she didn't have to be what everyone wanted her to be. A sister, a daughter, a future mother. Out here, she didn't have to be someone she wasn't.

"Another round," she said, pouring every ounce of her determination into it. The trembling in Foley's hand calmed, and Jesse smiled. "This one's on me."

CHAPTER VII
BEN

Ben tried not to harp on what had happened, tried not to shrink into his skin knowing that his partner had discovered the secret he'd been hoping to keep. It was dreadful fearsome to know that in such a short amount of time, it could all come unraveled.

It wasn't surprising. Disappointing, more like. Just more proof of how precarious his position was, balanced on the edge between safety and danger. If he wasn't careful, the slightest wind could knock him down.

Then again, ever since Murphy had clamped his jaw shut, stopped spouting defensive, irrelevant nonsense—ever since the furious flush had faded from his cheeks—he'd held up. He met Ben in the eye the same as before he'd found out, talked to him like a human being. He'd even worried on Ben's behalf about going into the bar— something no white stranger had ever done.

Was it worse, having Murphy around? Ben tried to imagine what this all would have been like, how it all would have wound up, if he'd been alone. If Stationmaster

Declan and Alexander Majors had only hired one rider. If he'd had to run from Randall alone, ended up in the thicket, seen the inexplicable snowstorm, the spectral monster. Heard that mourning, inhuman voice.

If he'd seen that ghostly, blue-eyed creature by himself, would he have believed himself afterward? Or would he have told himself he'd imagined it, since there would be no one else to pinch him and tell him he wasn't dreaming —like when he'd been a child and seen the things he'd thought he'd seen? No one had been with him then, so no one could tell him the truth.

"Been through a lot today, haven't we?" he murmured.

"Yeah."

Murphy was almost hunched over the bar, hiding in his shoulders, though Ben wasn't sure exactly what he was afraid of. Maybe he was still worried Ben would leave him, or pull the gun again. Ben didn't plan to, but he couldn't say as much so plainly. Fact was, after the ghost and with Randall somewhere close behind, he didn't want to be alone. It was selfish, and he knew it. Knew it and hated it but knew it all the same.

They'd seen something unbelievable together, and Murphy wasn't running from it. Could Ben trust him? He sighed. Only one way to find out.

"Randall—the gunman. He's my half brother," he said quickly and quietly. "My father died end of August and freed me in his will. Randall weren't happy 'bout it."

Murphy perked at the explanation. Not because he'd

been especially curious, Ben reckoned, but because he was seeing it for the olive branch it was.

"I'm sorry about your father," he said.

"I'm not," Ben replied.

A tepid silence followed. Ben left it that way, letting Murphy draw what conclusion he would. He didn't need to know the details of Ben's growing-up, his father and Penny. His father's wife, Grace. His birth mother, whose name he'd never known. None of that was Murphy's business. The only part that mattered was the part about Randall, and he hoped even that wouldn't matter for long.

"We'll lose him," Murphy said earnestly. Then his eyes went far-offish, and Ben could almost see him thinking about the blue ghost in the wood. "Randall, I mean. We'll do it together."

Murphy raised his glass. It was an apology and a promise all in one. Ben felt the restless form—that worm-shaped creature in his chest—twitch. Then it calmed, though it was still there, awake. Wary. But when he raised his glass against Murphy's, it didn't stir.

They paid with coins from their advances and left the bar near ten, joined the horses back at the station and had a light supper of bread, cheese, and jerky from their traveling packs. Ben pressed the back of his hand against his face, wondering if the warmth from the liquor was as visible on him as it was on Murphy, whose cheeks were rosy pink. A dreamy smile crept across the boy's face. Like a stray cat, lingering no matter how many times its owner tried to tell it off.

"What's got you so happy?" Ben asked.

"I've never been in a saloon before! Did you see me? I ordered a drink. They didn't even say anything!"

Murphy wasn't used to liquor, not like Ben was. That was clear enough.

"Why would they say anything? You got money."

"Yeah, but people like me aren't usually—you know, to be found at a bar . . ." Murphy's voice had been steadily creeping up in pitch and softening the more he spoke. At this last comment he seemed to hear it happening and closed his mouth round it, locking it inside. "Never mind. Let's find a place to drop and get some sleep."

The lantern had been put out inside, so all they could see was the dying orange light from the fire. In silence, they climbed the creaking stairs. Two bunks were laid out in the attic, just wood pallets with hay mattresses on top. The whole room chirped with crickets, in the walls and every nook and cranny.

Ben took one bed and Murphy dropped onto the other. The moon filled the room with silver light, and a cool breeze came down from the sky.

This had always been Ben's favorite time, when the world was asleep. When everything was quiet and still. Penny would wake him, or think she was waking him—he was always too excited to go to sleep—and together they would run through the field that surrounded his father's house. Lit by the stars in the big indigo sky and serenaded by the night bugs, he held her hand as they made the three-mile walk to the neighboring property. There, Penny would sit and sing and talk with the men and women who labored in the field, tend their sore limbs and the wounds delivered by the overseers. She gave them any medicine she could steal from Ben's father's cupboards, held their babies and soothed their souls. Those were Ben's favorite nights. His own soul feasting on moonlight as he and Penny climbed over fences and crossed through fields, to see other people who saw him.

Including Theodore. A couple years older, tall and handsome, with a chemist's mind for numbers and ounces, which he put to use with the secret bourbon still he kept in a hole dug beneath the floorboards of the shack where he slept. Ben learned to love the sting of the whiskey. Anything to earn any drop of time he could, listening to Theodore speak with such enthusiasm and passion.

He had known from the beginning that what he felt for Theodore could never be said. It was like being in a cold room with no windows or doors, where any words spoken were swallowed by stillness and silence. Not even Penny would enter that room. Not even when she knew he was in there, afraid and alone. It was just how things had to be, it seemed. For Ben, and . . .

What was it Murphy had said?

People like me.

Ben turned to peer through the dark. He could barely

see Murphy on his back, straight as a board, hands daintily folded across his chest and knees pressed together with his boots crossed at the ankle. As if the boy were protecting something of his own, buried inside him, all while trying to act natural.

He thought of a handful of other times Murphy's mannerisms had been a little queer—just something different about the way he held himself and spoke. Emotive and fluid, like his voice, beneath that fox-like edge.

"Hey, Murphy?"

"What." Apparently he wasn't asleep, either.

"You got a girl? Back home?"

"You mean my sister? Back in St. Joe's?"

"No. I mean a woman. Like the kind you marry."

"Me, marry a woman?" Murphy snorted a loud laugh that answered Ben's question more than a simple *yes* would have. In the awkward silence that followed, Murphy took in a sharp breath. Then he rolled away toward the wall. "Mind your own business."

Even if it was the end of the conversation, it felt more like Murphy had pulled a curtain between them than slammed a door. The lonely room suddenly felt less cold.

"Sorry about pulling a gun on you today," he said. But Murphy was either asleep or ignoring him and didn't answer.

Ben didn't realize he'd fallen asleep until he bolted awake at an explosion of dusty flapping and fluttering of wings. Murphy yelped from the other side of the dark room.

It was still night. The only evidence of the sound they'd heard was a dozen dirty black and gray feathers flitting down from the rafters.

"Hello!"

The voice came from the window. Perched on the sill was a girl, not more than ten years old. Ben made out bare feet, scuffed and dirty knees, a plain gray shift, and a round face punctuated by big, obsidian eyes that showed hardly any whites. Her thick black hair was tied in a ponytail, though that barely contained the wispy, feather-like locks that sprang like a fountain from the back of her head.

"Hello," Ben replied hesitantly.

"Oh. Were you sleeping?" The girl's voice was sharp like a poker, smart-witted and barbed. She reached into her shift pocket and took a stick from a pack of Black Jacks. The molasses candy looked like a skinny black cigarette, bobbing up and down as she chewed on it.

"Who are you?" Murphy asked.

The girl slid off the sill, straightened and crossed her arms, turning her nose up so that she could give a haughty little sniff. She wasn't more than four feet tall, yet she did everything she could to keep looking down at them. In the moonlight, her skin looked both dark and bright at the same time, with a peculiar shine to it. At first Ben thought she was just very dirty, which was also true—but under the soot and soil, her skin seemed to glow as if she were dusted with silver, like the wings of a moth.

"You may call me Mock, if you must," she said.

"All right then, Mock," Murphy said. "What's going on?"

"How should I know? I was promised sweets. But all that's here is flea-bag cats and you two lumps. Are we going to be on our way soon, then, or no?"

"On our way?"

"To California. Stationmaster Declan did tell you that you'd be taking me there, didn't he?"

"No, no. He said we were picking up a parcel," Ben said. "Not a person."

"He lied. Now hurry! The moon is waiting!"

Mock scampered down the stairs from the attic. Once she was out of sight, Ben exchanged a bewildered glance with Murphy.

"Is this really happening?" he asked. "Declan didn't say anything about transporting a person!"

Murphy chewed on the inside of his cheek, thinking. "He didn't say we *wouldn't* be," he said.

That was true enough. Mock's explanation, while unbelievable, in some way fit what the stationmaster had said—he had asked if they were willing to do what others weren't, after all. Alexander Majors wanted young, upstanding men to run his Pony Express. Men who would neither cheat nor drink nor swear. Ben and Murphy had done all those things they had sworn not to, and that, Ben imagined, was precisely why Darcy Declan had hired them. Talent to fit the task: the task of bringing a person, not a parcel, to California, no questions asked.

"This is all so strange," he murmured. He meant it as a general observation, but Murphy perked up with a competitive glint in his eye.

"If it's too strange for you, then why don't you quit?" he teased.

The levity dispelled the strangeness of the moment, and Ben snorted. "You wish."

They found Mock at the post where the horses were hitched. The beasts nickered at her, bending their noses down so she could give them scratches and kisses. She snatched up a ratty black cape that was draped over the hitch post and swung it over her shoulders before clambering up Morgan's stirrups, using both hands and feet like a squirrel. When she reached the saddle, she glowered down at the two of them.

"What's keeping you?"

Even if they had been prepared for an unconventional assignment, transporting a young girl across the country was risky business. Any number of things could come their way, from bandits to an injured horse. Having a child with them would only make things more difficult. And Ben didn't know anything about children or their care—he and his half brother were close enough in age that it had never been his job to care for Randall. Randall, who was undoubtedly still somewhere on their trail with a gun and an itching trigger finger. But if that was the job, and if Murphy was going to do it, so was Ben.

"What kind of name is Mock, anyway?" Murphy asked, putting his hands on his hips. "Is it short for something, or is it just what you'll do once you've tricked us into doing whatever it is you're up to?"

Mock kicked her feet once, curling her toes. "You *mock* your assignment, I think," she said. "Shame to think about what your employer might say if he knew his *two riders* were being so rude to me on this unprecedented *special assignment*."

Ben looked between his riding partner and the imp perched on Morgan's saddle. But Murphy was already un-hitching the horses. If he had any reservations about what they were doing, he didn't show it—in fact, he seemed bolder every time Ben hesitated. Like this was a game, and Ben had no choice but to play. But the stakes were high and he wasn't ready to fold yet.

"This is a disaster, I reckon," he said, hoisting himself into Dusky's saddle.

Murphy looked over his shoulder. For just a moment, Ben saw a serious look in his face. Something that said he would do whatever it took to get to California. With or without Ben.

Then the look brightened into a grin, and Murphy took hold of the saddle horn, swinging himself up behind Mock. And three rode out, the moon lighting their way.

CHAPTER VIII

JESSE

Night drenched the plains in rich blues and blacks, as if the sun had taken the green and gold with it when it went to bed. The stars twinkled white, and across the grass-covered hills, lightning bugs blinked in and out in an undulating veil of yellow-green sparkles. It was late in the season for them, Jesse reckoned, but then she was no expert in the lives of insects.

Her body was still aching after getting only a couple hours' sleep, but it was a small sacrifice to be back on the trail. Even if it was in the middle of the night.

At several points, she thought she heard distant hoofbeats and wondered if Foley's half brother had caught their scent. But it was impossible to see far behind them in the dark, and Jesse hoped it would be just as impossible for him to follow them.

Mock smelled of sage and wheatgrass, holding on to the saddle horn as they rode through meadow and stream. "I thought you were Express riders, hey?" she said.

Contrary to her chiding, they were galloping at top speed, Dusky keeping pace at their flank. Morgan was raring from the tonic in his nostrils, as fresh as a pony on the way to the county fair. He was energetic even for himself, keeping Jesse on her wits as he hurdled rocks and stumps and ditches. With every leap, Jesse expected Mock to go flying away into the brush, but she had the balance of a bird on the wind.

"What's Declan paying you for?" Mock chirped. "At this pace, I might as well walk!"

The gold in Jesse's satchel felt suddenly heavy.

"Then do," Jesse suggested wryly.

She checked her compass. By moonlight, it was easy enough to read, needle wavering westerly. She had no idea how far it was to the next station. There seemed to be nothing in their way but prairie and stars.

"Those old things!" Mock said, catching sight of the compass. "He gave them to you? My, my! Special, aren't we? Turn here! There's a stream. This way!"

Mock suddenly yanked the reins from Jesse's hands, leading Morgan sharply to the left. Jesse locked every muscle to stay in the saddle as he swerved.

"What? Where?" she cried. "The compass was pointing that way!"

Foley cursed and turned his horse after them. "Where are you going?" he shouted.

"This way!" Mock replied, mouth full of wind. She whooped and hollered.

"Come on! This isn't the time for games!" Jesse said.

"It's nearly the witching hour!" Mock shouted. She looked back over her shoulder and her black eyes were wide with wild glee. "It's the only time for games!"

The glittering of water snaked through the meadow. A river ran ahead, though how wide or deep was impossible to tell. Jesse snatched at the reins, but Mock clutched them tightly like a cat with a string in its claws.

"Mock! Give them back!"

"The witching hour!" Mock threw her head back and howled again with all her might: "*ALL BEHOLD THE WITCHING HOUR!*"

They reached the water and Morgan leapt. Jesse pushed Mock's hands forward to release the reins so the horse could extend his head into the jump. As they cleared it in a flash of silver and blue, Jesse caught sight of the moon's reflection in the slate surface of the water. Airborne, she felt dizzy for a moment, but the sensation vanished when Morgan's hooves struck earth again.

Jesse finally tore the reins from Mock's grabbing hands, slowing them to a stop. She resisted the urge to push the girl out of the saddle.

Foley came alongside them. "What the hell was that?"

"Alexander Majors doesn't like it when you swear," Mock chided. She kicked her feet out from the saddle and let out a giggle that was a touch wicked. "That was the tops! Oh, just the tops! Most boys fall out there, but you're both here, and in the saddle, hey? Oh, what fun we'll have!"

"Now listen here, little missy," Jesse said. "When you're riding double with me, you keep your hands *off* the reins. You got it?"

Mock leaned full back into her, fixing her with upside-down eyes that reflected the whole moon. With a sly grin, she extended a finger toward the dangling leather.

"Don't you dare," Jesse growled.

"...Touch."

Jesse took a handful of Mock's cape and pulled so hard the girl went toppling, rolling in a ball of skinny arms and legs until she came to a stop in the dirt and grass. A cloud of mosquitos blew up in a flurry, and by the time they dissipated, Mock was huddled with her face in her hands, shoulders shuddering. Jesse felt an angry pang of guilt in her gut.

"Now you've done it," muttered Foley. He hopped out of the saddle and hooked his thumbs on his belt, leaning over the shivering pile of black hair and cloak. "Hey. Are you hurt?"

A muffled noise bubbled up, growing louder until Jesse recognized it. She rolled her eyes. Mock wasn't crying—she was laughing. Jesse spat to eject a foul taste from her mouth.

"Are we going to waste all night rolling in the dirt?" she asked.

Mock uncurled like a roly-poly, flattening onto her back and staring up at the sky.

"I think I'm done for now," she said. "Let's make a campfire and count the stars!"

Jesse wanted to scream. She almost did. "We've barely ridden an hour! If this is all you wanted to do—I could be sleeping in a bed right now!"

Mock rolled onto her side so her back was facing them. She sniffed and turned her nose up—or sideways, as it were, since she was horizontal. Jesse clenched a fist.

"Get up. Back in the saddle," she ordered.

"I don't want to," Mock said disdainfully. "And you shan't make me."

"*Shan't?*" Foley repeated, arching a brow. It was his only contribution to the conversation, and Jesse clenched her other fist.

"Yes. It stands for shall not," Mock remarked. "Listen, you. I'll do whatever I want, and if I want to camp, then that's what we'll do, or I'll tell Stationmaster Declan that you weren't agreeable. Then he'll disemploy you, I reckon. Take back all the deposit he paid you and replace you with someone else straight away. So you see, you *shan't* do anything I don't wish!"

Jesse looked up at the moon. Now that she was awake, she wanted to keep riding. Maybe it was a desire born of sheer stubbornness, resentment for having been woken. Regardless, she refused to be ordered around by a child. She swung out of her saddle and grabbed Mock by the wrist, yanking her up to her feet.

"I'm the boss of this outfit, and I say we keep riding," she said sternly.

Mock cried out, piercingly, though Jesse knew her grip

wasn't hard enough to be painful. Mock was screaming just for the sake of screaming. Jesse held firm against the girl's writhing until it stopped. Mock slumped to her knees in the most melodramatic heap of defeat Jesse had ever seen.

"Tantrum done?" she asked. "Good. Back in the saddle."

"But . . . it . . ." Mock sniffled and threatened to cry, but Jesse had long become impervious to that tactic, thanks to Alice. "I just wanted to sit near a campfire under the stars with the two strapping lads who would rescue me from my awful fate. I wanted to enjoy it . . . my first eve in so long, being seen in the dayland."

"Dayland?" Jesse repeated. She glanced at Foley, but he avoided her gaze. His unwillingness to discipline Mock or otherwise help get them back on the road was frustrating, but not terribly surprising. Men weren't taught to rear children, and anything they did learn was forgotten quickly when it was convenient, which was most of the time. Children were women's work.

So be it.

"What'll it be, then, huh?" Jesse asked, pulling Mock's hand up so the girl was at least looking at her. "You going to be a royal highness on a high horse, or a poor bird hopping about with a broken wing?"

Mock tilted her head and smiled. "Oh. Why not both?"

Jesse had half a mind to pull on the girl's hand, then, when she wasn't expecting, toss her over the saddle like a bag of flour. But Foley was folding up his reins. The argument was over.

"Go find some firewood," he muttered. "I'll get set up for it."

Mock's smile broadened, which made Jesse even more reluctant to let go. Foley didn't seem to care either way, though, so she threw Mock's hand back at her and turned away. She followed a path where the tall grass was broken from the hooves of buffalo and deer, marching into the hills where a crop of trees had watched their exchange.

The whole thing stung. Was she the only one who cared about California?

As Jesse gathered twigs and sticks in the little grove, every thorn that pricked her seemed ten times as annoying as it might have had she been in fair spirits. Mosquitos hummed about her head. The insects had blossomed in the night, swarming in bloodsucking clouds. They landed on her cheeks and ears, but her arms were too full of damp, sap-covered kindling to do anything about it.

How easy it would be to return to Foley and Mock and quit right there. To take Morgan and ride onward to the end of the trail! Foley had wanted that, hadn't he, to be alone to finish their delivery himself? As long as Jesse had the tonic for Morgan, she wouldn't need a fresh horse at every station—the only reason she'd joined the damned Express to begin with. Thanks to whatever devilry had created the sparkling potion in the vial, she could be in

Carson City by the end of the week. It would mean abandoning Foley and breaking her word, of course, and that would mean a tarnished reputation. But it wasn't as though she'd ever need to be rehired by Alexander Majors and his company.

Before she went back, she stopped to take a piss while she had the privacy. Squatting in the cool night, she wished she had been born a boy. And not for the first time.

She froze when she heard whispering amongst the trees. The moon glimmered off the thousand leaves and million blades of grass, and she listened. Waited, both in fear of seeing spectral blue eyes in the dark, and with a deep, dark knowing that it *would* happen again—just not yet.

Wherever the strange intuition came from, it was right. In that moment, no snowflake drifted from the heavens, and no heavy breath of winter chilled the back of her neck. There were no whispers. Only wind.

When she returned to camp, she dropped the bundle of kindling and finally slapped dead the mosquito that had been sucking off the tip of her nose.

"Everything's wet from the dew," Foley said. He stooped over a pile of smoking brush, pack of matches in one hand. Mock knelt next to him, arms full of rocks, which she began to arrange with great care in a circle round the damp twigs. "I can't get it started, even with the match."

Jesse sighed, putting her hands on her hips. "Mock, go run out into the field and find some buffalo chips. I saw some that way, between here and the trees on the hill."

"Buffalo chips!" Mock cried with unbounded glee. She set down the last rock, completing the ring, and leapt up. It was the first time she'd done what Jesse'd told her, and apparently only because it involved buffalo dung.

"Buffalo chips?" Foley asked.

"They're flammable," Jesse said. She pulled the brush apart, minding where it was warm from trying to light. "Though they might be a bit soggy."

Foley cracked a little smile at the thought of what Mock was about to encounter. "You must have prepared for this trip a long time. You know every landmark and stop?"

Jesse shook her head, arranging the fire. "Not every one. But I did my research. My pa went before me and left his notes from when he prepared. Sketches and maps. I even got a copy of Joseph Ware's guide and memorized it. It's foolhardy to head out west without knowing what you're up against." She paused, but Foley didn't reply. Then she added, "But I guess not everyone has the liberty of planning how and when they start the journey. Or having someone who went before them."

Foley's silence softened, those hard eyes twinkling in the moonlight.

Mock came back with her arms full of lumpy, half-soggy chips. She was pleased with herself to have found such a pile, though it stuck to her arms and shift along with the undigested grass. She stank like it, too, and Jesse reckoned she would for days.

Still, it was what they needed. Jesse got it lit with only two matches, and the three watched the fire bloom into a happy orange flower.

Mock shivered with joy. She tugged Jesse's sleeve and Jesse tried to ignore the odor of buffalo droppings.

"Now I'm hungry," the girl declared. "What shall we have for supper?"

Though they had a fire, they had no food aside from the provisions Jesse and Foley had brought for themselves. Foley's gun—hidden in his mochila or under his vest, she wasn't sure—might bring them a rabbit for dinner, but Jesse didn't want to ask him to use it. They'd have to find that rabbit first, anyway, and hunting down a warren in the middle of the night would not be easy. And then there would be the hassle of cooking it, which Jesse supposed would fall on her shoulders, because she was probably the only one present who knew how to prepare a meal. She'd heard dozens of stories about men who'd gone west for gold and died of starvation simply because none of them knew how to cook.

Her stomach growled at the thought. Just as she was about to tell Mock there was no food for her and that she ought to get used to roughing it on the trail, Foley leaned over and offered the girl a roll. She accepted it without thanks, cramming it into her cheeks like a squirrel. Not a crumb hit the earth as the thing vanished into her face.

"Now that I've paid you in bread, might I ask some questions?" Foley said. As an extra incentive, he held out a little flask.

"What's this?" Mock asked. "Smells bitter."

"A libation. If it please your highness."

After a big gulp and a barely hidden retch, Mock wiped her mouth with the back of her hand. Jesse could tell the flavor didn't sit well with her from the wrinkle on her lips, but Mock didn't complain, apparently more interested in being treated like royalty. Wobbling slightly, she sat cross-legged, knobby knees poking out of the hem of her shift.

Foley put the flask away. "Is someone after you?"

Mock tucked a last crumb on her lip into her mouth with a pinky. "No. And no one has come before me, either. There is only me."

"All we want to know is if we should be looking over our shoulder," Jesse huffed impatiently, crossing her arms. "You know that's what he's asking!"

"You should always look over your shoulder," Mock replied. "It's how you know where you've come from. Well, I'm very tired now, and I wish to go to sleep. We will ride again at dawn. Good night." She pulled her cape round her shoulders and rolled onto her side. Within moments, she was snoring.

"Abrupt," Jesse remarked. When Foley stood, brushing

off his backside and kicking dirt onto the fire, she realized he might have had something to do with it. "What was in that flask?"

"Laudanum," he said. "Help me get her on the saddle, and let's get moving."

Jesse couldn't help but feel a spark of respect, rising to help him put out the fire. Perhaps Ben Foley wasn't the mild-mannered boy she'd thought he was.

CHAPTER IX

BEN

"Ready . . . and . . . lift!"

Mock was light as a feather. She didn't stir, just snored as they lifted her between the two of them, Ben at her ankles and Murphy under the arms.

"Morgan or Dusky?" Murphy asked.

"She seemed to fit well with you, if it's all the same." Ben kept out the part where he didn't want to be stuck with the girl if Randall came after him again. *When* Randall came after him, that was. It was only a matter of time.

Murphy shrugged. "It's all the same to me. Morgy it is."

Ben took a step toward Morgan but stopped when he felt resistance. "You coming?" he asked. If Murphy was just going to stand there, Ben might as well throw Mock over his shoulder and carry her himself. She was light enough.

But the annoyed frown on Murphy's face said the delay wasn't on purpose. "I'm trying! I think she's caught on something," he said.

They looked below her to see if her cloak had snagged on a tree root or rock, but it hadn't. It felt like the girl had a rope round her waist and the other end was tied to a boulder. Tug as they might, they could barely move her an inch closer to the horses. She was harnessed to the ground, like an ox to a field plow, dragging metal through the reluctant earth.

They gave up and set Mock back in the grass, where she mumbled incoherently and curled into a little sleeping ball. Ben felt a shiver in his bones, like he imagined birds felt when they knew a storm was coming. He doffed his hat and ran his hands over his head while Murphy kicked at rocks and swore, over and over.

"I don't understand," Murphy said. "It don't make any goddamned sense! None of this does! Little girls tied to the earth with invisible string. Magic compasses. Invincible horses! We saw dad-burned *ghosts* in that wood, Foley."

Ben didn't want to listen to it; hearing someone else repeat all the strange things they'd seen together made it harder to forget. Now Murphy was shouting it all across the world. Ben reckoned the caravan traveling the California Road, some miles south, might even be able to hear him if they listened hard enough.

Murphy settled down after a bit, thumping heavily to his posterior in the dirt and getting to work brushing earth off the still-smoldering fire.

"Sorry 'bout that," he said. "My sister says I have a temper."

Ben snorted. "Your sister is right."

They cleared the dirt from the fire together. Ben hoped some of the coals were still hot enough to light from. The next time they tried slipping a little girl laudanum, he reckoned they'd put out the fire last. Murphy grunted when he burned himself on one of the coals he'd uncovered, sticking his singed finger in his mouth and talking round it.

"You know what Alice'd say about all this? Magic. She says magic's behind everything she can't explain. Magic and God, anyway. Or the Devil."

Ben wondered if Murphy's sister was anything like Randall. Magic *was* the Devil, so far as Ben's father had been concerned, and Randall believed the Gospel with all his heart. Ben had never been so sure, but he'd learned that if he showed he loved God enough, his father would sometimes teach him to read out of the Bible. Sometimes, even better, he'd take him to church on Sundays, where he sat still beside a fidgeting Randall, enraptured by the steepled building and all the people who had come together within it to worship.

Penny had often told Ben to keep faith. She had told him faith was the key to enduring hardship—that it was part of his magic power. But if his faith was magic, and magic was the work of the Devil, then what did that make him?

A cluster of leaves caught against a gray, cracked ember. They nurtured the tiny flame, Murphy feeding it twigs while Ben leaned in and blew gently. As if by their combined will, the fire crackled back to life.

"I reckon it's all the same, one way or the other," Ben said finally.

A crawl of nerves rushed over his back when he noticed that the horses had gone still, ears up, alert. He heard it, barely masked by the wind, faint: voices that rose up from the very earth itself. Even the infant fire cowered, dying almost to hot coals again, smoke pouring from the trembling flames like a living black serpent. The temperature dropped, though not yet enough to bring snow or frost.

"What do we do?" Murphy whispered, taking hold of Ben's arm. "Is that *thing* coming again?"

"You ask like I know!"

If that blue, spectral being came to them, all antlers and eerie whispers, they would not be able to escape this time, out in the open as they were. And even if they hadn't been, they couldn't get Mock on a horse. He still didn't know how he felt about their ward, let alone how Murphy did, but Ben had a feeling that even if they were pushed to it, neither of them would be able to leave her behind.

Murphy dug his fingernails into Ben's skin. The expanse of the rugged prairie was as impenetrable and shifting as the waters of the Platte. But Murphy had seen something, and now Ben saw it, too: silhouettes, even darker than the shadows. And then footsteps, soft, careful, like deer treading through the brush.

They were not alone.

Ben wondered if Randall had found them. Or maybe the trappers from the bar had not been trappers but bandits or slave catchers. Maybe they'd seen his wanted poster, and had recognized him . . .

Four pairs of phosphoric lights broke the darkness. They hovered about where a man's eyes might, though the twisting shape in Ben's gut knew there was nothing *human* about what he was seeing. The shadows settled, the smoke cleared, and the moonlight fell upon the shoulders of four thin figures.

The first stepped into the globe of firelight, as if conjured from the smoke itself, a full cloak of swarthy feathers round his shoulders. His dark gray hair was long, gathered in a bun at the top of his head, dripping with thorns and bones. Everything about him was like a living shadow, and when he spoke the wind whistled overhead like a hawk circling prey. He held a spear, its entire length curved and thick like an enormous thorn, in a hand the color of the undulating coals in their campfire.

"Hello."

His voice was rich as blood, though it had a strange melodic quality to it as well, like the song of a piper leading an army to war. He peered over the thick collar of his cloak, smiling at Ben and Murphy as they crouched near the dying fire. His eyes were a vivid and iridescent yellow.

As the man—Ben didn't know how else to think of him —gazed at them with those unnerving eyes, the others emerged from the shadows. Like the one with the spear, they had two legs and two arms each, but their bodies were unnaturally slender, as if they were built from tree limbs instead of bones and flesh. They had long faces with slitted nostrils like a deer's, and jewel eyes with the horizontal pupils of a goat. Each had a pair of antlers protruding from their brow, but the twisted, whorled, swooping shapes were all different. Aside from simple ragged shifts, they were in varying states of nakedness, and the exposed skin of each was a different shade. One blue like a Mississippi jay. Another red like a cardinal. The fourth light brown and dappled like a sparrow.

In the full light of the fire Ben knew without a doubt they were not trappers or bandits. Despite how impossible it seemed, the truth was undeniable: the four strange figures *were not human.*

"Who are you?" Murphy asked. "What are you?"

"Ah, yes." Their leader bowed deeply, sweeping his cloak aside. His cohorts, though silent, did the same. "Forgive us for meeting this way. You may call me Shrike."

Murphy stood, dragging Ben up with him. Ben was struck again by the boy's brazen willingness to act despite not knowing what could come next.

"Where did you come from?" Murphy asked.

Shrike laughed, his white teeth in stark contrast with his black, hooked lips. "I have a very important question for the two of you," he said.

Shrike tapped the butt of his spear repeatedly against the earth. On the last tap, he thrust it down so hard it stuck, standing by itself like an unbreakable pillar. Then he clasped his hands together as if he'd caught an insect. When he opened them, a pile of gold nuggets spilled out. Shining and yellow, raw and pure, like the teeth of a dragon. They rippled in the firelight on his silver and black palms.

"Do either of you like . . . gold?"

Shrike's companions responded with the same hand-cupping motion. In moments, three more piles of raw gold nuggets were glittering at them. Ben had never seen so much money and wasn't likely to ever see it again in his whole life. It was a sudden, painful glimpse into an impossible future: enough to buy land and a house to put on it—enough to buy Penny's freedom.

The gold must have inspired a similar fantasy in Murphy's mind, because he reached out. As his fingers neared the peanut-shaped nuggets, Ben snagged his wrist and yanked it back.

Murphy glared. "He's offering!"

"But you don't know why!" Ben cried.

Shrike laughed. He spread his hands, letting the gold rain onto the earth. Ben tried not to watch, tried to keep his eyes on the mysterious man, who suddenly thrust a hand forward. Murphy went stiff, gulping as Shrike's thumb pressed into his forehead, leaving an oval smudge of black dust.

"It is done," Shrike said.

"What's done?" Ben shouted. "What did you do?"

Shrike tilted his head, as if weighing his answer. But before he could land on a reply, a cold wind swept through the campsite. His strange companions shrank into their shoulders, hissing and whispering in a language Ben couldn't understand. The air took on a blue glow, like the shine of a full moon on the first day of winter. The same chill Ben had felt yesterday, in the thicket, rippled through him.

"Curses," Shrike swore. "He comes."

Ben felt it before he saw it: the cold kiss of a snowflake on the back of his hand. Then the frost came, glittering white in the air and along the curled leaves and grasses of the earth.

The wind gusted hard, as if a door had been thrown open in the middle of January. It blew back Shrike's robes, baring his body for a moment so Ben could see the white and gray streaks up and down his torso, not paint or tattoo but the color of his skin. He looked out into the field, a hunter seeking prey. Ben turned to see what he was fixated on, clinging to Murphy's wrist against the freezing wind.

He didn't want to see the blue-and-white creature again. The creature that had whispered *oathbreakers* at them. But there it was.

It stood in the open field, the blowing, frosted grass shivering in the halo of its light. Its blue eyes shone through the mist like twin stars, alabaster antlers spreading into the sky like leafless branches.

"What is it?" Murphy asked.

A ghost, Ben wanted to say, but the word wouldn't come out.

Shrike stood tall, facing the wind without blinking. "He is winter. Do not worry about him. It is my duty to protect you from him, you see. And I will do that . . . I will protect you from everything, my precious double-goods."

The haunted blue thing swayed. Its cloaks flared, revealing a long, ivory bow. Before Ben knew what was happening, the creature drew an arrow, nocked it, and loosed it into the sky, as if aiming for the heavens themselves. The arrow blazed white like a shooting star, then gravity took hold and it came down.

"Begone!"

Shrike swung his spear up, blasting the arrow into shards of ice. But the shot had only been a warning. Preternaturally fast, the blue spirit charged across the field, a ghastly blur of blue and white. Shrike's companions screamed, rallying. The one with the azure skin raced forward, spear bared. Before they could meet their enemy halfway in the field, another arrow pierced their heart. They burst into stardust and ash, leaving neither bones nor flesh behind. Ben stared where the creature had been, biting back his surprise until he tasted blood. Beside him, Murphy was not so successful in stifling his reaction, letting out a startled moan low in his throat.

The blue spirit's bow disappeared and he drew a short blade. In moments he closed in on them, threatening to shatter the safe-seeming globe of golden light surrounding the fire. But just as he lunged, Shrike swooped between them. Knife met blackened spear, loosing a spray of black and gold starlight.

"We have to get Mock out of here!"

The voice was Murphy's. Ben still had hold of the boy's slender wrist, the one thing that made any sense. He nodded. It was the only response he could give.

They scrambled to Mock, through the air that was a wreck with flakes of ice and sparks as the cold knife came down against Shrike's spear again and again. He was so close Ben could see that the blue spirit—like Shrike—had a face. But it was shifting and undefined, like a dream on the brink of being forgotten, sometimes with a nose and a thin-lipped, grim mouth, and sometimes with no features at all aside from his sapphire eyes.

Shrike beat back the wintry ghost with his spear, deftly tossing the icy blade to the side time after time. The way he both moved defied gravity, as if he were flying without wings. Whenever his spear prong touched the blue spirit's body, its blue haziness wavered, as if it might blow apart at any moment.

Ben and Murphy reached Mock and grabbed her. It was less thought-out this time; Ben grabbed whatever limbs he could find, and then they pulled. They tugged and yanked, but whatever had tied the unconscious girl to the earth before was strong and fast as ever.

"I don't get it!" Murphy struck the earth with his fists. "It makes no sense! None of this makes any sense! Damn it!"

The blue spirit finally struck Shrike, casting him down with a bloody wound, though he didn't disintegrate like his fellow. A flurry of snow blew up as another of Shrike's companions came to rescue their master and died in a powder of chalk. In their wake, the blue spirit's moonlight gaze shifted, toward the sound of Murphy's cursing, and suddenly Ben felt the numbing chill of his eyes upon them.

No, not *them*, he realized. As the spirit's face came into focus, the focus of his gaze became clear.

"*Oathbreaker*," he said to Murphy.

All the voices in the clearing were silenced: Shrike and his remaining companion, Murphy's cursing. Even Ben's heart quieted its pounding in his ears.

Shrike rose, leaning on his spear and holding his guts in with his other hand. He sprayed blood when he shouted, "Look out! He comes for you!"

The spirit's stillness broke and he moved as if he were plummeting toward them, betraying the laws of the earth. When Shrike was unable to conquer his injury enough to protect them, he cried out and his third and last companion leapt . . . and died on the spirit's short blade, melting into a splash of water and an echoing howl.

Ben froze, petrified, though Murphy kept tugging at Mock's immovable body. All he could do was fixate on the silver blade.

Then Shrike jerked his hand toward the fire and it erupted, engulfing the blue spirit and spewing embers and flames in every direction, catching on the damp grass and their traveling packs. Ben felt a wash of heat. The earth tilted under his feet, the dirt glistening with morsels of gold. He heard a song-like bird's cry, felt the dusty touch of gray and white–striped feathers on his cheek.

Then, nothing.

CHAPTER X

JESSE

Jesse dreamed of an open plain. The wind pushed its fingers through his hair, and the rhythm of the beast running beneath him beat in time with his heart. Faster and faster, heavy and shuddering, driving his soul deeper into the earth. He was with Foley, or it seemed like he was. Even though he couldn't see the other boy, he could hear him, smell him—he was there, and not there.

They were escaping, the two of them. Racing through the twilight. Running. Behind them, Jesse heard the screaming of monsters, the cold winter, and the hunting calls of birds. He tasted blood on his tongue—Foley's. Jesse couldn't tell where he'd been wounded. Only that he was suffering.

Jesse woke with his—no, her ears ringing.

She still ached in her back, her thighs—all over, really —from riding in the saddle as hard and as long as they had. The sky was clear and blue, Morgan and Dusky grazing a ways off. Foley and Mock were nowhere to be seen.

Then she remembered. The fire. Mock. Shrike and his strange companions. The gold, the blue spirit, and . . .

The campsite was a mess. A fine layer of soot and ash caked the earth, but it was wet and heavy with dew. Everything was cold and damp and miserable. Worse yet was the sight of their incinerated packs and the charred remains of their supplies. Jesse was glad that they'd left the mochilas on the horses' saddles, or else they would've been burned up, too.

She felt something hard in the dirt. A single gold pellet was half buried there. She picked it up, remembering the look in Shrike's eyes when he'd reached out to press his finger into her forehead.

She rubbed her face with her sleeve and pocketed the gold. At least she could think of it as being compensated for all the trouble.

"Morning."

Foley trudged in from behind, carrying a bundle of twigs under one arm and a buffalo chip in the other.

"Don't know what you're planning to do with that," Jesse said. "Our matches all burned up."

Foley swore, soft and slow. He dropped the useless kindling in a pile and pinched the bridge of his nose.

"Where's Mock?" Jesse asked.

"Sent her to get water. Hoping she's got the wits not to bring back mosquito sludge."

Jesse picked up two sticks. Ware's guide didn't say anything about starting fires aside from the suggestion to use buffalo chips, but she'd done it with some sticks and a shoestring once. They had time, so she might as well try.

While they waited for Mock and Jesse spun one stick against the other, they didn't speak a word about what they'd seen. Maybe it didn't matter. Jesse didn't even know what it was they'd seen, anyway. After the shadow had erupted in front of the blue spirit's sword, everything was a blur. She didn't remember falling unconscious. She didn't remember anything clearly. Every time she tried to bring the terrifying, antlered shadow monsters to mind, trying to inspect them and identify any possible explanation, all her mind wanted to do was run. Be empty, reject the reality of what she had seen. She already had too much to do without fitting in this complication. She already had too much to feel, and her heart did not want to make room for monsters.

Then there was the dream she'd had. Jesse's cheeks grew hot. Nonsensical and unnatural, those dreams were —no, *unnatural* didn't even begin to describe them. Luckily they were safe in her mind where no one else could ever see them. See *him*. The secret person she'd been, if just for a moment.

One of the sticks snapped in Jesse's hands and she sighed.

"It was all a dream," she said. "We dreamt it, didn't we?"

Ever the killjoy, Foley said, "We didn't."

The sound of footsteps came moments before a little figure mounted the hill. It was Mock, all three of their water sacks strapped round her willowy torso. They jostled and swung with weight, giving the girl a bizarre, unbalanced gait. In the full daylight, Jesse could see that Mock's skin was indeed an earthy gray color. Not tan or brown or any other human shade, but a warm gray. Like the strange, spear-wielding Shrike.

"Look at you, toiling along with the rest of us peasants," Jesse chuckled.

"I know. It is shameful."

Even so, Mock bounced with unchecked pride, like a child praised for washing her dishes for the first time. She sat by the pile of wet wood and untangled herself from the flasks.

"So! What shall we eat for breakfast? Where's the fire?"

Jesse glanced at the charred remains of their packs.

"There won't be a fire, and no breakfast, neither, unless you want grass or tree bark," she said.

"What!" exclaimed Mock. Then again, with even more offense: "What!"

"See for yourself. All our supplies burned up."

Mock pounced on the bags and tore them open like a bear clawing for honey. Flakes of black and gray fabric shredded off in her fingers until she leaned back and let out a long, plaintive wail.

"But I'm so *hungry!*"

"We'd have food if it weren't for those strange fellows come out of the fire last night." Jesse leaned back on her heels and arched a brow at the girl. "You wouldn't happen to know anything about that, now, would you?"

At first Mock stiffened, every finger going straight. Foley, who'd been trying to wipe the remains of the buffalo dung from his hands and sleeve, paused to listen.

Mock folded her hands primly below her chin, sniffling away her hungry tears. "I don't know a thing about it, last night or anything. I was asleep."

Jesse couldn't tell whether the statement was spiteful or matter-of-fact, whether Mock knew she'd been drugged. Still, unconscious or not, it was obvious the little girl was wise to something. Jesse needed to figure out what, and how to get the information out of her.

"Either way, we won't be having breakfast until we make it to a station with provisions," she said. "So we ought to get cleaned up and back in the saddle."

"Without breakfast!" Mock cried again, so high-pitched Jesse thought she might throw a tantrum right there.

"There's *nothing* out here!" she shouted, gesturing beyond their ruined campsite.

Mock's eyes flashed with a sudden anger, as if she wanted to bite off Jesse's hand.

"There is *everything* out here," she said quietly. Then she turned her nose up and away. "Have it your way. Where is your next settler's station?"

The way she said *settler* made it sound like a bad thing, but Jesse ignored it. "If we were on the Overland proper, the next place to get supplies would be Fort Kearny, halfway between St. Joe's and Fort Laramie. But we hardly rode at all last night before you got tired and decided to go to sleep. Even if we ride hard, we won't make it to Kearny for another day, if we're lucky."

It was tough talk, but Jesse felt better when Mock looked down. This was the girl's fault, after all. Or at least, Jesse tried to tell herself it was. It had to be someone's.

Foley doffed his hat and ran his hand over his head, then sighed. "Well, we ought to get ready and moving, then."

He whistled Dusky over and lifted her saddle. The blanket beneath was grimy, and Jesse knew Morgan's would be the same. If they were going to do another hard day's ride on just the two horses, they ought to tend them properly.

"Here, give me the saddle blankets. I'll go rinse them in the stream," she said. She hoped she might also get some privacy to relieve her bladder.

Mock perked up. "I'll go with you! Maybe you'll catch me a fish to eat."

Jesse tried not to show her annoyance and nodded instead. Foley took Morgan's saddle off and Jesse folded both the saddle blankets in her arms, following Mock away from the camp. A nipping in the back of Jesse's mind asked what she'd do if Foley took off without her or, even worse, took both the horses and stranded her. Like he'd tried to do before.

He wouldn't do that. Not after what we've been through . . . right?

Jesse tried to agree with the voice in her head. The one that sounded like a boy and believed in Ben Foley. The one that didn't ask what Jesse would do if their positions were reversed. If Jesse had the chance to leave Foley behind.

"Say, Jesse Murphy. Would you say you'd do anything to reach California?"

Jesse glanced at the girl. Carson City was where Edward Murphy had gone, and that was miles before California, but Mock didn't need to know that. Both were so far away they might as well be the same until it mattered.

"Yes," she said.

"What about him?" Mock nodded back over her shoulder at Foley.

Jesse chewed on her cheek. "Ask him yourself."

The stream wasn't far. Jesse got to work shaking out the blankets and then scrubbing the horse sweat and dirt out with a river stone. Mock sat nearby, swinging her bare feet in the shallow water so her naked toes flicked droplets everywhere.

"If it came down to one of you to make it, but the other couldn't, or wouldn't, who do you think it would be?" Mock asked.

Jesse saw Alice. The baby. Their house, their land. She thought of their trial to win this ill-forsaken job. Yesterday morning she would've said her, without a doubt. But now that she was learning more about Foley, she wasn't sure.

Maybe that didn't matter. To this conversation, anyway.

"Me," she said.

Mock stretched out on her side in the grass, temple resting against the earth. Like a cat lounging in the sun. She watched Jesse draw the blankets from the stream and twist the water out of the thick things best she could. It was tough work with her bare hands.

"Never saw a boy so good at laundry."

Mock smiled when Jesse glared at her.

"My ma died, and my sister's no good at it," she said. She felt bad using those things as an excuse, but it wasn't harming anyone, and it would be worse if Mock and Foley found out her secret.

"I see! Women are quite unreliable, aren't they?"

Jesse didn't know how a boy would answer that question, so she just nodded.

They went back to camp and re-dressed the horses. Jesse got out the tonic and treated Morgan, who was eager as ever for his magic droplets. Only a day ago, if someone had told her he would ride at a gallop for a hundred twenty miles, she would've told them they were dreaming. Yet even after so little time, the strange tonic and its effects were already rolled into the rest of it all, natural as the sun rising and setting and the filling moon replacing it.

"Ready?" she asked. "Before the day gets away from us."

"I am," said Foley. He regarded Dusky's saddle for only an instant before getting up in it. "A day to Fort Kearny, you said?"

"I did. Mock, you ready to go?" Jesse called.

Mock was standing in the dirt and ash in the middle of their burnt camp, amid the evidence of what had happened the previous night. Charred proof of monsters with bows and arrows, spears and glowing eyes. Jesse wanted nothing more than to leave it all behind.

"No! Just one more thing!"

Mock took a running kick at the pile of soggy kindling. Her little foot smashed into it—*THOCK!*—and wet logs went flying. Then she threw her hands in the air and cheered.

The land was stripes of tan and white, green and red, as they rode west. The plains could not make up their mind, and long stretches of flat, grass-covered field were suddenly broken by bluffs that erupted into crooked, hunched mountains casting broad pools of blue shadow. Far, far away, like a fence between the earth and sky, was a line of blue mountains.

Closer ahead, and a few miles south of their trail, a striking rock formation protruded from the orange and green, jabbing up like a thorn into the sky. From so far away, Jesse couldn't tell how big it was, but its shape brought to mind a few of the landmark descriptions in Ware's guide—Court House Rock, Chimney Rock, Scott's Bluffs. But those waypoints were much further along the journey, at least two days out, if not more. They hadn't even made their first crossing of the Platte yet.

Jesse watched the narrow pillar as they passed it. She had expected such formations to be rare out here, and thus easy to recognize. It was difficult to imagine another rock that so closely matched Ware's description: "a tall column-like projection near its centre resembling a chimney." But perhaps the real Chimney Rock would be so much taller, so much more column- and chimney-like— so much more obvious and grand—that she would laugh at herself for thinking this was anything like it.

After riding most of the day, they let the horses take their time mounting a hill, but when they reached the top, Jesse had to stop to take it in.

A wide, curving river ran through the hills, reflecting the sky like a line of paint. In the crook of its elbow was an orderly collection of buildings and houses, arranged round a rectangular main parade on which a small company of soldiers ran drills in two straight lines. Scattered round the fort's perimeter, across the river in the dry grass and clusters of prickly pear cactus, were white and tan tipis. People gathered there, too—the Native people who came to trade and sell to the foreigners coming through.

And come through they did. An endless line of settlers carved their trail toward California. They entered from the north and east and left to the west, scarring the soft earth with the ruts of hundreds of creaking wagon wheels. It was late in the season, so the lines were thin, but even from afar, Jesse could hear the bellowing of the oxen.

"I thought you said Fort Kearny was a day out," Foley said.

Jesse didn't answer right away, unable to stop staring. All the different parts of the scene made sense: the fort, the slow-moving river, the blue mountains behind it all. She could understand those things and make sense of them one at a time, but seeing them all together had made it difficult for her to speak.

"That's not Fort Kearny," she managed finally, though she still couldn't find the words to say what it was, even though she knew. Just like she'd known Chimney Rock when she'd seen it, but hadn't been able to say its name, even to herself, because . . . "This is impossible."

"What do you mean?" Foley asked.

The miles and hours stacked up in Jesse's head as she tried to make the math work. How far they'd ridden, and how fast, taking into account all the lollygagging they'd done thanks to Mock. The distance from St. Joe's to Fort Laramie might take an Express rider three or four days, twelve hours in the saddle every day. By wagon, with a family and livestock, it could take months.

"Cottington was just inside the Nebraska Territory

border. Even at the good pace we've kept since this morning, we shouldn't be able to see the Laramie Mountains already." *Yet they'd been staring at them all day.* "And if those are the Laramies, then the fort is . . ."

It really didn't matter how she added it up, or how fast the horses had run. The truth was right in front of them.

"*Fort* Laramie?" Foley asked.

Anyone fixing to head west should know of the place. The two of them gazed down at the white buildings, the soldiers, the Natives, and the travelers of the California Road. Foley's voice seemed to stick in his throat, and Jesse's felt the same.

"But isn't that even further west than Fort Kearny?" he choked out at last.

"It's at least six days' travel from St. Joe's," she agreed. "And somehow we've reached it after only two."

It felt stupid, to sit there on their standstill horses, unwilling to believe what was plain to see in front of them. They should be charging ahead to the next station, but Jesse could only stare at the fort and try to tell herself it wasn't what it obviously was.

"Well . . . at the very least, we could restock our supplies."

Foley's practical suggestion broke her out of her daze. He was right. If it really was Fort Laramie down there, that meant a sutler's store. Food, yes, but more importantly, emergency supplies—bandages and the like—and matches. After seeing how meagerly stocked the

Nightland stations were, Jesse was loath to continue without any of it. Only one night of getting lost in the unforgiving cold could mean the end of them.

Even as she considered it, a rider came racing down the road on his pony, galloping alongside the pioneers and into the fort. A tan mochila fluttered beneath his thighs—filled with mail. Jesse frowned. They had sworn an oath not to disclose their assignment to other Express riders. How would they be able to hide their ward if another rider approached them? Did it count if the other rider saw what—or rather, who—they were transporting, even if they said nothing?

"Wretched place."

Mock hadn't said anything about the fort or their arrival until that moment, and now she crossed her arms and legs and pressed herself back against Jesse as if that would keep them from moving. Then again, Jesse remembered how immoveable she'd been the previous night—or had that been a dream? She didn't want to think about it.

"What?" Jesse asked.

"That fort is a desecration. A foothold stolen from the land so greedy giants can dig their hands into the sacred soil."

"Sacred lands!" Jesse rolled her eyes. "This isn't Zion. Without Fort Laramie, settlers would have nowhere to resupply."

"You are stupid," Mock snapped. Jesse hadn't yet seen her so serious, her tongue so sharp. "The Black Hills were here long before the Mormons. If you must go, you must go, but I shan't step foot inside those walls."

"Well, all our rations burned to a crisp. So if you want to eat on the remainder of our trip to California, we'll have to."

"I shan't! I shan't, I shan't, I shan't—"

Jesse clamped a hand over Mock's mouth before she started screaming. She yelped when the girl's sharp teeth chomped down on her fingers.

"Why you—!"

"*I shan't!*"

"Then I'll go," Foley said. "If she doesn't want to go inside, don't make her. You two go round to the west gate as soon as you stop bickering. I'll stop at the sutler's and meet you there, and we'll be off."

Jesse held her hand where Mock's teeth marks were still pressed into her skin. Words tumbled out, awkward and worried. "That's a fort full of soldiers. What if someone recognizes you?"

"Life can't wait for what-ifs. Let's just get it over with."

Foley gave her a half smile. She'd seen it before when they'd gone into the saloon. But this time she saw that his eyes didn't shine, and the corners of his mouth were flat. It was a mask of confidence. Well practiced, flawless. Alert and brave.

"Foley . . ."

"If you want to learn something, learn this, Jesse Murphy: if you want something done, you have to do it."

Before she could finish, he tapped his heels against Dusky's sides and led the way down the hill, toward the river of westward settlers.

CHAPTER XI

BEN

Ben left Dusky with Murphy and Mock outside the fort.

Inside the perimeter, the place stank of sweat and bodies, human and livestock together. The slow movement of the Overland journeyers was like the Platte itself. Gradual, endless, slow, inevitable. Even so late into autumn, when the incoming winter could make the journey deadly. Ben pulled his hat down, counted broken wagon wheels, suffering oxen, enslaved people, and crying babies. Settlers wracked with maladies, usually the terrible cough of the consumption. Fresh horses being sold and lame ones being put out of their misery. The trail was brutal, and the evidence was on every face Ben passed. It was as if the land itself were trying to fight the migration, and Ben wasn't sure which side was winning.

Soldiers marched along the parade and lingered at every corner, impossible to avoid. Ben wondered if the wanted poster had gotten this far west yet. If it had, how many of these rifle-slinging, uniformed white men had seen it? Maybe it had been a mistake to split up, leaving

Mock with Murphy. If Murphy wanted to leave him behind, he couldn't have asked for a more perfect opportunity than to strand him in the middle of the continent, surrounded by armed soldiers. Ben felt the slithering in his stomach come alive with a vengeance. It had been asleep, and now its tail rattled in warning.

The sutler's store was modest, a sturdy structure flanked by two less permanent trading-post shops selling beaver and other pelts, tanned leathers, and Indian-made goods. It was stone on the outside with a nice long, peaked roof. Ben gathered himself up. All he had to do was get in the store and get out as quickly as possible. Some supplies purchased with the ample gold he'd already been paid, and then he could be gone from this dangerous place.

He stopped in front of the dirty window glass to check that he'd put on his father's face and went inside.

It was dim and cramped and smelled of sweat and tobacco and manure tracked in on boots. Seemed once the stink came in, it never left. Ben waited his turn at the counter.

"Yes, *hazel eyes*, it said. Can you imagine that?"

Ben's ears burned as the words touched them, whispered from a white woman to her friend, both huddling in line ahead of him. The hems of their skirts were stained with mud, and they wrung their hands though the air was hardly chilly.

"I didn't even know they could have light-colored eyes," said the second woman. "It must be strangely beautiful. I should like to see something like it."

The first woman sniffed. "I, for one, wouldn't want to get close enough. I'm glad at least here in the fort we have so many soldiers for our protection."

Ben's heart hammered, the tangled, twisting shape roiling inside him. Wanting him to run, or to say something. Wanting him to clear his throat so they looked at him, saw his hazel eyes, and ran for the protection of the armed men waiting outside. But they probably wouldn't. He would be as invisible then as he was to them now.

"I can see you have it right there!"

All the other idle conversation ceased at the loud outburst from the man at the front of the line. He wore a pale blue coat and carried a hat under his elbow. The clerk didn't even look to where the man was pointing, at a row of amber bottles.

"I don't like the look of your money," the clerk said.

"My gold's as good as theirs," the man cried, turning and gesturing to the two women behind him. They gasped and stepped back, as if he had threatened them. "I earned this. As I earned my freedom. Please, sir. My wife has the consumption. Just let me buy the calomel!"

The clerk drew himself up, moving his hand to a practiced spot below the counter. "I think you'd best take your leave, *sir*."

Quiet crept over the tiny store like ice on a barely frozen lake. Then the man took the other items he had purchased and shouldered his way out, boots raising clouds of dust from the floorboards as he left.

Ben kept to himself while the women made their order and took away their goods. When it was his turn, he asked for bread, canned beans, and matches. As when he had waited on the women, the clerk barely looked back from the shelves as he filled the order.

Taking care not to flash it widely, Ben took a gold coin from his pocket. It didn't even feel real. Even a piece so small could be bright enough to attract the attention of everyone in the fort, if the light hit it right. His heart thumped as he ran his thumb along the flattened edge. The creature in his gut coiled, ready to snap.

"One more thing," he told the clerk. "Calomel, please. If you have it."

The clerk placed the amber vial on the counter. The same bottle the freedman had requested, delivered without a second glance. That was the kind of place this was, Ben thought. No surprises there.

No sooner had the bottle touched the wood than Ben palmed it, gathered his other purchases, and left, hoping the coin he'd left on the counter would distract the clerk long enough that he might never be able to identify the man who'd left it.

Back in the streets, he kept his pace quick. His heart hammered as if he'd stolen something, though he'd vastly overpaid. He clenched the vial of medicine and searched the yard, the walkways, in between the buildings. When he saw the dusty blue coat, he jogged over as quickly as he dared.

"Sir," he called. "Sir, excuse me. You dropped something."

The man turned with a defensive but well-practiced speed that Ben recognized—fast enough to protect himself from imminent danger but careful not to seem that way. Ben held out his hand in peace, the amber bottle tucked in his thumb. When the man saw it, his expression changed from fear to distaste.

"I don't need your charity," he said. But all the same, his eyes were fixed to the bottle. He needed it, and Ben wanted him to take it. But they were both afraid in this place. Why did even his own acts seem to belong to the armed men who might try to stop him?

"It's not . . ." Ben began. He lowered his hand and offered it, the whole while worried someone might see them. But even if someone saw them, then what? What was wrong with giving another man medicine? And yet the creature in him warned him that was enough. Enough that it could get them hurt. He licked his lips and spoke to the man in the way that Penny spoke to him. In the way he and Theodore had spoken to one another.

"Ain't no charity, sir," he whispered. "It's what my momma would've had me do."

The man peered closer at him, like he'd seen something but couldn't tell if he was imagining it. Then he took the bottle and put it in his pocket.

"Thank you," he said. "And thank you to your momma, too."

Ben nodded, and they parted ways without another word.

The walk to the gate where he had planned to meet Murphy seemed miles and miles, though the whole of the fort probably didn't occupy much more than twenty acres. *Occupy* was certainly the right word, Ben thought as he passed within sight of the soldiers lining up on the parade.

He stepped back between two buildings as the drums began and the white men marched, shouldering their rifles and stomping across the lawn in their heavy boots. Horns and a pipe joined the drum, and the soldiers arranged and rearranged themselves for no apparent reason other than the time of day.

"Explain."

The word landed different with the nose of a gun punctuating it, jabbed into Ben's kidney from behind. Ben wished for everything that he'd left when he'd had the chance.

"Explain what, Randall?" he whispered.

Hidden in the shadow between two of the fort's structures, with the parade ongoing, no one could see or hear Randall Foley as he came round, the gun never leaving Ben's torso. His movements came stilted, with a limp Ben hadn't seen before, when they'd run from him. He'd been on horseback then.

"What's wrong with your feet?" Ben asked.

"Last night we'd just entered Nebraska. Now we're in Fort Laramie," Randall snapped, spraying spittle. Some of the droplets caught on his mustache and stayed there, thick and beady. "I tracked you all night, but there's no way! What devilry is this?"

A mix of emotions filled Ben's chest. A bit of pride that he had come to terms with their supernatural circumstances, at least enough that he was not still reeling as Randall was. A strange unpinching of relief that someone besides Murphy and Mock was witnessing what had happened to them. A pang of regret when he realized he'd left his gun back in Dusky's mochila.

"Just that, I suppose," Ben said. "Devilry. And now I'm afraid you're in hell."

"Give me your papers."

Ben willed himself not to reach for the folded papers in his breast pocket. He didn't want Randall to know where they were. His heart raced, beating with the rattling in his core. The soldiers on the parade had captured everyone else's attention. Out in the sun, where they had no reason to look back into the shadows. All Randall had to do was pull the trigger, bury one bullet in Ben's gut, and that would be the end of him.

"I know you have them. I know you stole them from pa's will. So now you're going to give them to me and I'm going to destroy them, and then I'm dragging you back to Louisville off my saddle. Pray you die off't because worse will be waiting for you when we get home."

Usually, a threat about Penny would follow. Ben waited for it. He feared pain and he feared death, but he was willing to face those things to a point—so long as they were weapons only aimed at him.

But that threat never came. Neither did a bullet. Randall shoved with the gun until Ben's back was against the stone of the building behind him. They were so close now, Ben saw a red creeping up Randall's neck. At first he thought it was a flush of rage, but as he looked closer he saw blisters and pus. It was a burn, and a recent one at that. More of it spread across Randall's hand on the same side.

"What happened to you?" Ben asked.

"You want to know?" Randall hissed. Near panted. "You want to know what's coming to you? That she-devil set the house on fire. Stole my shoes. When I ran to put the fire out and chase her down, she'd crushed those damned blue bottles all in the mud and grass. I barely got out alive!"

Randall's voice was drowned out by a swelling in Ben's skull. A heady, light feeling. Distantly familiar, like the shape of a cloud on a windy day.

"She ran," he whispered. He didn't even care if Randall heard him.

"Why would she do that?" Randall asked, shaking the gun. He leaned in even closer, nearly pressing his forehead against Ben's. Like they'd done when they were children, before they'd known anything. When they'd just been brothers. His breath was rancid in Ben's nostrils, growing hotter and hotter. "Our father built that house!

That was her house, too! Why would she burn it down? *Why would she do that?"*

Ben closed his eyes, shutting Randall out. Saw Penny gathering kindling and matches. Quietly crushing glass from the bottle-tree in a flour sack at night. Glass that trapped evil, she'd always told him. He imagined the swirling of the smoke as his father's house billowed into flame in a ring of glittering blue shards.

For how long had she prepared? If he'd looked closer in the shack they shared, in the shadow of his father's house, would he have found evidence of her plan long before the funeral?

Don't you worry about me.

When she'd sent him away, she'd known. Ben smiled.

"She shouldn't have run," Randall said. He stepped back, holding Ben at arm's length again, his desperation simmering down after boiling over. "After what she's done, she'll have a target on her back until the end of her days. I sent the sheriff after her. A couple slave catchers, too. The whole of Louisville is looking for her. And I didn't ask for her alive. She'll get what she deserves. Now you give me those papers, Ben."

The vision of Penny's escape in the night was like a panacea, a cure to all the heavy weight in Ben's limbs. He wondered if she'd gone to the others across the cornfield, if they'd sent that plantation up in flames, too. The thought soothed the slithering fear in his core, though the shape of it did not go away completely. The road his mother walked now, by moonlight in between roads and fields, was a long and difficult one. But she walked it free.

"The papers," Randall said again. He cocked the hammer.

Without his papers, Ben would have no proof of his freedom—the only inheritance granted from his father, aside from his face, his skin, his eyes. And the bruises and scars, though they were hidden. Ben took the folded sheets out from his breast pocket. They seemed so fragile, so insubstantial. And yet they were everything, weren't they? His only protection.

Randall lunged at them like a starving dog, but Ben held them away.

"Give them to me," Randall said. "Or I'll shoot. And don't you even think about running—I'll call runaway and you'll have twenty soldiers' rifles down your back in an instant. They won't think twice if I tell them what you really are."

"And what am I, really?" Ben asked. He felt fire, strength, crackling in his soul. The flames of the house burning, the roof and boards falling away until only its skeleton was left, laid bare.

"Property," Randall growled. "My. *Property.*"

Ben turned his head so the last syllable of spittle hit his cheek. He raised his fist where he clenched the document that detailed his freedom. Or rather, his exception. For without it, the default law—both written and unwritten—would apply, so long as there was someone to apply it. He imagined his greatest fear: being caught. Would the papers mean anything to a slave catcher? Would the words on the flimsy pieces of paper protect him from being sold back into slavery?

Cast in that light, Ben realized, the papers were just another appendage of the same ugly beast.

"I suppose you'll chase me to the ends of the earth for these," he said.

"Yes," Randall said, reaching out.

Ben took the corners in his other hand and pulled, tearing the sheets in half. The first rip was the hardest, knowing what he was destroying. Knowing what he was throwing away.

He folded and tore again. And again, and again, feeling the tiny soft edges brush like feathers against his palms and wrists as they fell to the mud at his boots. Randall stared, uncomprehending at first of what had happened. A low moan came out of his throat, the grim noise of a temper that had never been tamed. The uncontrollable wrath of someone who always got what he wanted. It boiled up from his gut and he raised his gun.

But when he fired, the bullet struck stone. Ben was already gone, running for his life.

CHAPTER XII

JESSE

"I'm not sorry I bit you. You deserved it."

Jesse ignored Mock. They waited a short distance outside the western gate posts along the stone wall, watching the overland journeyers leave in an endless pattern of calico and leather. She had picked a spot close enough that Ben could find them while still far enough away, she hoped, that no one would take note of the strange little girl in Morgan's saddle.

"Where is that boy?" she muttered.

"We could just leave him," Mock suggested in a singsong voice. When Jesse snorted, she broke into a smile. "Playing fun, of course. Playing fun!"

Hoping Foley would join them soon, Jesse went into her vest for Morgan's cooling tonic, thankful the little vial had been with her when the rest of their things had gone up in flames. Morgan stretched his neck, lips reaching and nostrils flaring eagerly.

"Well! Now here I was thinking folks was imagining things when they said they saw another Pony rider come in."

Jesse finished administering the drops and shoved the vial in her pocket as a man approached. He was dressed in a tan leather jacket and dusty black riding boots. Jesse didn't recognize him, but she did recognize the red neckerchief round his collar. He seemed too tall and weighty to be an Express rider, and he smelled like sweat and a little liquor.

"What's your name, kid?"

"My name?" Jesse echoed, trying to buy time to think. What harm could her name do? "Murphy. Jesse Murphy. And you are . . . ?"

"*I'm* an Express rider," he spat. As he got closer she could see his name was embroidered on his coat pocket: *JENNINGS*.

"So am I. So what's the problem?"

There was a thin line between close enough to have a civil conversation and *too* close, and Jennings crossed it with one big, lanky stride. Jesse didn't want to give ground, but she stepped back, putting herself between him and Morgan. The closer he was, the more she had to crane her neck. She hated not looking a man in the eye.

Mock wriggled and fidgeted in the saddle but kept quiet. Jesse hoped she'd stay that way; this was not a time to have to deal with the girl running her mouth.

Jennings leaned close and sneered. "The problem is I got called to run this route because old Hod Russell said there was no riders to run it. Now here I am when I meant to be trapping and I hear tell of two fresh riders come in from the east. So what is it, no riders or two?"

"You a relief rider or something?" Jesse asked. "Shouldn't you just be glad for some employment?"

Jennings opened his mouth to retort but stopped to look Jesse up and down. "Now hold on. I been riding Deer Creek to Fort Laramie for months and I don't think I never saw your face before. And who's this on your old Morgan horse? A friendly companion?"

"Go away!" said Mock.

Jesse took Morgan's reins. She became painfully aware of the gold she had stowed in her mochila, and how easy it would be for Jennings to steal it once he wised up to its existence. *This* was a man Alexander Majors had hired?

"If you'll excuse me, I got a route to run," she said.

Jennings stayed where he was, putting his hands on his belt and spitting onto the ground. It was the color of black mud. "What you say your name is again? Murphy? Ain't you a queer little thing. What station you ride out of—Julesburg?"

"Yes, Julesburg," Jesse agreed immediately, hoping to end the interrogation. But Jennings let out a laugh that turned mean at the end. He stepped in, nearly pinning her against Morgan's side.

"There *are* no Pony riders who do Julesburg to Fort Laramie," he said. "And certainly not with *females* accompanying them. Now tell me who you really are and why you're impersonating a Pony rider, or I'll have you arrested and turned in to Alexander Majors himself."

Jesse felt as if she were clutching a hot coal in her fist, she so badly wanted to punch him. But he was so big and dense she doubted it would do anything.

"You're welcome to notify Mr. Majors about me, but I've got an important delivery to make, so I'll be running ahead. I'm sure he'll be glad to know I'm making my route on time when your news reaches him."

Jesse turned to get up in the saddle, but Jennings snagged the back of her shirt, pulled her down, and spun her so she was facing him again.

"Don't you turn away from me, little brat!" he growled.

"Let go!"

He grabbed the front of her shirt with his big bear paws, and the binding undershirt she'd sewn tore at the seams. It was only an inch of thread ripping, but it felt like her own skin splitting.

Jennings' eyes widened when he heard the noise. Before Jesse could stop him, he yanked the buttons of her shirt open, baring the undershirt and gasping.

"You're a—"

The last time a man had grabbed her and moved her against her will, it had been when John Quinn decided he wanted to dance with her at his cousin's wedding. He'd pulled her up and against him before she could say no. Round and round the fire he'd taken her, grinding his hips against her. Worse, when she'd finally gotten away, he'd found her behind the shop while she tried to snitch a sip from her flask. Put his drunken hands round her waist and held her while she pushed and pushed him away. He'd kissed her, drunk and sloppy and disgusting, rubbing the soggy lump in his trousers against her until she'd finally pushed him back enough to run, humiliated and enraged.

When she'd gotten home, all Alice could say was that it was mean, what she'd done to poor Johnny. That all he wanted was her affection. Couldn't Jesse just be *normal* once in a while? Pay attention to the men who came calling so that maybe she might not die a spinster?

Never again.

"Don't touch me," she growled. Her anger sparked at him like a match near a fuse, but she didn't care. She'd rather lose all her teeth than be moved by a man's hands again.

Jennings saw her fists and raised his own.

"You gonna fight me?" He sneered in disgust. "Wait 'til Majors finds out. A female dressed up like a man! What are you, some kind of freak?"

"Jesse—"

"Stay out of this, Mock."

"But—"

Jennings threw the first punch, and it hit Jesse in the cheek. She saw stars, a flash of light, red and black. Then pain, but she hadn't gone down. She'd never been hit before and didn't know what to expect. But now she had, and she was still on her feet. The pain didn't matter.

He couldn't move her.

Jesse made a fist and struck back. This, she had practiced—against pillows and her bedroom wall, sometimes
trees that left her knuckles bloody. Hundreds of times,
every time the anger inside her boiled so hot it couldn't be
kept in anymore, had to come out whistling and scalding.
She hit Jennings in the chin, straight up from below. Her
fist smarted, but her spirit soared when he stumbled.

She slugged him again, square in the chest, hard as she
could. The wind coughed out of him like a pigeon flying
the coop.

"Jesse!"

Little hands pulled her back, tangling in her shirt and
vest. Mock wrapped her arms round Jesse's waist, and despite the girl's size, her embrace felt as though she were
ten times as big. Jesse couldn't move. Couldn't charge forward to strike at Jennings again and again. She felt as
though she were dragging a boulder with a rope, her
boots digging troughs in the dirt.

"Let me fight him!"

"No!" Mock cried. "I've been trying to tell you! He's
here!"

A shadow fell over them and Jesse stopped struggling.

Shrike's feathered cloak swept the dirt at his feet, the
spear in his hand casting a deadly silhouette on the red
and brown earth. In the evening light she realized he was
barefoot, like Mock, with long-nailed toes that reminded
her of a bird's the way they spread against the ground
when he walked.

"You!"

Jesse had tried to pretend he didn't exist. That he'd just been an apparition in the moonlight and the chaos of the smoke. A nightmare. Yet now, here he was in the light of day.

"Me," Shrike agreed.

"What the—who the hell are you?"

Shrike ignored Jennings' question as if it were a dog asking.

"Jesse Murphy," he said. "I will take care of this inconvenience for you. You would like that, wouldn't you, my friend?" He smiled over his wind-ruffled collar and Jesse shivered.

"Take care of who?" Jennings stammered. He reached into his vest, but he was not fast enough. Shrike moved like a trick of the light, coal-colored hand darting out like a snake. Jennings' revolver went flying, but Shrike's eyes never left Jesse's. Any moment, she expected someone from the long line of settlers to see what was happening, to scream and point and draw the attention of the soldiers, but no one did. It was as if they couldn't see what was happening along the stone wall outside the solemn fort.

Her heart hammered as she tried to measure every possible threat at hand, tried feverishly to set them in order from least to most dangerous.

"So? Shall I rectify this inconvenience for you?"

She wanted Jennings out of the way, but when Shrike said *rectify this inconvenience* all Jesse heard was *kill*.

Fighting was one thing, but killing was another. Shrike drew back his spear and adjusted his footing. It was all happening so fast—he hadn't given her enough time to answer!

"Wait!" she cried as he lunged. "Don't kill him!"

The spear stopped inches from Jennings' heaving chest. Jesse coughed out the rest of the breath she'd been holding.

"It would be the most lasting solution," Shrike said. He smiled again, but it was touched with bloodlust. Jesse took in his spear, just a plain sharpened stick. It would be certain death to be impaled upon it, but a slow one, and painful. Not like the mercy of a bullet. Who was this man, and where had he come from that he was so ready to murder on her behalf?

"It would—it would get me in trouble!" Jesse exclaimed. Part of her cringed; would that seem weak to Jennings, not being willing to kill him? Would he do the same in her position, or was it part of a man's code to finish what he started, even if it meant death? Either way, Jennings wasn't complaining.

Shrike retracted his spear and the lump in Jennings' throat bobbed up and down in an angry, nervous gulp.

"I certainly wouldn't want you to be in trouble," Shrike said. He uttered the next part in Mock's direction, lowly and under his breath: "After all, we all have jobs to do. Places we're supposed to go. Whether we want to or not."

Mock clenched her hands and said nothing.

"Majors will hear about this," Jennings growled. "Majors and every stationmaster between St. Joe's and Sacramento. You and whatever bandit gang you're working with, posing as the Pony Express—"

Shrike turned so his spear was down and his empty hand was out, palm facing Jennings' forehead. A flash of glittering black exploded from it, striking Jennings in the face and knocking him to the ground, where he lay, unmoving except for the slow rise and fall of his chest. Bathed in the gold of the sunset, Shrike's hooked nose and slicked-back, feathery hair resembled the bird whose name he bore. A bird, Jesse reflected, known for driving the bodies of its prey on thorns.

He faced her and smiled. "When he wakes, he'll remember none of this. Consider it an example of what I am willing to do for you."

Jesse had no idea what she'd just seen. After everything else that had happened in the last two days, however, it didn't seem that out of place. There was a nagging, gnawing sensation in the back of her mind. It sounded like Alice's voice, singing to herself in the copse behind their house. Singing of Faerie and the little folk as she lit candles and left out berries and cream.

Jesse pushed the memory away. She didn't have time for it. She got back in Morgan's saddle, feeling the safety of the hard, polished leather and the horse's agitated, restless shifting. He didn't know what he'd seen either. Like her, all he wanted was to run.

Shrike stood over Jennings' unconscious body, stamping the butt of his spear into the earth like a stick on a drum. Jesse wasn't sure if he would disappear again, as he had the previous night, or if he still had more to say to her. More to say and offer. For the time being, he seemed preoccupied with what he'd done to Jennings, like a cat admiring a kill.

Where the blazes was Foley?

"You'll be getting a real mouser there, Murphy," Mock said, leaning back into Jesse. The gesture had felt overly intimate before, but now when the girl reached up and tugged Jesse's collar, then touched her bruising cheek and eye, Jesse felt a swell of protectiveness. "Gonna look real tough when it shines up. Our friend Foley will be jealous his face is not half as tough as yours."

Gunfire rang from within the fort. Then shouts. Shrike turned his head to take in the loudening commotion.

"Do you hear that?" he asked. "I believe your partner is on his way here, and he's bringing a guest."

"A guest?"

Shrike cupped a hand round his ear, lifting his growing grin as if taking in the sounds of a magnificent orchestra. "Yes. A man who shares his blood. A brother. Come with a gun. I smell smoke and blood. I hear hatred and anger. They are coming this way."

Randall.

"He got here, too? How'd he get here so fast?"

"Same way we did, I reckon," Mock whispered. "Shall we go?"

"Not without Foley."

Jesse's mind sharpened, focusing. Foley, her partner. Foley, pursued by his half brother. Shrike, who was thirsting for violence and to help Jesse—though why, she still wasn't sure. But perhaps she could use his enthusiasm after all.

"Hey. You. You're willing to take care of things for me?" she asked. "People, I mean?"

Shrike turned, almost too quickly, flashing a smile full of devilish teeth. "Yes. I want what you want."

Jesse nodded. She felt a tiny wave of vertigo, as if she were standing on the precipice of hell. But she'd never get to Carson City to find her father if she didn't take action when it was needed. She didn't know how or why she'd earned this mysterious, unearthly man's deadly service, but perhaps she could put him to use.

But that would mean believing something was happening here that couldn't be explained. That Shrike had truly appeared out of thin air with his entourage of strange, inhuman creatures. That the ghostly blue monster made of ice and snow had truly seen them, had come upon them, and was out there somewhere waiting for them.

The wind whistled, and Jesse heard Alice's song again, clearer than ever.

CHAPTER XIII

BEN

Ben left Randall's hollering behind him, flinching as another gunshot echoed off the buildings. Shouts of surprise and dismay fell as a backdrop for his escape as groups of travelers parted before him and hid behind their wagons, many calling for the soldiers. In moments, Randall's tantrum would bring every armed soldier to the yard, and Ben could not recall a single occasion where strife between them had favored him and not his brother.

Tantrum. As if something so potentially fatal could be compared to a baby's wailing.

Ben ducked round a corner and paused for just a second to catch his breath, Randall's shouting muffled by the buildings and distance between them. Thanks to Penny's blue glass, it would be easy to outrun him—on foot, at least. Once they were on horses, it would be another matter. Ben let the fire in his belly launch him forward again, sprinting as quickly as he could without being seen down the alley between the back row of buildings and the stone wall that circled the encampment. Even if he could outrun Randall, the same might not be true of the soldiers, who would any moment be running down the lanes and crowding the gates. He had to get out.

He found the west exit. Waning sunlight fell on his shoulders as he broke into the open, dashing for it. He could see Murphy and Mock in Morgan's saddle, Dusky waiting. He was almost there.

"Foley, what the—?"

"There he is! Fire!"

Shots rang, this time from soldiers' cap rifles. Murphy's eyes went big as Ben flew into Dusky's saddle, kicking hard. Then they were galloping away from the gate, away from the fort, as soldiers fired after them.

"What the hell?" Murphy cried.

"Randall! I'll explain later—*go!*"

"Ben! I'll have your hide!"

Ben risked a glance over his shoulder. Randall was breaking through the line of soldiers, digging his spurs in. He waved his gun wildly and fired, the bullet flying off wide.

But the next few might not be so careless. Ben snapped Dusky's reins and they pulled ahead, as they had before, their invincible horses like locomotives. Randall's horse was a powerful beast, but the Nightland horses were primed for speed. In a fair race, he could never overtake them.

"He's about to eat dirt!" Murphy shouted. Ben took a second glance at his partner's face, which was shiny on one side, growing swollen and puffy.

"What the hell happened to you?"

"An inconvenience." Murphy chuckled. "God! How can I laugh at a time like this?"

Ben felt the wind rushing over his tear-damp cheeks, the pumping of Dusky's gallop pounding up through his ankles and knees. Felt a peculiar smile on his face despite the fact they were running for their lives. He glanced over again. Beneath the blackening eye, Murphy's grin was unmistakable. He looked the way Ben felt.

"It's a magic power," Ben said.

Murphy laughed again. The sound was so good Ben had to laugh, too. They heard another *pop!* behind them and a clod of dirt sprang up to Ben's left. Still, it seemed like nothing. He barely cared.

"How many shots you think he's got left?" Murphy asked.

"No idea," Ben said. "But if he keeps shooting clouds like that I reckon he'll be empty soon enough."

The earth was thick with grass fed from the Platte, prickly pears and turf flying out from under the horses' hooves. They sped away from the fort, following the river.

"This way!" Mock pointed, having apparently learned her lesson from grabbing Morgan's reins out of Murphy's grasp the previous night. She tugged at Murphy's sleeve and pointed again, dead into the middle of the Platte's green waters. "Into the river!"

"What?" Murphy cried.

Randall shot again, and this time the bullet burned

through the air nearby, too close for comfort. Either he was gaining or his aim was improving, and neither was good. Mock appealed to Ben next, pointing harder as if it would explain better.

"We can't be here when he comes! Not around so many people—magic won't hide what is going to happen!"

"When who comes?"

But Mock didn't answer. Ben thought of when she'd led them in a sudden, strange direction on their first ride together. During the witching hour, she'd called it, just west of Cottington.

He stood in his stirrups. They didn't have much of a choice. A yank of the reins and they turned away from the settlers on the trail, heading for the river where it twisted round the fort.

"You better know what you're doing!" he called to Mock.

"Have I told you wrong before?" she replied. "There! Into the water! That spot!"

Ben could hear Randall's horse squealing. In minutes he'd be on them. Ben got the revolver from his mochila and checked the chambers, then shoved it into his belt and took Dusky's reins in both hands. She didn't seem hesitant about the river when he pointed her at it, so he gave her a tap of leather and she went right in.

Murphy let out a groan of exasperation, but in a moment Ben heard Morgan splash in behind them. As he did, Ben took a second look at the blue and green waves.

The reflection of the moon, rising as the sun set, rested on the dappled surface of the swift current. The water shimmered, breaking the image in two, like a window into another world. Lapping at his knees, cold and heavy.

And he *felt* something.

Heady and light, like what he'd felt the night before when they'd flown through the Nebraska countryside. What he'd felt when Randall had told him what Penny had done, of her defiant escape. What he'd felt long ago, as a child, when he'd tried to leave this world behind in search of a safer one.

The other place . . .

"Sharp. Now we're trapped," Murphy said, pressing his hand against his swollen temple. "He promised to help!"

Who? Ben almost asked again, but decided if either of them wanted to tell him they would.

Mock took the reins from Murphy's hands, gently this time, and Murphy allowed it. The little girl confidently guided Morgan deeper into the river. Ben heard Randall up on the shore. In a moment, at this pace, they'd be easy as ducks to pick off. The only blessing was how fast the sun was sinking, bathing them in the safety of darkness.

"Will he give chase?" Mock asked. Moonlight glinted in her eyes when she glanced over at Randall, whose horse was balking at entering the river. Ben swallowed and nodded.

"Until one of us is dead."

"Good."

Randall fired but was yards short. How had it gotten so dark, so fast? Wasn't it only moments ago the sky had been on fire with the setting sun?

The dizzy sensation surged, and Ben turned toward it. Dusky followed, and the sun blinked in the sky, as if a shadow had fallen and risen again when he hadn't been looking. The air changed, turning cold and thin, and Ben wondered if a storm front was moving in.

Randall cursed. Fired again, missed again. Then Ben heard splashing as he forced his horse down into the water.

"Here he comes," Mock said. Her little voice was pleased. Full of shadows.

The dizziness faded. Ben jerked in the saddle and blinked, hard. But it didn't change what he saw.

The river was gone.

So was Fort Laramie.

The horses broke into a gallop, charging through a flat expanse of hard earth toward a long, steep ridge. Sagebrush swarmed them on all sides like an endless army of silver-green goblins brandishing spears, tangled hair whipped by the hard wind. The sun had dropped below the tall horizon, steeping them in sudden twilight.

Ben's head swam. What had just happened?

"What the . . ." Murphy gasped. "Where are we?"

Ben looked over his shoulder, but there was no sign of the scene at Fort Laramie. Instead, he saw a huge mound of red stone, smooth like the carapace of an enormous tortoise. Ben didn't know as much about the California Road as Murphy did, but even he knew Independence Rock when he saw it—the landmark pioneers had to reach by Independence Day if they had any hope of making it to California before winter. The halfway point between the east and the west.

"Hurry!"

Mock kicked at Morgan's sides. They raced hard through the sagebrush and cold air, every hoofbeat jarring Ben's bones.

"Shrike!" Murphy called suddenly. "Can he follow, too?"

Shrike? Was that the *he* they'd been talking about?

Mock gripped the pommel and called back to Murphy. "I'm counting on it, after what you've asked him to do."

"You saw Shrike?" Ben asked.

Murphy's jaw stiffened. "He helped me. Back at Fort Laramie."

"And what exactly did you ask him to do?"

The boy answered with a warning glare. It was particularly daunting shadowed by his black eye, shining in the burgeoning moonlight.

The ridge grew steady ahead. As their arcing path took them nearer, Ben made out a notch in its face. No, not a notch—as Mock pulled Morgan into a straight run at it, Ben saw it was a narrow gorge, cutting through the ridge as though a giant had cleaved it with an ax. The rocks along either side looked like faces, gazing down into the pass, where a river ran, glinting under the rising moon.

"Devil's Gate," Murphy exclaimed. "The Sweetwater!"

"Fort Laramie to Independence Rock and Devil's Gate," Ben panted, gripping Dusky's reins. "That can't be!"

But Mock's furtive gaze told him it could.

An unholy wind whispered at their backs. Ben could swear he heard laughter, like that of children, high-pitched giggles that tickled his ears. Eyes were on them, watching. Waiting. Ben's wits crawled across his skin, every hair alert. He wished that just for a moment they could be still, their horses not crashing through the rocky land, so he could look and listen. He felt they were surrounded, but by who—or what—he didn't know.

Ben shoved down a yelp when he saw a little figure crouching near a cluster of sagebrush, a long, curled tail drooping from its naked rear end. It vanished as Dusky raced past.

"Murphy—" he began. But he didn't know how to finish. "There was a little man. With a tail. Right back there ... but ..."

Mock shook her head. "It was not a man."

"What was *that*?" Murphy cried, voice cracking. He'd seen something, too.

All Mock said was, "The others."

She leaned to the side and Ben glanced back, too.

"Here he comes," Mock said. She smacked Morgan's shoulder. "Give it your best. Dusky, Morgan!"

Hooves thundered out of thin air, as if bursting

through a stable door. Randall crashed out of nothing behind them, in the place where they'd appeared only moments ago. He was swearing and sweating, holding reins in one hand and waving his gun with the other. He fired it in surprise when he saw he was no longer in the Platte River.

Ben snapped Dusky's reins. He didn't know how to reconcile what he'd seen, what they'd just done. If it bought them time to get away from Randall, he'd take it. But this path led into open terrain, where no shadows could hide them from the moonlight. It was only a matter of time before one of Randall's deadly lead balls found one of them or their horses. The only advantage they had was speed, to bring them under the cover of the ridge called Devil's Gate.

Why would Mock take them here, to this open, rocky place where there was nowhere to hide?

"You want him to chase us?" Ben cried.

Randall shouted and fired another shot, this one zipping and burning through the air right off Dusky's hide. Mock pressed her lips in a line.

"Jesse Murphy asked for Shrike to come. We should make the best of it. When Shrike feeds . . ."

She didn't finish, and Ben didn't want her to. He stared through the night to Devil's Gate. Spruce and sagebrush covered its rocky body like tufts of fur. He strained his eyes through the dim, making out dark forms as they came into view on the ridge. At first he thought they were more trees.

But then they moved.

Awakening, coming to life with glowing white eyes. Walking, creeping, crawling, on two legs and four and six, along the jagged rocks of the ridge. From so far away Ben couldn't see if they were man or beast, feathered or furred or scaled. Whatever they were, they swarmed across the rocky cliffs of Devil's Gate, flooding the narrow pass with their whispers.

A beacon of pale blue flashed, filling the pass with cold light. It froze the river and lit the throng of monsters, casting their shadows across the walls of Devil's Gate. Ben felt the full force of the dizzy sensation there, like a doorway into another place. A place he'd known once long ago and since lost hope of finding again.

But though he'd found the door again, passing through would not be as easy as it had been in the past.

"Oh no," Murphy said.

Standing in the light that filled the gorge was the blue spirit, solid and vivid. As they closed the distance Ben could make out a cloak lined with fur, long white hair and a crown of antlers. As light touched rock and tree and water, it was suddenly winter, snow falling and frost sweeping across the faces of the blue rocks like lichen on tree bark. The curving Sweetwater, now a bridge of rippled, thick ice, was their only avenue through the gorge.

Ben heard the *CRACK* of Randall's revolver just before

pain lanced through his side. His vision flashed, and he lost time. One moment he was holding tightly to Dusky's reins; the next his hands were empty, the blue light in the gorge spiraling overhead as he fell from the saddle.

CHAPTER XIV

JESSE

Jesse heard Foley cry out. She turned in time to see Dusky scream, jerking to one side. Foley fell, hitting the ground with a spin and a sickening *POP*. Jesse pulled on Morgan's reins and nearly fell out of the saddle herself, diving for Foley where he lay in a pile on the hard earth even as Randall raced toward them on his laboring black mount.

"Foley! Goddammit, Foley!"

His arm was all messed up, dislocated from the fall, but that wasn't the worst of it. His side was cut open, gushing blood. His head was bloody from hitting the rock, too, and he was barely conscious.

Jesse got her feet under her and Foley's arm round her shoulders, lifting him even as he winced and swore. Dusky had not run, nostrils flared and eyes wide as though she might have seen action on the field before. Not Morgan, though; every muscle in his body was strung to bolt, and only Mock's grip on the reins kept him steady.

"Hurry, hurry!" Mock cried. "We must get into the gate before Shrike comes!"

"God, it hurts," Foley wheezed. "It hurts so bad . . ."

Jesse could barely see over him, but she could hear Randall's horse thundering toward them. There was no escape. She let Foley slide off her back, hoping he wouldn't just bleed out right there, and tore through his clothes, finally finding his revolver.

Where was Shrike? Hadn't he promised to help?

If you want something done, you have to do it.

She pointed the gun. Randall's horse was nearly dead on its hooves, rider just as frothed round the mouth as his steed. Jesse tried not to think of it as killing a man. She stared into his spit-stained face and imagined he was a rabid dog. An animal to be put down for its own sake, and the sake of others.

"Don't kill him."

It was Foley talking, but he hardly knew what he was saying, bleeding all over the dirt.

"Don't look," Jesse whispered.

She tried to remember what her ma'd taught her about shooting. *Both eyes open, lean into it, be ready for the kick. Don't put your finger on the trigger 'til you mean to shoot. 'Til you know it could kill and you're ready for that stain on your soul until you die.*

Randall hadn't fired on her yet, all his efforts tied up trying to control his horse. When she could make out the moonlight off his teeth, Jesse's finger slipped to the trigger.

Ready.

She ducked when a burst of feathers showered them like rain. Pinions raked across the back of her head and she threw herself over Foley, hoping against hope that she might protect them both.

Randall screamed.

Something warm and thick splattered across Jesse's shoulder. Red spilled onto the dirt and rocks, followed by a sickening crunch and then Randall's voice in a strained, broken gurgle.

Jesse looked up.

Randall's boots dangled in the air. They were as far off the ground as they'd been in the stirrups, but his horse was running off without him. At first Jesse thought he was hovering in midair, arms fallen straight to the side and head hanging back so his open-jawed face stared at the sky. But then she saw the blackened spear point jutting out of his cracked chest, holding him aloft.

Standing at the foot of the spear where its butt drove into the earth was Shrike, red with blood. He was breathing hard as a wolf on the hunt, hand wrapping and rewrapping round the base of the spear like he wanted to plunge it into body after body.

This isn't what I asked for, Jesse wanted to say, but her mouth felt sewn shut as she beheld the piercing eyes in the strange man's face. *What have I done?*

The horror did not end there. Before Jesse could wipe away the blood that dripped down her cheek, Shrike's cloak spread and bulged, seeping out of his body like dark in a room when the fire dies. The blood on his face and neck dissolved, disappearing into his skin.

Then he began to grow.

Jesse shrank back, clutching Foley, as Shrike's body arched overhead, the surface of his skin all shadows and roiling layers of black and gray feathers. He had arms and legs, but also wings and antlers. Cruel talons and raven feathers, every one as sharp as a knife.

He grabbed the spear on which Randall was impaled and pulled it from the earth, holding him like a skewer of rabbit. Randall whimpered; it was the only sound he could make with his broken body and blood-filled mouth. Just a sad, confused, dying whimper.

Shrike's mouth split open, bigger and bigger, transforming into a hooked and shining black bird's beak. He tilted his head back and hoisted Randall overhead, cracking open his horrible maw still further. His voice was no longer human when he spoke.

"Thank you, oathbreaker."

Then he devoured Randall whole.

Jesse felt Foley slipping from her grasp. She couldn't look away as Randall disappeared down Shrike's billowing gullet.

A dull instinct fired in her belly: *run.*

"Come on," she whispered. "Foley. Ben."

He was plenty thin and wiry, like every Express rider, but he was still taller and heavier than Jesse. She tried to put the awful crunching of bones behind her. The moment the sound stopped Shrike would be reaching for his next bite. Foley groaned at his first name, so she tried it again, trying to keep the terrified quaver from her voice. Had she not had to save him she might rather have given in to the fear, laid down and died of it.

But not when he was depending on her.

"Come on, Ben. Good ol' Ben, you can do it, you big baby."

Foley's weight lifted. Mock had come, jumped off Morgan and grabbed under Foley's other arm.

"We have to go!"

Mock bit her lower lip and blew a piercing whistle— Dusky came prancing over, eager to leave this awful place. Through nothing less than a miracle, they got Foley into her saddle and Mock climbed up with him. The same moment Jesse's rear hit Morgan's saddle leather, Shrike let out a disgusting, earth-shaking *burrrrrruuppp!*

"Up ahead!" Mock cried. "Lead him to the Devil's Gate!"

"I thought he was helping us!"

Mock's gaze was fixed ahead. Grim.

"Not everything is so clear," she said.

The blue spirit and his shadows had watched the bloody ordeal from the protected rocks of the gorge. His following had grown into a small army of the eerie shadow soldiers that covered the steep cliff walls, pouring down from the top of the ridge.

Over the pounding of the horses' hooves, Jesse heard another sound like the rumbling of boulders, of earth being turned inside out. She looked over her shoulder, and it was a mistake.

Shrike had finished with Randall. When he saw the gathering of shadow beings in the path of Devil's Gate, his blood-wet smile could have eclipsed the moon. He snatched his spear and straightened, a twenty-foot mountain in a cloak of black and gray feathers.

Then he lunged, lifting off the ground and shooting toward them without a foot touching the earth. Chasing them as they raced into the gorge to meet the deadly spirit that waited there. All at once, Jesse understood.

"You think that blue thing can stop him?" she cried.

Mock crouched on the saddle, Foley's body pinned between her ankles, entire body perfectly in tune with Dusky's powerful gallop. She didn't answer, and Jesse could barely care anymore. The wind chilled her face where it struck her sweating brow and hair.

The blue spirit drew his bow as they entered the shadow of the gorge. The rocky walls of the narrow pass pressed in on them from both sides. Behind them, Shrike was gaining fast. There was nowhere to go but through.

"Go, Morgan, *go!*"

Morgan charged.

The shadow beings exploded left and right as he plowed into them. They weren't human, as Mock had said; some had animal faces, tails and wings and claws. Jesse smacked at the wretched, long-nailed fingers that clawed and snatched at them as they navigated the frozen surface of the river.

"Get off! Get off of me, you terrible little things!"

Suddenly the shadow beings parted. In their wake, the blue spirit waited, his cold light filling the gorge as they neared. He notched a shining arrow and raised his bow. But when he loosed it, they were not the target.

Instead, Jesse's gaze followed the arrow as it arced over them and plunged between Shrike's hungry eyes.

The blow brought him down, crashing against the cliffside and dropping his spear. He thrashed in pain and let out a roar that shook the cliffs, but he did not die. He grasped at the glowing arrow that had pierced his bloated forehead, yanking it out with a spray of black gore. Then he grabbed one of the nearest screaming shadows. With a swift jerk, he thrust the little wailing creature onto the fallen arrow and it dissolved into dust. Then Shrike snapped the arrow in his talons and tossed it aside.

"Snow," he bellowed. "Snow of the Twilight! First Snow of the Winter! Coldest bringer of the Slender Moon! Come now. Come at me! Show me your power in this dividing realm, and I will show you mine!"

Shrike's challenge scared off the grabbing shadow beings in droves. They fled, cowered in the nooks and crannies of the cliffs, shivering and crying in amorphous huddles. Only the blue spirit—Snow, Shrike had called him—stood unafraid.

Snow stepped forward, nocking another arrow. They were so close Jesse could see the details of his indigo face. He was beautiful, with long, silver hair braided with winter pine. His antlers were velvety, entwined with ivy and white flowers. As Morgan and Dusky passed on either side of him, hooves struggling on the solid ice, he glanced at Jesse with ultramarine eyes.

"I will not forget this," he said. His voice was as cold as the frozen Sweetwater.

Then he turned away from Jesse and Mock, striding toward the monster that waited for him. Shrike howled in challenge. Jesse looked back to see him grab a clawfull of fleeing shadow beings, dumping them in his hooked gullet and chewing them with limb-crushing glee.

They cleared the gorge. The horses eagerly climbed off the ice and up onto the grassy bank.

"We have to go, now," Mock said in a quick, desperate whisper. "While he's occupied with Shrike. We have to go south, off the trail of the Nightland."

Without waiting for Jesse to agree, she clucked at Dusky. Jesse nudged Morgan after them, fleeing the gorge that echoed and flashed with the cries and lights of the spirits that warred within it. The horses broke into a gallop again and Jesse realized, as the wind hit her face, that there were tears on her cheeks.

Shrike screamed again and the noise was followed by a *boom* and a flash, but she didn't look back again. She wiped the tears and focused ahead. Ahead, and away from the carnage behind them.

"Off the trail?" Jesse asked. "Why?"

Mock rested her hand where Dusky's coat was dripping with Foley's blood. It ran in sheets from her shoulders to her tail. Mock tightened her grip on the reins and urged the horse onward. She stared solidly into the southwest and said, "If we don't, Ben Foley will die."

CHAPTER XV

BEN

Ben thought it strange that Mock would say he was dying. He felt fine.

As she led the way west, he flew alongside them. Morgan's and Dusky's coats sheened with moonlight, and their hooves plowed through the dry, hard earth. Ben felt as light as the air as he rode with them, leaving the monsters from Devil's Gate behind.

What was behind him didn't matter. None of this mattered. He was finally going back to the other place.

"Wake up. Wake up, Ben Foley!"

Mock's voice sounded loud in his ear even though he was floating higher and higher above them. Free. To join the stars in the sky. To go home.

He saw her talking to a heavy shape draped over Dusky's saddle. She leaned over the body again.

"Wake up!"

He felt it then, the shuddering of Dusky's hooves as she galloped. The terrible wetness of his blood leaving his body. Then the dizzying pain.

The sky pitched and spun and he fell, out of the sky, right into the sad sack of flesh and bone in the saddle. Right into the puddle of memories he'd almost left behind.

"I don't want to go," he mumbled, the words tumbling from his mouth and rolling off Dusky's shoulders.

Then stay, came a voice from above. *For just a little while.*

Then nothing.

The floorboards of the shack were thin, missing altogether in some places, so the packed dirt showed through. Ben stooped over one such place, staring into the rectangle of caked mud. Not even grass could grow here because the sun could never reach it through the single, paneless window.

Ben hated that window. He wished the thin wall went unbroken. A window was supposed to let in the light and the breeze. Make the outside closer to the inside. Let you see it even if you couldn't go there.

But this window had been built too close to the roof, so the sun could never reach in, and the wind blew by and never through. The only thing the window did was let in the sounds.

Ben's ears hurt beneath his fingernails, but he didn't let go. He stared at the dirt. The floor was a better window than the window. At least he could touch the earth through it.

He pressed his bare toes into the soil. He pretended that he was a worm and could burrow away. Deep into the lap of the earth, where he could hear nothing but the breathing of the planet. The deep and gentle hum, like when Penny sang to him. He closed his eyes.

The pain in his ears went away. The sounds faded, too, as if someone had finally closed that cruel, lying window. He opened his eyes.

The shack was gone. Walls, drooping roof, broken floor and all—vanished. He crouched in a thick forest, feet tickled by a carpet of fallen leaves. In the air round him were glowing lights, pink and blue and gold, green and white. They danced like lightning bugs, whispered amongst themselves.

Where am I?

The lights didn't answer. Ben felt the coiled shape in his chest relax. He heard birds and saw the stars twinkling through the trees above. All was calm. All was safe. Though he didn't know where he'd gone, he knew he belonged there. He knew it was a place where no one could harm him. After some time, he closed his eyes and fell asleep in a bed of leaves and moss.

He woke to the sound of Penny humming. His cheek was in her skirts, her hand on his head.

"I went somewhere nice," he said.

"Where did you go, baby?" she asked.

He told her about the other place. She listened and stroked his temple, then touched his ears where he'd been clutching them, soothing the little crescent-shaped bites left by his fingernails.

"I want to go back there," he told her.

"Then you do that," she replied. "Whenever you are frightened. Whenever your daddy calls me into the yard with that voice. Go to that wonderful place and stay there as long as you can manage. In that place, you are free. In that place, we all are free."

"Are you crying, Penny?" he asked, and yawned.

"No," she said. "Don't you worry about me."

He liked that he fit in her lap so nicely, that her arm could wrap all the way round him. If it were up to him, he would never grow big. He pulled her skirts round his shoulders like a blanket and listened to the gentle chiming of the blue glass on the bottle-tree in the yard.

In that place, you are free.

The scent of fresh water brought him to a pool. He could hear Penny calling to him from the bottom of the lake. He followed her voice as the light of his mind ebbed.

She was there, sparkling like cobalt-blue glass. He saw her reflection in the water. Walking through the woods in the hands of the night. She was not alone. And as the moonlight broke through the leaves, he saw a smile on her face.

We all are free.

When the light came again, he was awake.

It was evening. Murphy was sitting next to him, biting his nails. Standing on his other side was a stranger. His age, dressed in a buttoned, peach-colored calico dress, wringing a washcloth into a basin with strong, square hands before putting the cloth on Ben's forehead. Murphy jumped up. His swollen eye looked like Ben felt.

"You're alive!"

"Give him space," the stranger said, waving Murphy back.

Ben was on a cot, safe, it seemed, though he felt certain if he tried to move he wouldn't be able to sit up. His whole body throbbed in pain, and he felt hot on his skin and frozen in his bones. Murphy sat, just far enough to avoid another scolding, leaning forward with his hands in his lap.

They were in a cabin, its single room plain and furnished with a chair, a bed, a stove, and a pile of books and maps stacked on a large worktable. A black kettle sat on the stove. Outside, Ben could faintly hear wagons and people, cattle and bells. On top of it all were the clanging, grinding, banging sounds of a structure being erected somewhere in the distance.

"Where . . ."

"Salt. Lake. Valley," Murphy answered, emphasizing every word. "Mock took us through another . . . doorway. After Devil's Gate, near Split Rock. She says the mountains are full of them. We came out here. Nelly is Mock's friend. She's going to fix you . . ."

The rest of Murphy's words were overwhelming, melting in Ben's ears 'til they were nothing but an incomprehensible blur. Salt Lake Valley was impossible. At least, that's what he would have said the day before. Now he couldn't protest any of it. Not even if they'd crossed all of the Rockies in a night. They could no longer look the other way, not anymore. Ben might not be able to understand it or explain it, but he couldn't deny it. Something had happened to them. Something that had changed them forever.

"Mock?" he asked, hoping Murphy had stopped talking.

"On the roof. Keeping watch."

The girl—Nelly—gave a little snort. "The others won't come here, not with all the clanging. Not anymore. It's only us human mortals now."

Ben wondered for a moment what she meant, but in the back of his mind he knew she could only mean what she'd said: the *others*. The ones they'd seen clustered round the blue spirit, in the shadow of Devil's Gate. They hadn't been human, but without knowing what they were, there was nothing else to call them.

"You know about them?" he asked weakly.

"About who? The forest dwellers? The spirit folk? Or do you mean the people eaters?" She shook her head and turned her back on him, going to pour water from the hot kettle.

The names echoed in Ben's head, loud and clear but meaning nothing. He had believed those things to be only myth, but he had seen too much now to think anything was myth anymore.

His side was bandaged where he'd been shot, the wound stinking of copper and dirt. Murphy saw him taking note and smiled weakly.

"We stitched your side up just fine," he said. "But your arm . . ."

Ben followed Murphy's glance to the tools resting by the fire: shears, sinew, and needles for sewing. He didn't mind having missed that operation and wished he could miss what was coming next. He remembered seeing a boy fall off a horse in his childhood, knocking his elbow out of place so it jutted out backward, strange and abnormal, until the doctor came. The boy had screamed bloody murder through the whole thing. Just thinking about it made Ben light-headed. He tried not to. Tried focusing on the good.

"I'm surprised you're here," he said.

Murphy leaned back half an inch, a flurry of miniature expressions passing across his freckled cheeks in hurried succession: confusion, surprise, relief, defiance, and finally the same old aloof smugness.

"I don't know what you mean. Of course I am."

"I mean you got off Morgan to try and save me when you could've just left me behind. That . . . thing . . . could've eaten you. You're here anyway."

A shadow fell across Murphy's nose. "Yeah. Well, if it hadn't been for me, Shrike wouldn't have . . ."

He didn't finish, and that was fine. Ben didn't know what had happened to Randall, exactly, but from the aftermath, he could guess. The only thing he did remember, groggily, was what he'd said to Murphy.

Don't kill him.

What a thing to come out of his mouth at a time like that. After all Randall had done.

Mock came swinging in through the open window. She scampered round the room and hopped onto a counter that butted up against Ben's cot. It rocked him only slightly, but it was enough to send bolts of pain up his shoulder.

"How are you, Ben Foley?" she asked. "I thought you were good as dead!"

Nelly joined them round the cot. It made Ben feel like a hospital patient, though he couldn't have been further from a doctor except if he'd been back out in the mountains. She rolled up her sleeves, putting her fists on her hips.

Mock strung her hands through one of Nelly's elbows, hanging off her.

"Will he die, Nelly?" Mock asked.

"Hell if I know."

"Have you ever done this?" Murphy asked. Ben didn't know if Murphy was talking to him or Nelly, though he expected the answer for both of them was *no*.

"I watched it once," Nelly said. "Well, we might as well get it done. Say *ah*."

Ben opened his mouth, though he felt so dizzy no *ah* came out. Nelly put a stick between his teeth and he bit down on it, anticipating the pain before she'd even done anything. How bad would it be? Worse than when it had happened? He didn't even remember falling out of the saddle. Maybe he wouldn't remember this, either, after it was over.

Nelly started pressing her hands into his body, against his shoulder, feeling where his bones had come apart. Every touch was a new kind of unbearable, and then she put her hand under his elbow and said, "Up."

He tried, but between the pain and the knowing that his joint had come undone, he couldn't bring himself to do anything but whimper. An awful, shameful sound.

"Come on, white boy," Nelly urged. "It'll be over soon. Up!"

White boy. The misdemeanor seemed small against the pain. He tried. His shoulder screamed in protest, but he tried. He felt like he was falling. Losing his purchase on reality, slipping back into that dream world he'd tasted so briefly. He clenched his teeth, groped for something to hold on to before he slipped unconscious again.

"Ben."

Murphy was there, locked in his sight, and Ben wasn't falling anymore. The pain ebbed, all the different voices of it—sharp, blunt, straining, burning—blending into one bone-shaking blare that Ben yearned to forget.

"Anyway, if you aren't going to die," Mock chirped, as if nothing were happening. "I've decided that after all we've seen the last two nights, there's something vital I must share with you. With the both of you."

Nelly slowly helped Ben rotate his arm, touching his shoulder the whole time, probing into his bones with her fingers. He could tell she didn't know exactly what she was doing, but he didn't have a choice but to let her do it. Everything hurt already, so how much different was this? All the nerves in his arm were firing or dead anyway. All he could bear to do was stare into Murphy's eyes. Sweat dripped from his forehead, and he worried any moment Murphy would grow uncomfortable and break away. Then Ben would be lost again, down the bottomless pit of pain and unconsciousness.

He didn't. Those copper eyes were steady as ever, and willing. Murphy didn't break their gaze when he answered Mock.

"I reckon you do owe us some answers," he said calmly.

Ben's vision swam, his whole body feeling like he was swinging in the air, alternating cold and hot. This wasn't the feeling of going to the other place or traveling through the moonlight gates. This was his spirit trying to leave his body behind.

"I think I got it," Nelly said. She bent his arm and held it by the elbow. He could feel his bones grinding against each other, and tears squeezed out of his eyes. "Ready?"

Murphy reached out and grabbed Ben's good arm, finding healthy nerves and squeezing. It felt like flowers in summer compared to the glacier of hurt from his other arm that was slowly pushing him off a cliff.

"I've got you," Murphy said.

"I'm a Faerie," Mock blurted finally. "So are Shrike and Snow. We're all Faeries!"

Nelly yanked up—*POP!*—unleashing a flood of pain. Ben's joints smashed back into place and he fell, tumbling again into nothingness.

CHAPTER XVI

JESSE

"We're all Faeries!"

Foley went limp under Jesse's hands, his head falling back into the pillow, but his arm no longer bulged in all the wrong places. Mock's words seemed to echo, but Jesse couldn't quite catch hold of them no matter how many times they passed by. Even though she knew what they meant, and knew, in the pushed-down part of her that knew such things, that they were true and explained everything that had happened.

"Did you hear what I said?"

Mock tucked her knees under her chin, her hands and feet a tangle of knobby gray digits as she wove her fingers between her toes. Her hunched shoulders were shy, but her pinched brows were angry, and Jesse realized she had no idea how to read the girl's body language at all.

Nelly went to the door and pulled on a man's deerskin coat. It was strange, but somehow right, on top of her calico dress. Pretty and practical. Handsome. She dipped her hands under her collar and flipped her dark hair out so it rested just above her shoulders. It was a daring look for a young woman, but Nelly owned herself without an ounce of doubt. Jesse swelled with envy.

"I think his shoulder'll be fine. But that wound in his side, I don't know. I'll go into town for opium to make the pain bearable."

"Thanks," Jesse said. It was all she could think of to say.

Nelly fixed her dead in the eye but said nothing. Then she left and the house was silent again except for the snapping of the coals in the stove and the uncomfortable, unnamed feeling smoldering deep in Jesse's belly.

"I said, did you hear what I said?" Mock demanded, putting her feet down and pounding her little fists on the counter she was perched upon.

Of course Jesse'd heard what she'd said. It was impossible to have missed it. But Faeries were myths. Explanations of the unexplainable. For children, to frighten them into coming home before dark. For Alice.

Yet a dreadful chill rattled her spine. Nothing else could explain what she'd seen, what they'd done. How they were in Salt Lake Valley after only two days' travel, on horses that seemed to neither feel the miles nor fear the shadow beings that had torn at their manes and tails.

Jesse held on to Foley's shirt, though it was now for her benefit rather than his since he was unconscious. Lucky him. He didn't have to deal with the egg Mock'd laid, now that it was hatching. She thought about every tale

Aunt Mary had told. Every story Alice had committed to memory about the Fae: the little folk from Faerie, a separate world hidden by a magical veil. That they were tricksters, always trouble. Childlike, impish, self-centered, pure. The spirits of the earth, the children of the land. Gnomes and elves, leprechauns, sprites, and pixies—Jesse had heard it all. The Murphys were a good Irish family, as Stationmaster Declan had so prudently noted. Aunt Mary was no exception, Jesse's father's sister, who'd brought the tales of her grandparents across the Atlantic to Kansas City.

Even still, they were only tales. Tales Jesse had believed as a child. Tales she had grown out of when her mother had died. When she'd realized her father would inevitably leave her. When he finally had, and she'd set aside her childish fantasies and risen to the task of caring for Alice and the remains of their family.

But what other explanation made more sense? They had seen ghosts. Magic. Leapt through the air and been transported miles. Seen monsters. Shrike. Snow, with his frosted antlers and shadow court, gathered at Devil's Gate, growing in number as the night flowered.

"Yeah," Jesse said at last. "I heard you."

"Then won't you say the words? 'That can't be true, those kinds of things don't exist!' And so on! I've heard it before, so we might as well get it over with."

"I thought . . ." Jesse grasped for words. She'd wanted an explanation and now she had it. Her gut and her bones were telling her it was the truth. A secret part of her, in fact, was rebelliously excited by it. So why was it so difficult for her mind to accept, even after everything she'd seen?

"I've done something. Maybe something bad," Mock said. Jesse let her talk. Maybe the story would fall apart. "And now Snow is trying to kill me. That's all you need to know. Anyway, it doesn't matter whether you want to believe me or not. The fact is that you *have* to."

"That a threat?" Jesse asked.

Mock hopped down from the counter and crossed Jesse's path to the cot where Foley lay, fixing Jesse with a side-eye the whole way. She took ahold of the gauze shoved up against Foley's side that was feebly trying to hold his blood in. Jesse looked away when Mock peeled the cloth back, covering her nose with her hand. It stank of purple blood and something worse, the leaking of organs that had been blown open by Randall's bullet.

"Look!" Mock said impatiently, so Jesse bit back her nausea and did.

She'd told Foley he'd be fine, but even after stitching and cleaning, it had been far from the truth. The bullet hadn't made a clean wound ready for sewing up. Until now, Jesse had only heard about the splintered, smashed-open ruinations caused by the soft lead bullets; now she saw the torn skin for herself and heard the flies buzzing, drawn to the ripening flesh.

"He's going to die," Mock said. "Unless we do something."

She pressed the gauze back, hiding the terrible face of the wound. Jesse had tried to tell herself it wasn't that bad, and that Nelly's help meant Foley would make it, but seeing it up close was making it mighty hard to keep believing. Were they really going to lose him?

Her voice came out half whispered when she spoke.

"Nelly's gone to get drugs. There isn't anything else we can do."

"Haven't you been listening?" Mock shouted. "The spirit world! What you call *Faerie*, Jesse Murphy! There is a fruit from that world that heals all ills with a single drop of nectar. If we get it, we can heal him. He will live."

"If he eats or drinks anything from Faerie, he'll be trapped there forever!"

Jesse clamped her mouth shut before anything else came out. Mock tilted her head.

"So you *have* heard something of other worlds," Mock said.

"It's—that's common knowledge," Jesse stammered. "One of those things old crones tell from their creaky rocking chairs. Like leprechauns and pixies and that kind of nonsense."

"Crones don't know everything, and not all of us are leprechauns and pixies."

Jesse felt hope before she felt doubt. Magic was the only thing that could possibly save someone with a wound like Foley's, but magic wasn't real. Just like Faerie and the Fae, little folk and Mock. But if it were true . . .

"So he won't be trapped in Faerie?"

"Do you believe or don't you?"

"I can't just . . . *believe* in Faeries!"

"Then you're leaving him behind to die?"

If Jesse'd had hackles they would've gone straight up. "What kind of person do you think I am?" she demanded. Mock shrugged.

"You did say you'd do anything to get to California. You're certainly not getting there with him like this," Mock said. She crossed her arms and turned her nose up. "I guess believing me will just have to be one of those anythings you'll do."

It was a damned predicament. All the songs and rhymes from childhood came creeping back, like water in the creek during a heavy rain. The stories that said the Fae held many courts and took just as many forms. Some with wings and the ears and eyes of animals, others that grew from trees and mud and rocks. That they drew power from the night and the full moon, stole babies and delighted in bewitching mortals and luring them into the wood.

But the stories didn't describe the monsters Jesse had seen. Not completely. Alice had never spoken of a blue spirit named Snow with velvet antlers and a beautiful midnight face. Or of a feather-skinned, man-eating bird spirit that could conjure gold. Jesse shivered; she'd have remembered a story about Shrike.

Not all of us are leprechauns and pixies.

She touched Foley's forehead. It was slick with sweat,

but it seemed he'd kept off a fever, at least for now. But he was far from out of the woods.

Jesse sighed. Unconscious, he was so vulnerable; all that stoic, square-shouldered confidence melted under thick lashes and full lips that had fallen partly open in his sleep. She wiped the sweat from his brow with one of the towels. He had seen so much, this boy. Lived a life Jesse couldn't imagine. Had seemed so strong, as if nothing could scare or hurt him.

Yet in the end he was flesh and blood. Just a boy like her. She vowed quietly to protect him.

She turned to Mock and stood, smoothing down her trousers and kicking the sand into the toe of her boots.

"All right," she said. "Show me where we get this Faerie fruit."

Mock's entire body swayed when she let out a big sigh of relief. "This way. Outside. Under the moonlight. This way!"

Nelly's property was built atop a hill in the sprawling Utah desert. To the north, Salt Lake Valley was a dim glitter of lights. It was somewhere out here, Jesse knew, that the route in Ware's guide split off, heading north into Washington Territory along the Oregon Trail. A twinge of concern worked its way up her throat, but she swallowed it. Without the handbook to guide her, all that was left were the tales. Stories of an arid land full of gold and Indians, danger spread far and wide round little pockets of water and civilization. Before she'd left St. Joe's, Jesse had thought those tales would be sufficient to lead where the guide left off. But now, swathed in the skins of the awakening night, the land swallowed all the tales alive, drowning them in an infinite desert of stars.

The words at the end of the guide flitted through Jesse's memory like a goodbye.

A word before we part, you are now in a country different from that which you left.

"Nelly's people have lived here a long time," Mock said. "We used to play. Over there by that rock."

Jesse glanced back at the building on the hill behind them, rectangular and made of granite brick and mortar.

"I didn't realize they lived in cabins," she said. She only heard what she was saying after she said it, and frowned. Mock scrunched her nose as if she smelled something terrible. "I mean . . ."

"*They?*" Mock repeated, the wrinkle across her face spreading to her lips and tongue. Jesse's cheeks burned.

"I mean her people. What should I call them?"

"Your people call her people Shoshone Indian. It's not my place to give you the name they use for themselves. You just *say things* sometimes, don't you?"

"I just meant—I just meant it wasn't what I expected!"

"Why?"

Jesse shut up. Mock skipped out into the desert, her feet slapping the hard rock and sand. Jesse followed her, hoping they wouldn't have to go too far. She chewed on the inside of her cheek and changed the subject.

"I don't see any cactuses or anything. What kind of a

plant does this Faerie fruit grow on, anyway, out in the—what the hell are you doing?"

Mock was shimmying out of her cloak and shift. Naked as the day she was born—were Faeries born?—she kicked her clothing to the side and leapt onto a rock that stood in the middle of the desert. "Now you!"

The heat of Jesse's blush smothered the chill that was setting in. "What?"

"The spirit fruit is from the spirit world, *obviously*," Mock said, punctuating her explanation with a pert, annoyed sigh. "But I can't just bring it here willy-nilly. That takes power. I need your . . . what do your people call it . . . *faeth*."

"My faith? For what! And I'm sure you'll explain why you need me to undress for it," Jesse said, crossing her arms. Aside from the terror of being naked in the cold air under the moon and stars and all of the heavens, Jesse's clothes were the only thing that hid her secret.

"Not faith, *faeth*—oh, maybe it is the same thing," Mock muttered. Then, "Clothes are a shroud! I need your belief. In me. Belief, honest and true. Your faeth in me, pure and genuine. It is power for spirit people. Power for magic, so we can make bountiful crops and sunny days and rainbows. With faeth, I can bring the Faerie fruit here so we can heal Ben Foley."

A fruit that he would die without, if Jesse were to believe it all.

"What if I don't believe?" she asked.

"Then you'll wait for him to get better and find that he doesn't," Mock replied. "Or leave him behind, to find your father in Carson City."

It felt like a slap in the face.

"How do you know about my father?"

"I know a lot about you, Jesse Murphy. Perhaps more than you know about yourself. Now . . . do you want to save Ben Foley or not?"

Mock shone with the challenge, her lithe body outlined in the light of the gibbous moon. She was unashamed, unabashed. A creature of the night with the knowing expression of someone far older than she appeared.

What she was asking of Jesse was indecent. Mock seeing who she was beneath her clothes could put her entire assignment with the Express at risk. But if what Mock was saying was true, Foley would die. And even if what she was saying wasn't true, was Jesse really going to risk her partner—her friend!—over one lousy secret that was bordering on expiring anyway?

"If I do what you're asking," Jesse began, "give me your word you won't tell Foley about what you see. Or anyone. Your word is your bond, isn't it?"

Mock nodded solemnly. "*My* oaths are not for breaking."

"Then swear it. You won't share what you see with another soul living—or unliving, for that matter."

Mock nodded, though from the shine in her eye Jesse

wondered if she already knew. "I swear it."

Fighting every schooled instinct in her body, Jesse forced her hands to her collar for the first button. When she fumbled, she swore and forced the little wooden disc through its eyelet. It felt like she'd never undressed before, not in the history of her life, as she undid the buttons one at a time. Mock watched like nothing was the matter, crossing her arms and tapping her foot.

Off came the shirt and vest. Jesse waited for a gasp of surprise when Mock saw the binding undershirt, but the girl only yawned. Off came the belt and trousers. The sound of them hitting the ground round her ankles was so loud Jesse was surprised it didn't start an earthquake.

Then she hesitated. Up to this point, she could maybe still pass for a boy.

"We haven't got all night!" Mock cried.

"Why?" Jesse asked. Almost pleaded. "Why do I have to do this? What is faeth?"

Mock deflated with a big sigh. "Belief," she said. "Sacrifice. Trust with a secret. Do you understand now?"

Her secret.

Jesse pressed her face into her hands. There really was no way round it, then.

For Ben.

The undershirt came off. She'd almost forgotten what it felt like to breathe. Then it was time for her drawers. She'd stolen them from a boy north of town when his mother had left them outside to dry. She'd spent weeks looking for a family to nick them from, one with a son who'd be near her size but far from where she lived. One afternoon she'd ridden Morgan by, kneed him fast into jumping the family's property fence. They'd raced through the yard and she'd snagged two pairs. Morgan had jumped the fence on the other side before anyone noticed.

Now they came off. The cold air hit every inch of her skin, reminding her of all the body parts she'd tried to forget were attached to her. It was purely awful, standing there in the body she'd been born in, the body she'd worked so hard to hide.

"There. The secret's yours," she said.

Jesse wished she had more hands to cover herself with, though she wasn't sure which was worse, the embarrassment of her nakedness or the cold touch of the night.

"So what's the secret?" Mock asked.

What a stupid question. Had she known all along? Jesse wanted to run. Mock could see the truth in front of her eyes and even then wanted her to say it out loud.

"I'm a—a girl, all right? Look at me!"

Jesse hated how the words came out in a stammer, but she didn't know what else to say. She had a girl's body. That made her a girl. So why was it so difficult to say out loud? *I'm a girl.* The words felt like a lie. Like confessing to a theft she hadn't committed. But how could she say otherwise when she was standing there naked, truth clear and plain?

"Oh, Jesse." Mock rubbed her cheek with her knuckles. "That's not your secret."

Jesse's heart pounded. She didn't know what to think, especially in the face of Mock's complete nonchalance. She hadn't realized how reluctant she'd been about it. Now it felt like her mind was taking on all the clothing she'd shed, wrapping itself in a different protection. Reinforcing what she really wanted.

"It's okay," Mock said softly. "Tell me."

Jesse thought about the drawers. She'd stolen them months ahead of joining the Express, for the purpose of doing just that. But after she brought them home she'd worn them under her skirts every day. Dreamed of cutting her hair, dressing the way she wanted. Flirting with girls and them flirting back the way they flirted with boys.

It had made her happy, dreaming of it all. Dreaming of the fantasy.

It had made her the happiest, most unnatural sixteen-year-old in Clay County.

"I'm not a girl," Jesse whispered.

Mock hopped down, beckoning. Unsure, but not knowing what else to do, Jesse pried her hands away from her body—the body she'd felt sure would betray her—and took Mock's. The little girl pulled their hands together into a single mound of fingers and palms. Her eyes, for the first time Jesse could remember, were kind.

"There it is, Jesse Murphy. Your secret. Your power. And because of it, look what we have brought into this world."

She opened her hands round Jesse's, spreading like the petals of a flower blooming. Jesse opened hers and drew in a short, quick breath. Cupped in her hands was a fruit, fleshy and soft and shaped like a plum or a persimmon. It glowed slightly, the warm red of fresh blood. Jesse knew for a fact Mock hadn't slipped it into her hands when they'd touched. It was simpler than that: one moment it hadn't existed, and the next it had. For a moment, the cold air didn't seem to touch her skin at all.

"Very good," Mock remarked, stepping back. She snatched her shift from the sandy earth and draped it over her shoulder. "Now, let's go and get Ben Foley well and back on his horse."

CHAPTER XVII
BEN

Ben awoke refreshed, though a nagging part of his mind was surprised that he'd woken up at all. He didn't move at first, focusing on the morning sunlight coming through the open window. He knew that once he moved, the pain would come, and for just a moment he wanted to enjoy the comfort of stillness, the solace of the golden beams highlighting the speckles of slow-moving dust and a single lazy, fluttering moth.

"Good morning."

Nelly was sitting right beside him. She had a shawl draped across her shoulders and a book in her lap. The sliding of the pages between her fingers was the only sound in the quiet cabin.

"Thank you for letting me spend the night," Ben said. He knew words could hardly make up for the space he'd occupied in her home and the sheets he'd likely ruined with his blood.

He tried to raise himself, his forehead ready with a wince . . . but no pain came. The sheets fell to his lap as he sat up, his shoulder feeling fine and spry. A sling kept his arm in place, as it was supposed to, but it didn't hide any swelling or discomfort.

He lifted his shirt and gasped. The bullet wound in his side was nothing more than a red, glossy stripe. Panic filled his lungs.

"How long was I . . ."

"Just the night," Nelly replied. "You were healed by powerful magic. I believe your friend made a great sacrifice to save you, so you won't have to try your luck with any of these." She gestured to the stack of blue and amber medicine bottles waiting on the bedside table.

"A sacrifice? Which—Murphy?"

Ben didn't know what kind of sacrifice could even have led to his recovery so quickly, but he knew what kind of hothead Murphy was. Though hearing Nelly call the boy Ben's *friend* was strangely comforting. She nodded on her way to the stove.

"The other two went into town for supplies," she went on. "I think they plan to leave again this afternoon, provided you're well enough to get back on the spirit horse."

Spirit horse. Ben wasn't sure whether Nelly was speaking metaphorically or literally, though Dusky seemed like the least supernatural thing he'd encountered recently. He would have expected all the talk of magic and spirits to be difficult to swallow, but all it felt was natural. As if finally hearing aloud the word for the nameless, velvety, earthy thing in the night. He couldn't yet pronounce the word with his own tongue, but at least now he knew it existed.

"So you already knew?" he asked. "About Mock—and what she said?"

Nelly shrugged. "I've known Mock a long time. I presume that's why she brought you here and not to a doctor."

She let the rest explain itself in silence. Ben didn't know what else she could say, anyway. He'd seen what he'd seen, felt what he'd felt. The strangest part of it all was that he didn't feel surprised. That was how it was supposed to work, wasn't it? Surprise, shock, denial. But he didn't feel any of that. And it felt equally comfortable to find that Nelly didn't need convincing, either. If she'd known of Mock and all of this for a while, maybe she could answer some of his questions.

If only he could figure out how to ask them. He wet his lips.

"Nelly, is there . . . another place?"

She poured a mug of tea and tilted her head at him. She sat down in the log chair beside the bed, inhaling the steam.

"I don't know," she said. "I reckon Mock came from somewhere."

Ben nodded. Made sense. Another memory resurfaced from the previous day. Something Nelly had said, linked to the feeling of paper in his fingers as he tore them to shreds in front of Randall's nose.

"I'm not white," he said.

"Eh?"

"Yesterday, you called me white boy. I'm not white. I'm mixed."

Ben had never said it aloud to a stranger like that before. In fact, he wasn't sure he'd ever said it aloud at all. He'd spent too long trying to be one thing or the other. Trying to fit in. He was just tired of it.

"I'm sorry I mistook you," Nelly said. Then she added, "So am I. My whole life my parents argued over where I should live and who should raise me. In the end, I live out here, and look after myself."

The story was familiar; they were strangers, and yet they had this thing in common. But Ben didn't know how to close the gap. He looked into her eyes, and for a long while they said nothing, Ben imagining Nelly's life, knowing she was imagining his. Neither picture could be complete with how little they had told one another. Yet Ben was struck by a deep comfort. It touched him, soothed him in a way that, at first, felt unimaginably complex. But as they sat in the quiet together, he realized it was actually very simple. It was comforting because it meant he was not alone.

"It's not easy, is it?" Nelly asked.

"No," he said. "But it's a little easier now."

Hooves, then two sets of feet, came just before a knock on the door. Murphy and Mock came in, the former with a bag round with rations. Mock bounced over to him, spritely and dirty as ever.

"So you're a Faerie?" he asked.

The word settled, and Mock's whole face squinted with a half smile. She slapped her hands together.

"Goody! You remember. So we don't have to tell you again. Do you think you can get up in the saddle today? If we ride hard we can make Carson City by tomorrow night!"

"Leave him alone. Can't you see he's tired?"

Mock hunkered down when Murphy scolded her, nose dipping below the side of the cot. She shuffled away, just the pitter-patter of bare feet on the floorboards. A moment later the flicker of her shadow disappeared out the door.

"Carson City!" she cried, followed by a cacophonic peal of laughter.

Murphy put the sack of rations on the worktable and unpacked it. When Nelly rose and joined him, standing close enough to inventory the cans and boxes, the freckled boy's cheeks turned pink. There was something different about him from before, though Ben couldn't place it. Or maybe it was just that Ben could still remember how Murphy had stayed by his side when Nelly had wrested his broken body back into place.

He rolled his shoulder against the sling, waiting for any twinges of pain, but none came. Curiously, he slipped it off and discovered what he expected: he didn't need it.

"I picked up some extra things," Murphy said to Nelly. "For you, since you're living here all alone . . ." He cleared his throat, cheeks reddening even more. "It's the least I could do after you let us stay in your house and took care of Ben."

Ben. The sound of his first name coming out of Murphy's mouth was surprisingly welcome. He pushed off the blankets and put his feet on the floor. His side didn't hurt at all, his arm just sore round the shoulder. He sought out his socks and boots, keeping busy while Murphy tried to make nice with their hostess.

Nelly took up the peppers and other vegetables he had bought, putting them away in groups of two and three.

"It ain't my house, but I accept the gesture," she said.

"Yeah, well, it was built it on your land, right? So it was yours to begin with. Your tribe's."

Ben, who was now used to Murphy's occasional foot-in-mouth affliction, coughed. Just because he was used to it didn't mean it wasn't uncomfortable. Murphy was trying, but it just came out so wrong sometimes. To Ben's surprise, Nelly sighed. When she spoke it was with level sternness.

"Let's put it like this: A man builds a house. Who owns the house?"

Ben pulled on his boots while Murphy squirmed. Where was Nelly going with this?

"The man," Murphy answered.

"But now you learn that the man is enslaved. He built the house for another man because he'd get whipped if he didn't. Now who owns the house?"

Ben had asked himself the same question, hundreds of times. Black men and women worked the fields and built the houses, tended the animals and even fed their white master's children. But who laid claim to it, in the end? Even if Lincoln were able to do away with slavery, there would be nothing for newly free men and women to inherit. They wouldn't have the right to a single brick they'd laid in their master's homes with their own bare hands.

"I . . . I don't know," Murphy stammered. "I suppose, according to the law, the master . . . but that ain't right."

Nelly barely acknowledged the response. "And the stones and timber the enslaved man built the house with, for the man with the whip—the stones and timber came from the Black Hills. A place sacred to many tribes, land known by them for thousands of years. Now who owns the house?"

"I don't know," Murphy whispered.

"And the Black Hills are the place where the rock bleeds into the land to give life to all things. The timber was trees that grow from the earth, drink the water of the rivers, breathe the air of the sky. The stones from the earth, hot with fire."

Ben had never thought of that. Never thought that the land he'd worked for his father had ever been anything but his father's meager land. He hadn't had the time to think of it, or the heart. All he could think of at the time was the daydream of running to California, where, it was told, a man could own as much land as he could grab. Where the valley was an unending bounty for the taking. Where he could take, and finally have, a place where he belonged. That was the dream he'd had, for him and Penny. Now, he wasn't sure. The tradition of taking and owning was all he'd ever known. It was hard to imagine anything else.

Nelly let the silence in the little cabin settle, heavy and cold. Then she said, "*Now* who owns the house, Jesse Murphy?"

Murphy said nothing. His eyes fell lower and lower until he was looking at his boots. He let out a sigh and shook his head. When he met Nelly's gaze again, his face had changed. He didn't have an answer, and he didn't try to give one.

Ben stood, drawing their attention. The tension drained slow, like blood from a blister. He cleared his throat gently.

"There's no simple answer," he said. "Yet the house stands. It's up to us to decide what to do with it now."

The answer didn't seem to totally satisfy Nelly, but she nodded anyway.

She saw them to the door, where soon they would say goodbye. The three of them looked across the dirt lot where Mock played with the horses, dancing between them, her little gray body powdered with yellow and red dust from the road.

"My little Mockingbird," Nelly said.

Her cloak in black and slate, like Shrike, splashed with white stripes. Ben had seen a bird like that before, a little gray thing. When it flew, the white flashed against its wing feathers.

Murphy whistled softly, seeing what he saw. "Mockingbird."

"Has she always been like this?" Ben asked.

Nelly nodded. A fond smile crossed her face, then faded. "Always. And that is why I worry. They're not like us . . . People can adapt. Learn. We endure and we change, even out of balance—or we try." She glanced at Ben. "But the spirits are different. They don't know how to change. But now they must, or they will die."

Ben watched Mock. When he'd first met her, he hadn't seen much in her that was different from any waif on the streets of Louisville. Now he saw something else: A desperate fighter. An orphan of old ways.

"We were chased here by spirits," he said quietly. Claiming the experience felt like trying on a hat for the first time, one that was two sizes too big. "One was a gray and black bird called Shrike. The other one was blue, with antlers, made of snow. We met him in Devil's Gate."

"Shrike is the butcher bird. And Snow, eh?" Nelly looked up, tapping her chin with a finger. "Winter has killed many near Devil's Gate . . . '56 was especially bad. I reckon he is very strong there indeed."

That was it, then. She acknowledged the monsters were real, but what were they supposed to do? If the blue spirit that was after Mock was truly the ghost of winter, then how could they stop him? Winter was inevitable.

"Well, then, we ought to leave you to it," Murphy said. He rubbed his nose with the back of his hand. "I'm, uh, sorry again. For being so ignorant. I just . . . don't know what to do. I left Missouri thinking I had it all figured out, but turns out I don't know anything."

"So learn your own history," Nelly replied. "It's the only way to keep from making the same mistakes."

Ben tilted his head. What had Mock said, that first night? *Look over your shoulder. It's how you know where you've come from.* Murphy cleared his throat and turned away, shoving his thumbs in his pockets. Then he turned back and held out his hand.

"Thank you."

Nelly hesitated, then accepted the gesture.

Ben held his breath, watching Murphy go to the horses. "Nelly, I . . ."

He felt as if he had a thousand things to say, but nothing would come out. Part of him wanted to stay there with her. To learn her story and tell her his. But there wasn't enough time. Maybe one day, after he had found his place in the West, he could visit.

She pushed a pair of medicine bottles into his hand and said, "In case of emergency." He pocketed the drugs and bowed his head goodbye.

Mock perked up as Ben joined her and Murphy. She'd stowed food in the mochilas, though not very well. Apples bulged lopsidedly and sticks of dried meat poked out of the pockets.

"So? Carson City?" she asked.

"Yep," Ben agreed. He put his body to the test and hoisted himself up into Dusky's saddle. Nothing hurt. In fact, he felt more refreshed than ever.

He turned back to wave at Nelly, but the stoop was empty. She'd already gone inside.

Murphy gave Morgan a sniff of his tonic before making room for Mock in the saddle, though he didn't say anything. Ben didn't know what he was preoccupied with, though he wondered—worried—that it had to do with whatever his partner had done to get the medicine that had healed him.

A great sacrifice, Nelly had said.

Whatever it was, he reckoned Murphy wouldn't tell him until he wanted, which could very well be never. Even as the regular Pony Express ran, Sacramento was only a few days away, and with Mock's magic gateways, they could be there sooner. What would happen when they reached the end and said goodbye? Would they all part ways, each burdened with their own slice of what they'd learned about the world and the little folk that apparently lived in it? Somehow Ben thought not.

"Carson City," he said, hoping to get a reaction—any reaction—out of his partner. Anything that might give him insight into what the boy was thinking or feeling. "Think we can make it there by tomorrow night, Murphy?"

Murphy took so long to answer that at first Ben thought he hadn't heard him. Then he shrugged and turned Morgan so the rising sun hit the back of his shoulders.

"Yeah," he said finally. "And call me Jesse."

Then he snapped the reins, leaving Ben in the cloud of sand that exploded beneath Morgan's hooves.

CHAPTER XVIII

JESSE

The remaining bit of northern Utah Territory was an area many reckoned to be the most dangerous part of the route. The last gauntlet, a final stretch between the red and yellow of Salt Lake Valley and the promise of green in California.

It was quiet. Desolate and deadly, if the travel guides were to be taken at their word. The only consolation Jesse had was that it was remote. At least, for her. Far away from the world Jesse had come from. Far enough that while they rode in silence, Jesse practiced thinking of herself as a boy.

No . . . thinking of *himself* as a boy.

It felt uncomfortable, even in the privacy of her—of *his*—own mind. He'd caught himself doing it before, by accident, sometimes in dreams. So now that he'd made the decision, why was it so difficult? Everyone else called Jesse *him*, ever since the stable yard back in St. Joe's. So why couldn't she—*he!*—do it himself?

Because he'd known himself the longest, he reckoned. It wouldn't be easy for someone like Alice or his father to think of him as a boy. But he'd just met Foley and Mock, Alexander Majors and Darcy Declan. Even Nelly, though something about the girl made Jesse think she knew the truth about him anyway.

What truth there was to know, Jesse wasn't sure. He didn't even completely understand himself. All he knew was he felt good, and right, for the first time in a long time. Even if Alice would say there was nothing natural about it. No social provision for it, no course of action. No explanation from the law, nor the Bible, and Jesse could only guess where a pastor might say someone like her would end up.

There was that *her* again. Him. *Him!*

Jesse gave up after a while, from sheer mental exhaustion. Sometimes it felt right and sometimes it didn't. She guessed it would only work when she was trying the least. When it made the most sense and her mind settled on a decision.

Or maybe it's not the kind of thing that ever fully settles, she thought, and shrugged. *So be it.*

The next station wasn't more than a tiny log shack with a stone foundation, hardly a building, though not much less so than other stations they'd seen along the way. The station keeper, a tiny man, gave them water and directions to the next stop even though the compasses could've shown them the way. No sooner had Jesse felt the shade of the roof on her brow than they were off again. The quickness gave her a taste of what the Overland Pony riders did, riding their hundred-mile routes.

Jumping from saddle to saddle with only a moment to swap mochilas and take a sip of cold water.

And so the desert passed them slowly, wide and yellow, their progress marked by the stations and the steady, watchful movement of the sun overhead.

"What do you call those places we can jump through? Gates?" she asked Mock after they left the third station west of Salt Lake Valley.

"Gates," Mock agreed.

"And are there any gates between here and Carson City?"

"You're sounding spoilt, Jesse Murphy. You've been out of Missouri less than a week, already run past the Great Salt Lakes, and you're complaining?"

"Let's just say I wouldn't complain if we'd had the gates in the desert instead of the shade-filled Rockies rife with streams and game. The basin is a dead land."

Mock shrugged. "We can't always have what we wouldn't complain about. And also, shut your mouth. This is no dead land. There is life here. Ancient life—more than you could imagine. You just need to look harder."

Foley had overheard, apparently, and called out, "It would have taken us a week to get here at full speed without the gates, and we wouldn't have been able to sleep as much. If at all."

He was mostly teasing, and right, but it rubbed Jesse the wrong way.

"I'm not complaining," he snapped. "I was just asking."

Mock chuckled and patted Jesse's knee. "They only open when the moon touches them, Jesse Murphy. I thought you might have noticed that by now."

Of course. Jesse felt like a fool for not putting it together sooner. Thinking back, he remembered seeing the moon's reflection in every place they'd visited. Even the very first time, before he'd known they were using magic gates.

"Anyway," Mock went on, "you're in luck. There's a gate past Fish Springs. Then we ride a hundred miles to Carson City. You can rest your tender bottom there."

Jesse shut up after that. *Ancient life*, Mock had said. Jesse didn't see any, but as they rode through the endless-seeming land, pale gold and salmon under a deep blue sky, he tried to set aside his feelings. Tried, as he'd begun to learn to. With Foley and with Nelly. Shut his own mouth and listen. Stop thinking he knew what he was seeing and really look.

White grass softened the sweeping landscape, broken by yellow marigolds and dusty aqua sagebrush that blossomed in clusters across the pointed, rolling hills. Birds sang from somewhere, and rattlesnakes slithered. A herd of orange pronghorn picked their way through the brush, ignoring Dusky's and Morgan's powerful forms from afar as they raced by.

It was still quiet. Still deadly. But Jesse noticed he, too, was thriving in the desert's powerful hand, and he realized Mock was right after all.

He went stiff in the saddle when he felt eyes on his shoulder. On a hill maybe twenty miles away, he saw four figures on horseback. Watching them, rifles at their side. Mock saw Jesse noticing and nodded with her chin.

"Paiute," she said.

"How long have they been there?" Jesse asked.

"Thousands of years," Mock replied.

"That's not what I meant. We're not in danger, are we? I mean, things were settled in June is what the papers said."

"I think they have more reason to be wary of us than we them," Foley remarked.

Jesse bristled. That wasn't what he'd meant, either. But he remembered what Nelly had asked him to do—to listen—and kept his mouth shut. Maybe he didn't know what he was trying to say.

"But the Express just carries mail," he said finally, unable to help himself.

"Nearly every word of that is uniquely wrong," Mock replied.

Jesse groaned. "I get it," he said. "This is their land! We're the trespassers."

"It's not that simple," Mock insisted. "And you're just saying that because of how Nelly dressed you down."

"No, I'm not. I'm trying to show I'm listening."

"Trying to show you're doing something and actually doing it are very different. *I've* been telling you these things since we left Missouri."

Jesse felt a chill despite the warm, arid climate. And though he couldn't see Mock's face from where he sat behind her, he knew the shape on her lips was one of sadness.

The sun began to set as their route took them toward a mountain that Mock called Ibapah Peak. It was whiter than the rest of the desert and overgrown with spruce and fir. As they neared it, the land suddenly bloomed with life —a wetland, in the middle of the desert, lush and green. Grasses and other wildflowers sprang out of its shade, a patch of cool moisture amid the dry yellow warmth. As the horses waded through the shallows, a flock of blackbirds erupted across their path.

"What is this?" Jesse asked.

"Fish Springs. The gate's just ahead. That rock. Can you feel it, double-good?"

Jesse didn't know what any of that meant. But Foley apparently did.

"Yeah," he said. "This way."

Jesse led Morgan after Foley and Dusky, who took them off the trail of the compasses and deeper into the springs. Jesse searched the grasses for the crouched, spindly shapes of the little folk he'd seen before, but if they were there, they were hiding. He didn't feel anything calling to him, birds or gates or otherwise, but Foley had his head up, like he could hear something.

They slowed the horses to a walk and Mock stood in the saddle, leaning back against Jesse's shoulder and hanging her arms round his neck as had become her habit. As much as he'd never admit it out loud, he'd come to like the gesture.

"Should we be worried at all about the blue spirit?" Jesse asked while they followed Foley. "Did Shrike beat him at Devil's Gate?"

"I don't think so. Although Shrike was wild with power, strong from consuming Randall . . . Snow is rich with faeth. As is his right, for his nature is easy for humans to believe. Devil's Gate is a stronghold of his."

Mock's explanation was uncharacteristically reserved. It came as a bit of a surprise to Jesse, who would've expected the girl's enthusiasm to go unbridled now that her secret was out.

"That's why you wanted us to lead Shrike there," Foley murmured. "In the hopes he would be fat on Randall by the time he went up against Snow."

He waited for Mock's confirmation, but it never came. As much as it made sense—that Mock would want Shrike to defeat the winter spirit that had been hunting her—her silence didn't have that flavor. Jesse thought of how Shrike had scolded her at Fort Laramie, how apprehensive she was round him. Was she running from him, too?

"What did you hope would happen there?" Jesse asked.

Again, the little girl didn't answer.

The face of the moon glittered in the water swirling round the horses' knees as they neared the big stone. Tall marsh reeds grew up round it, limber bodies bent to its shape like a wreath. Jesse heard skittering and looked, only to see a tiny foot disappear round the backside of the stone.

When the silver faded, the marsh was gone, though Jesse could still feel the give of Morgan's hooves on the soft, wet turf. The sky felt bigger, somehow, and the only mountains nearby were broad and blue, off in the southeastern distance, facing the sunset.

Mock hopped down from the saddle and Jesse took in a deep breath. The air was moist and smelled faintly of sulfur.

"Here we are!" Mock said. As if Jesse hadn't asked her any questions and she hadn't answered with bottomless silence. "A treat for my human friends, for believing in me and taking me this far."

Jesse dismounted. The ground under his boots was boggy and marshy and difficult to stand on, but it was better than being in the saddle. Mock had run off toward a pool of clear, green water. In the cooling dusk, he could see steam rising.

"A hot spring?" Jesse asked.

Mock was already stripping. In moments she was naked and leaping into the steaming water. When she emerged, standing in the shallow pool, she grinned.

"Come in! It's sublime!"

Jesse felt a surge of excitement—he hadn't had a hot bath in ages—but the feeling plummeted earthside right away. As Foley pulled off his shirt and belt, hesitating only a moment before stripping completely and wading into the water, Jesse was suddenly a girl again, hiding in her clothes. Blushing at the candid nakedness of her companions. To be a girl in the company of a naked boy was obscene. But if she'd been a boy . . . Her grimy, dust-encrusted hands ached for the feeling of hot water.

It wasn't fair. That was the petty sentiment that jabbed at him.

Her. Whatever.

"It's hot," Foley said, up to his chest. "It feels amazing, Jess! Come in!"

How bad would it really be if Foley found out? Was all this anguish for nothing? Maybe he already knew—but no, he would've said something. Wouldn't he? She'd kept *his* secret this whole time; that didn't mean he owed her anything, of course, but she hoped it might mean that he'd understand when the time came . . . though exactly *what* there was to understand, she still wasn't completely sure. After nakedly confessing to Mock the secret she had been keeping even from herself, she didn't know if she understood it all.

Jesse clenched a fist and looked at the water. Then she took off her boots and waded in, clothes on and everything.

The dirt and dust clouded the pristine emerald water lit by the watchful face of the moon in the darkening sky. Foley tilted his head and looked at her, and Jesse froze up, waiting for him to notice something where it shouldn't be. But the other boy didn't react except to say, "With your clothes on?"

"Thought they could use a rinse, too."

It wasn't as satisfying as it would've been naked, but it was still divine. The water was as hot as a bath fresh heated—a rare luxury in the Murphy household. Jesse sank in to her neck, body concealed by the ballooning clothes, and rinsed her hair and face. She swished her arms back and forth and watched the miles of filth disintegrate into the endlessly pure water. After a minute, Foley climbed out to bring his clothes into the water, too, giving Jesse a flash of his muscular backside, slick from the water and shining in the moonlight. Then he turned round, clothes gathered in his arms, and she looked away before he noticed.

When they'd had enough, they took the opportunity to unsaddle the horses and brush the grit out of their hides, splashing them with water from the spring. Then they sat out on the rocks that rose at the back of the pool, waiting for their clothes to dry. Mock didn't bother getting dressed, moonbathing shamelessly. Alice had often said that shame and embarrassment were products of human nature and that the spirits, like children, had no sense of such inconsequential emotions whatsoever.

Foley lounged in his drawers, stretched out on his back with his arms behind his head under the night sky. Still wet, the folds of the fabric clung to his body so tightly he might've still been naked, outlining the bulge between his legs.

Do I really want that? Jesse thought, trying not to stare. *Is that what it means to be a man?* But it was like asking the question into an empty room. Part of her was still clenched and tense, worried any moment he would notice the way her shirt clung to her chest, but he never did.

"What will you do when you reach California?" she asked.

Her partner paused, as if weighing a slice of night air on his tongue. "I don't know. When I left Louisville, it was because I had to get away. I told myself that I would find somewhere in California to live, and that after I built a house there I would go back and find Penny—my momma, I suppose—and my friends, and bring them all out to a place where we could just . . . live."

It had never occurred to Jesse, somehow, that Foley had a family. Or rather, she assumed he must have one, but she couldn't picture what that looked like. Randall didn't seem to qualify. But he had a mother that he'd left behind. Friends, too, maybe.

Friends . . . Jesse wondered suddenly if she was one of them, now.

"Just live?" she echoed.

Ben looked at his feet stretched out in front of him.

"Yeah, you know. Just have a place to be happy. When I was little, Penny used to take me to the neighboring property. Those were some of the best nights of my life. But even then, I still didn't always feel like I belonged."

Jesse felt a pull in her chest. In her heart, where it resonated, almost painfully.

"Me too," she said. Foley didn't seem to notice the squeak in her voice, and she was glad.

"There was this boy," he said, almost absent-mindedly. "Theodore. He made moonshine. I really loved . . . being around him. I wanted to give him a gift, so I stole him this book about chemistry and distilling from my father's library. I gave it to him, but he didn't seem to like it. Later I found out he'd burned it to ash."

"What? But . . . why?"

Foley gave a sad half smile. "I didn't know for a long time. Then I realized he didn't know how to read. And what's more than that, if anyone found him with a book and suspected he could read it, he would be in dangerous trouble. I should've known better. But I didn't."

A hot, sick chill crept up Jesse's neck and she looked away. "Oh . . . I'm so sorry." *About everything.*

"I'm not trying to tell you a sad story. I just mean to say . . . We were from two different worlds," Foley went on. "But I don't know which world is mine. All I know is I've never felt like I fit in. No matter where I go."

I understand, Jesse wanted to say. But she feared not only what he might do if she told him why but that maybe, in the end, no matter how much she tried, she might never truly understand.

Before they had wasted too much more time, and Foley's clothes were dry enough to put on again, he and Mock got dressed and readied themselves to head out. Jesse's were still damp in her armpits, crotch, and waist, but it was evaporating quickly. As they left, Jesse cast a longing look back at the green waters fading in the distance. Once she said her goodbyes to Foley and Mock, she would use the gold from the stationmaster to buy a bath at a fancy hotel and luxuriate in it as long as she wanted.

Once she said her goodbyes. It was going to happen so soon.

"What did you do, anyway, that Snow wants you so badly?" she asked Mock as they rode on. "Can you tell us, now that we know what you are?"

Mock opened her mouth to reply, though first she shrugged bitterly, as if it meant all the world and at the same time she didn't care.

"I want to save our world. Snow does not."

Jesse didn't know what to make of that. Mock's little body drooped with a solemnness that weighed upon her like her heavy cloak, and Jesse thought of what Nelly had told them, that the spirits couldn't change. That they were dying because of it.

She remembered something else.

"Why did he call us *oathbreakers*?"

Mock's back straightened like an arrow, then relaxed. "Oh . . . that's what we call humans," she said.

"It didn't feel like . . . just that," Jesse muttered.

"You are so self-centered, Jesse Murphy. Leave it be. It doesn't matter. You are nothing special."

"Do you swear it, little one?" Jesse asked, meaning it seriously but asking as if to tease. He wished he could see Mock's expression. "Do you swear I'm nothing special?"

Mock squirmed in irritation, then slapped Jesse's thigh with a stinging *smack*. "Leave it be, Jesse Murphy! The next station's already up ahead."

Indeed it was: one more broken-down shack in the middle of the silver desert. Jesse's thigh smarted where Mock had struck it, the echo of his unanswered request. He let his interest fade with the pain, quickly and without trace. Many of his questions would go unanswered at this rate. Within days they would reach the California border, and Mock, Shrike, Snow—even Foley—would all be behind him. Behind him and gone, and with them all the supernatural inconveniences and monstrous danger they'd brought to what should have been a straightforward, if daring, adventure.

A pang of unexpected sadness tugged at Jesse when he caught a glimpse of the horizon far to the west. A reluctance, despite his eagerness to arrive. As dangerous as their adventure had been, he realized he had never felt so alive as he had the last few nights with Foley and Mock and the horses. Despite the spirits. Despite the humility of unlearning what he thought he knew about the world, one day at a time. He had never felt so free. Never felt so much like himself.

Himself.

For the first time it didn't matter. At least, he wished for it not to matter, with all his might. Wished that even if Foley learned about him . . . whatever it was that there was to know . . . it wouldn't change anything. That he would accept Jesse for who he was. That he would understand. And that they could go on like this forever, racing under the stars, below the open sky and into the wild nightland.

Jesse felt eyes on his shoulder and glanced back, just in time to see Foley looking away.

CHAPTER XIX

BEN

They rode late into the night, stopping at stations every twenty-five miles or so. The stations came into view out of the hills of infinite sagebrush, one single-room shack after another. Built of red and black rocks that Ben guessed would dissolve into the desert before a decade had passed. When he'd first imagined being a rider for the Express, he'd thought every station would have a special character, something intrinsic about it that felt like progress. That they'd smell more like California the closer they got.

In practice, though, all the stations felt the same, giving him the feeling he was running the same twenty-five miles over and over again. If not for the drastically different landscape, Ben might have thought himself still in Nebraska, where he ought to have been without Mock's moonlight gates.

He wondered what the world would be like if anyone could open the gates. If he had thought to try, as a child, could he have learned to harness the moonlight and open those doors? Penny had always said he had a magic power. The power to walk in both worlds, she'd said. To know the man-made halls of his father's house that stood in the day—but also to know the footpath to the neighboring field that was only safe at night.

And what about Randall? He'd known only one world, and now none. A casualty of a hidden war, a villain slain by a monster. Slain at the request of a friend. But which war was the one that had brought him to an end—the war that had seeded hate in his heart where it had gone on to fester and flourish, or the war that had brought Jesse Murphy to invoke the supernatural to stop him?

They reached a river and slowed to a trot at the sight of the station that rested along its banks. They had been riding for hours, but Ben felt invigorated as he had when they'd left the hot spring.

"Mock says this is the Carson River," Jesse said. "Hear that? Carson River, just like Carson City. Only ten miles away." He held the reins loosely in his right hand, left hand propped on his thigh. The station attendant hadn't come out to greet them, but Ben felt he could use a couple minutes' break. "We oughta fill our water sacks here while we have the chance."

Mock slipped out of Morgan's saddle without her usual energy. Ben had half expected her to make some perky comment about arriving, but she said nothing, walking to sit on a pile of unused stone bricks and folding her arms round her knees.

"We must be getting close, huh?" Jesse asked, apparently also noticing Mock's change in temper.

His attempt to reignite any of her enthusiasm failed, though. All Mock said was "Very," and so Jesse shrugged and Ben followed him inside.

The tiny cabin reeked of rye. The scent emanated from a hairy man marinating in his own liquor-stained beard, dozing in a rocking chair near the rear window. A shotgun leaned against the wall behind him, easily in reach in case of bandits, Ben reckoned. He wondered if a gun could stop a Faerie.

"This does not seem to satisfy the oath of an Express station," Jesse remarked. "Oh well. Let's see if he's got a well or water barrels somewhere and be on our way."

The rest of the shack was stuffed full of deteriorating wood crates and sacks of potatoes. Ben poked around gingerly, hoping not to wake the attendant if he could help it. The man would probably vomit the instant he awoke, and there would be no more lovely desert springs to wash in.

When he thought of the hot spring, something nagged at his mind, like a mouse nibbling a stalk of corn. Why hadn't Jesse come in stripped, like the rest of them? Especially in the desert. Selfishly, Ben might have liked to see what Jesse looked like without all the layers of clothes. He shook his head. He'd never seen Jesse take a piss, either. Maybe the boy was just shy.

The rummaging noises ceased on Jesse's half of the cabin. Ben's heart sank when he saw that he was shifting through a few broadsides and other sheets of paper, brows knotted together. He remembered a similar pile from the first station they'd ever stopped at.

"What's that?" Ben asked, though he had a rotten feeling he already knew. "Listen, if it's one of those damned posters . . ."

He crossed the room, but when he reached to take the papers, Jesse yanked them back. Clutched them to his chest, eyes flashing.

"Stop!"

"What's the matter with you?"

The pain of betrayal in Jesse's face was all wrong, and Ben felt like he'd caught a stone full in the chest. Why, when he already knew? A tiny flare of anger burned at the soles of his feet, and he reached out again. Jesse stepped back, so Ben lunged, grabbing a fistful of paper and yanking.

"No!" Jesse cried.

Ben tore the papers from his grasp and at the same time heard the click of a shotgun hammer. Cold metal touched the back of his neck.

"Drop the papers and turn round."

Ben turned, raising his hands, dropping the paper in a crumpled, half-torn wad. His own face, or some version of it, stared up at him from the floor. The station attendant, still oozing the scent of whiskey, gestured at Jesse with his rifle.

"You too, mister."

Jesse's fist trembled, just as reluctantly releasing the sheet of paper in his hands. It fell to the ground beside the wanted poster, and Ben's heart stopped.

It was a portrait of two girls, though it had been folded to center the younger. She was about fourteen years old, in a blouse with a long braid draped over her shoulder. Despite the sepia tone, Ben knew her hair was auburn, her cheeks peach with freckles. Her eyes electric copper, her voice like fresh autumn apples.

His heart lurched back into motion, pounding so hard he thought he might die. Shouting at him with every beat, shaking up every moment he'd thought something was different about Jesse. Handsome, brave. Ready to be right and learning to be wrong. Compassionate and strange . . . strange and wonderful.

When Ben had first seen his wanted poster in the relay station that first day, he'd thought it was meant to be a warning for the attendant. But now he wondered, had he looked through the papers on that table a minute longer, if he would have found the portrait of the girl. If copies of the two papers with the two familiar faces had been delivered to every Nightland station, to identify the riders who would be coming through. Ready to risk death daily on their special assignment. A wanted poster and a family portrait.

One for him. And one for Jesse.

The station attendant squeezed his eyes shut, then opened them again. He compared their faces to pieces of paper on the dirt floor, confirming what Ben had begun to guess, and lowered his gun.

"Oh. It's you two," the attendant said. "You're a bit late. I was expectin' you this afternoon, and then . . ."

He turned away and cast about, his footing unsteady. When he saw what he wanted—a bottle of liquor—he went for it as if he'd already forgotten they were there.

Ben got one last glimpse of the photograph on the floor before Jesse snatched it, crushing it into a ball and throwing it into the open fire.

"Jesse," he whispered. "You're . . ."

Jesse didn't stay for the rest. He stormed out the station door, leaving Ben to stare at the other face on the floor—the unsightly face the artist had drawn, imagining what a runaway looked like, based on Randall's instruction.

Ben reached down and picked up the wanted poster. The paper trembled as he held it, a fragile and furious reminder of what Randall had thought he was. He tore it in half, then in half again, leaving it in pieces before joining the others outside.

Jesse was already mounted, and from Morgan's antsy prancing, Ben could tell he'd already gotten a dose of his cooling tonic. Mock was sitting in Dusky's saddle.

"Jesse is feeling a loner," she said as Ben got up behind her. "He has a case of the mighty grumps."

"Are we going or what?" Jesse barked. Then he kicked hard at Morgan's sides. Ben clucked at Dusky to follow.

Without any more discussion of what had happened in the cabin—and without the water and rations they'd hoped to gain by stopping—they were galloping westward once again.

Ben had no particular love of the desert, but Jesse drove harder than he ever had before. Even Morgan complained, trying to slow, but Jesse wouldn't allow it.

Ben watched his back as they rode, trying to understand what had happened. What he'd found out, and what it all meant. He tried to force the idea that Jesse was a girl on top of what he saw, but it felt impossible. What he saw was a boy.

But that wasn't fair to a girl, was it? To prefer to think of her as a boy? He was unsure about everything, now. He didn't know why it even mattered so much, whether Jesse was a boy or a girl. It didn't change anything Jesse had done. It made plenty of sense, even. Girls weren't hardly allowed to leave home alone, so how could he expect to get hired by an outfit like the Overland, much less travel across the country?

"Jesse! Slow down!" Ben called. A froth was starting on Dusky's coat. They must have been coming on fifty miles to the hour, a pace some horses could only sustain for short times and some others couldn't approach at all. "Jesse!"

Jesse didn't answer. He drove Morgan faster into the desert. Ben called out to him twice more, to the same empty response. When Morgan's hoof hit a rock and he stumbled, nearly going down, Ben reached into his belt for the revolver and fired it into the air. The sound startled Morgan and he veered, nearly throwing Jesse. Then he stopped altogether, screaming and rearing when Jesse tried kicking him into motion again.

Ben jumped out of Dusky's saddle, firing the revolver again.

"Enough!"

"Don't you tell me what to do!" Jesse spat. "God damn it, Morgan!"

Morgan kicked and bucked, throwing his mane and tail and screaming, spraying spit. Jesse finally kicked his boots out of the stirrups and jumped off, swearing again as Morgan bolted, running a short way out into the desert before stopping and glaring back at them, ears back.

"Now look what you did!" Jesse shouted. "He's fine! We're all fine! What's wrong with you?"

"What's wrong with *me*? That horse is near invincible from magic tonic and you're still gonna run him dead!"

"You think you know my horse better than me? Go to hell!"

Jesse turned, stomping off after Morgan through the gritty sand. Ben didn't know what to say or do, but for some reason he blurted, "I already knew!"

It wasn't the truth. Not even close. But maybe if Jesse thought he'd known the whole time and accepted it—been willing to pretend Jesse was a boy without protest—maybe Jesse wouldn't be afraid.

Jesse stopped. He balled his hands into fists, but he didn't argue or run, so Ben went on.

"I figured it out at the station before Cottington. They had your photo with my wanted poster. I didn't say anything because I didn't want you to feel . . . to feel scared. So it's okay. That you're a . . . a girl. I don't mind."

Jesse stiffened. That wasn't the reaction Ben had hoped for. He'd hoped for a sigh, the relief of a burden lifted. Now Jesse could just be herself, for the rest of their time together. Wasn't that what she would want?

"I'm not a girl," Jesse said.

What?

"Listen, I know what it's like," Ben said, trying to understand even as he told Jesse how he already did. "You know I understand! Having to pretend. Having to be alone. But now you don't have to. Neither of us do. Nothing has to change. We can still be—"

"I'm not. A *girl*." Jesse turned. His fists were clenched.

"Of course you're a girl. I saw the photo. It's okay—"

"*It's not okay!* I'm not a girl!"

Ben's cheeks burned.

"So you're a boy?" he asked hotly. They shouldn't be fighting about this. Everything was falling apart. He felt his body tensing for a fight and he hated it.

"No!"

Ben wasn't sure what Jesse was saying. He'd heard of babies born with both boy and girl parts, or different parts, or none at all. He didn't know what became of them. Or was Jesse like Ben, a boy who liked boys? His head spun.

"You're not a girl, but you're not a boy—which is it?"

"Which is it?" Jesse repeated, rife with angry disbelief.

"No, I mean—what's wrong with you?"

That wasn't what he'd meant to say, but it was too late. Jesse exploded.

"First I'm crazy to be a girl who wants to dress like a boy. Then I'm called queer if I'm a boy who looks like a girl. And now *you*, of all people, asking me *which I am*—I didn't ask you which *you* were when I found out you'd run away and were *pretending to be white!*"

The shape in Ben's chest flinched, then coiled, wrapping on itself in knots. Reflexively preparing to strike.

As if they were the same.

"You wear trousers and masquerade as a man and the worst that happens is people call you crazy?" he asked, his voice rising.

Jesse clamped his mouth shut and went bright red, turning away, but it was too late. Days, weeks, months. Years of anger that had been pushed in Ben's gut boiled up. Each rancid memory, buried, but not deep enough. The day Grace found him helping Randall with his writing. His father turning away when Ben's cries tore through the yard, ripped out by Grace's switch. Randall, watching his mother, learning that there was indeed a difference between him and Ben. A difference not in the color of their blood but in what happened when it spilled.

After that first day, it had never been the same. Every day after filled with evidence that truth seemed to have no place in this world.

It all erupted forth, like bones dug up by coyotes from shallow graves.

"I can't take off this skin when things get bad, Jesse Murphy!" he shouted. "I can't let this blood! No matter how far I run. No matter how fast. There's no escape. They laugh at you, but they are killing me. In the streets and in the fields. On the side of the road. Tied together, torn apart. For nothing. You think it's the same? You think *we're* the same? My God! All *you'd* have to do is put on a *goddamned dress*."

Jesse whirled and threw something; it struck Ben in the chest and knocked the air out of his lungs before hitting the barren desert road with a thud. It was his Pony Express Bible.

"Go to hell," Jesse said again with all the darkness of the night. "I quit."

Then he grabbed Morgan's reins and hauled himself into the saddle, wheeling and disappearing into the desert.

CHAPTER XX

JESSE

As the sun rose slowly at his back, Jesse would have given anything to chase down the night and ride its twilight embrace backward in time.

He thought about pulling up on the reins and waiting. Apologizing when Ben caught up. Sitting down and explaining everything. But what would explaining do? If Jesse could temper his pride enough to admit there were things he had misunderstood, then Ben ought to have the decency to do the same.

What's wrong with you?

It'd been a low blow, the thing about the dress. Ben didn't know what it was like to wear a dress, of course—how restricting it was, how difficult it was to move. To get away. To breathe. Being in a dress meant being a woman, and that was hardly *safe*.

Even so, Jesse felt teeth in his gut, gnawing at him. Telling him that even though Ben had been wrong, Jesse had been wronger. It was easier for him to hide his secret. Maybe even as easy as changing clothes. He wanted to tell Ben that he understood that much, at least. That if the South took the North to war, he would put on the blue coat. Prove his words with his actions. It was the least he could do.

But what did that matter now?

He urged Morgan forward. The horse didn't care whether Jesse was a boy or a girl. Creatures of the earth were more pure than humans. They only cared about what mattered: whether they were in danger, whether they would eat soon or at all. Whether their human was kind to them. They didn't care about body parts or family portraits.

"Thattaboy, Morgy. It's just you and me now."

The air grew moist and Jesse tasted the fleeting odor of pine. Through the clear, he saw the glitter of firelight. A town was up ahead, probably about five hundred inhabitants based on the number of lights. Carson City.

Jesse let Morgan stop for a breath, regarding the city in the distance. In his dreams, he had raced, alone on a horse, a patriotic American hero. Delivering mail to loved ones—letters and cards and the like. Dashed in through Carson City, along the home stretch to Sacramento. When he passed through town in this dream, his father was standing there. Ashamed, apologetic. Ready to come home.

Now here he was with Morgan and without so much as a letter, stamping hoof marks across a land that didn't belong to him or anyone like him.

The alone part had come true, anyway.

He nudged Morgan onward. Ben and Mock would come this way eventually—soon, even—still on their way to Sacramento. Jesse had no interest in being here when they did. He'd quit now. Was a disgrace. But what else was there to do, if Ben was going to look at him that way? Like everybody else.

"Ben can deliver Mock and claim the glory for himself for all I care," Jesse said. Morgan snorted, and Jesse patted the side of his neck. "I'm sorry about before. I was worried about what . . . what Ben thought, after he saw that. Turns out I was right to be worried. But it doesn't matter now. It's just you and me, and we'll have a grand old time together, just the two of us. No stations, no little folk. No spirits."

Morgan breathed hard, his steps coming out of cadence, though it seemed like he'd had his tonic not too long ago. Jesse looked from the rising sun in the east back to the lights of Carson City.

"All right, then. A rest, for both of us. I'll buy you all the oats you can eat."

Carson City was the most town Jesse'd stepped in since Fort Laramie, all thanks to the gold found buried in the area and all around. It had a proper main street and everything, a thoroughfare with a general store and a farrier, a blacksmith and a carpenter. A tavern, Jesse hoped. He was starving and hadn't slept in a bed since leaving home, and a real one sounded delicious. Not a chair. Not a cot. Not the hard dirt. A bed with a pillow, like the ones he imagined furnished the plush rooms of the Patee House back in St. Joe's. He'd find a room with a bed, and a pillow, and a *bath*.

And there it was, down Carson Street: a three-story saloon with lights on upstairs. Jesse tied Morgan out front and paid the stableboy a whole gold coin.

"Keep him eating 'til I come back, and all the water he can guzzle," he instructed, and went inside with the hopes of achieving the same for himself.

He ordered supper, bought a room, and found it. When his food arrived he ate, and the instant his cheek touched the pillow, he slept. He dreamed about Shrike and Randall, Snow and Mock. And, of course, Ben.

When he woke, it was to the sound of Alice's singing.

It was evening. He could see the sun setting out the window, lighting the street with its brilliant reds. He waited for Alice's voice to fade away with the rest of the dream, but it didn't. It only grew clearer, wafting up through the floor from the tavern below.

It wasn't Alice's, Jesse realized, as the last touch of sleep left him. But it was close. Hungry and curious, he put on his boots and went to see what was going on.

The tavern was a little friendlier than the one in Cottington. Aside from the bar and the drinking, there were tables and men eating. But to Jesse's surprise, there was also a woman. With pretty walnut hair, no more than nineteen, standing in front of a piano while an old man played. She had her hands clasped across the front of her bar apron, singing a slow rendition of a song Jesse had learned as a girl:

Meet me by moonlight alone
And then I will tell you a tale
That must be told by the moonlight alone.
In the grove at the end of the vale
You must propose to come, for I said
I would show the night flowers their Queen
Nay, turn not away thy sweet head
'Tis you that are the loveliest thing.
Oh, meet me by moonlight alone
Meet me by moonlight alone.

Jesse took a stool at the bar, signaling for the tender to fill his neighbor's glass when he brought the bottle over. The girl's voice was sweet, lilting along the notes of the refrain, enchanting the ear of every man in the place. She reminded Jesse of Alice in some ways, with a white, round face, clear complexioned without a single freckle. Jesse wondered if Alice could have been this peaceful, happy girl, were it not for the hard times brought on by their father, and the father of her unborn, bastard child.

So meet me by moonlight alone
Meet me by moonlight alone.

Jesse applauded as the song ended, though his view of the girl was blocked when the man beside him at the bar leapt out of his stool to cheer and whistle. He was easily the most enthusiastic in the whole bar. The saloon girl gave a shy curtsy before tightening her apron and walking off the stage.

Jesse sipped from his glass tumbler as she trotted up to the cheering man, who wrapped her up in a tight, eager hug that was too familiar to be considered decent in public. The display soured the whole experience for Jesse; the man was easily thirty years older than the girl. He lifted her and kissed her on the cheek, then set her down, his hand going to his back pocket. Jesse watched his backside as he withdrew a couple gold coins from a lambskin pouch. He put the coins in the girl's hand and folded her fingers over them. Then he leaned down and said, "For last night, my darling."

Jesse nearly vomited into his glass. Not just because he was witnessing a man paying a debt to a whore young enough to be his daughter, but because his gravelly Missouri voice was deadly familiar. Jesse took a large swallow of bourbon as the man sent the girl off with a grin and turned back to the bar, showing his face for the first time.

"Oh! You refilled my glass. Why, thank you, young man. Chivalry is not dead."

His sun-weathered face was splattered with ruddy freckles, his auburn hair graying at the temples and in the edges of his beard. It was the face that had looked down on Jesse when he'd been a babe in the bassinet, and the face that had looked back twice, promising he'd be back after he'd found fortune in the West, before pounding off along the California Road. Jesse didn't know what trick of fate had brought them together so soon, but he found himself face to face with Edward Murphy.

His father raised his glass with a half-drunk smile. Jesse tried to lift his to do the proper thing, clink the butts of their glasses together, but his tumbler felt like it was nailed to the counter. He finally got it in the air enough for the most gingerly of *clinks*, then emptied the rest of it into his suddenly parched throat.

"You're a bit young to be at a bar, though, ain'tcha?" Edward asked. "Ahh, that's okay. Start 'em young. You got the election to worry about, I reckon. Wouldn't want no man walking into that battle sober."

Jesse felt like he was suffocating, all the words throwing themselves up his throat at the same time and blocking out all the air. His father didn't recognize him, not even from a foot away. And after seeing what he just had, with the saloon girl and dirty coins, Jesse wasn't sure he wanted to be made. What kind of rotten man had Edward Murphy become? Breaking his promises to return to his children—only to be spending all his time in a bar with a whore the age of one of his daughters?

Jesse had been silent a long time, but Edward didn't seem to have noticed, lost in his cup. Quietly, hoping not to attract any more attention lest he be recognized after all, Jesse paid and slid off his stool. The bar went loud with music again as he crossed to the door, this time with a fiddler alongside the pianist, but it was all silent inside Jesse's mind. He emerged onto the street, barely lit by the light from inside the tavern.

Sharp, lily-livered shame split his sides, and for a second he thought about turning round and storming back in there, grabbing Edward by the back of the collar and slugging him the way he'd imagined doing thousands of times. But as much as he wanted, as much as he'd practiced, Jesse couldn't turn his boots, like he was chained to the earth. Like Mock, dragging her invisible magic weight. He hadn't been ready, and now the moment had passed. That sacred first reunion that could never come again. And instead of shock, or regret, or anger, Edward had felt nothing. He didn't even know it had happened. Just like when he'd left and never come back, Jesse was standing alone, out in the cold, while his father enjoyed his new life in ignorant bliss.

"You all right?"

It was the saloon girl, her voice just as melodious speaking as singing. She'd taken off her apron, left on her conservative dress buttoned all the way up to her chin. Jesse'd never seen a saloon girl in person; he'd never seen the inside of a saloon before joining the Express. Somehow he'd pictured saloon girls and all the other ladies of the night to show more skin. All long legs and jiggling breasts, laughing and drunk. But this girl was just a girl, human same as him, only in a dress instead of breeches. And it occurred to him that even if she had been showing more, or laughing more, or drinking more, it wouldn't change that fact.

Then again, she'd taken Edward Murphy as a customer, and Jesse had learned in his own way that clothes didn't always betray what someone was like under them.

"Yeah. Fine," Jesse said.

The girl's whole body tilted, trying to get round to see Jesse's face. He turned, embarrassed by her inspection.

"Boy, and you are *young* to be out in Carson City," the girl said. Then she smiled. "Handsome, too."

Jesse's cheeks warmed. He wasn't going to be afraid of a girl. Up close he could see she did have a few freckles, and one beauty mark just northwest of her lips. Probably Irish, he reckoned, from her wavy brunette hair and light complexion. She was pretty—prettier still when she called him *handsome*.

"You're not hard on the eyes yourself," Jesse said. "What's your name?"

"Daisy. You?"

"Jesse."

Daisy smiled. "I knew a Jesse back in Little Dixie, where my mama come from. He was just a babe, but already fiery as all hell . . ." She smiled some more. "Think it comes with the name?"

Jesse wasn't sure what that meant, *fiery*. Was she flirting with him? As she had his father, he reminded himself—it was shameful work, soliciting a father and his offspring on the same night. Was she the reason Edward had never come back? For a big moment Jesse hated her and everything she was, everything she'd done. If it hadn't been for her, Jesse wouldn't even have been out here. Would never have met Ben and would never have fought with him. When it came down to it, this stranger was responsible for ruining his entire life.

"Maybe so," he said quickly. "You got something to put that fire out?"

Daisy smiled. "I might. Come with me."

Jesse followed her. She took a stairway round the back of the tavern, hitching her skirts so he could see her slender, naked ankles. She led him inside, down a hall and into a room. Jesse stepped in and Daisy closed the door behind him, lighting a lamp before circling round him.

"Oh, yes. Very handsome."

Jesse tried not to swell. A girl had never said such a thing to him, but now that one had, all he could think was that she was expecting to be paid to. He took two gold coins from his pocket where he'd stowed some of his advance and put the money on the chest at the foot of the bed. Daisy's eyes went wide as moons when she saw them, her face paling at the stupendous amount. Jesse had never paid for a woman before—he'd barely ever even flirted with one—but he knew the coins he'd put down were enough to make any girl afraid for what was about to be asked of her.

"Ain't that the usual?" Jesse asked hotly. "How much a different man gave you tonight, anyway. You've got expensive tastes, and I ain't about to get a second-rate service."

Daisy's cheeks flushed.

"Maybe I was wrong about you, Jesse," she said quietly. "I think you should leave."

But Jesse was in motion now. A steam engine that couldn't stop on a dime. The words tumbled out of his chest like an avalanche. Daisy didn't care. Edward didn't care. And neither did Ben. All any of them wanted was for Jesse to leave.

"So you'll take Edward Murphy's money and not mine? His money and his life! You know he had a family that you stole him from?"

Daisy balled her hands into fists. "Please, get out," she said. When Jesse didn't, she stood and made a move for the door. She cried out as Jesse grabbed her, swinging her roughly onto the bed.

"You think you can walk out, all unaccountable?" he shouted. "For ruining my life? How dare you!"

He wanted her to fight, wanted her to scream and shout back. But Daisy just sat there, every muscle rigid, knees locked together beneath her skirts, pale with fear and anger. His hand was still warm where he'd grabbed her, his fingers still tasting the fabric of her sleeve. One moment she'd been trying to get away from him, and now she was on the bed. Not of her own will.

He realized what he'd done.

He'd put her there. He'd *moved* her.

"I'm—I'm sorry," he stammered.

Heavy steps thundered down the hallway, and a moment later the door crashed open without a knock. Edward Murphy, holding a shotgun, stood in the doorway ready to shoot. He took aim on Jesse and swiftly moved between him and Daisy.

"He hurt you?" he demanded. "Did he touch you?"

"I'm fine," Daisy said, though all the wind sounded pressed up inside her. Her hands were clenched in her lap, her cheeks pale, her eyes red round the rims.

Edward turned his sights on Jesse, who was suddenly a ten-year-old girl again, being scolded for riding astride. A fourteen-year-old, trying to scrub John Quinn's drool from her collar. A fifteen-year-old learning she was going to be an aunt. And now a sixteen-year-old wishing more than ever that she'd never been born. Not into this life or any other. She wanted to dissolve into desert sand, fall through the cracks of the floor planks and blow away into nothingness.

Her father lowered the shotgun, moving his finger off the trigger. In the bright lamplight, Jesse felt worse than naked and more ashamed than ever, even more than when she'd stood under the cold moon to pledge her belief to Mock. More than when Ben had seen her picture. Seen the girl she had been forced to be.

But now, what kind of man had she become?

The gun dropped until it was pointed straight down to hell, where Jesse figured she belonged.

"Jessamine?" Edward whispered. "Is that you?"

CHAPTER XXI
BEN

Ben wanted to chase after Jesse and make things right, but Mock took his hand when he lurched toward Dusky. He had forgotten about the mysterious quality she had, her steadfastness to the earth. As long as she kept her feet planted, he couldn't move her, and so long as she held his hand, he couldn't move himself, either. He realized now it had to be spirit magic. Some kind of power or spell, and a potent one at that.

"Let him go," Mock said.

Once Jesse's silhouette disappeared into the dark, Mock released him. He took off his hat and threw it at the ground as hard as he could, running his hands over his head and wishing the moon had the answers. It didn't.

"We should wait, for him to make time on us," Mock said. She climbed up to sit sidesaddle across Dusky's leather, clenching and unclenching her toes.

Him.

"You knew? About Jesse?" Ben asked.

"About Jesse what?"

The three simple words confounded him. What *about* Jesse? He'd never heard of such a thing—someone who wasn't a girl or a boy—but Ben was privately relieved. He'd been trying to do it right, to think of Jesse as a girl. But it had felt wrong, like calling a cat by a dog's name. And then Jesse had said . . .

"That he's a boy. Born a girl."

"I don't know why you're obsessing over trivial matters," Mock replied. It wasn't an answer to Ben's question, and Ben figured it didn't matter anyway whether Mock had known. He just wanted to know who Jesse was—but maybe being a boy or a girl had nothing to do with that.

"I think I hurt him pretty badly," he said. "Maybe I was wrong."

"You weren't wrong. Jesse Murphy wasn't wrong. Or you were both wrong. You can both be not-wrong or wrong and still hurt each other. That's the awful way humans are."

Ben sighed. He took the reading off his compass. West, it read. Always west. Always away.

He wondered where Penny was now. Hoped she had managed to stay in the moonlight. Had she gone north? If she found a place to go—a place, maybe, to stay—he wasn't sure he would ever see her again. Even though he'd promised to.

How far was left to Sacramento?

"Carson City is next?" he asked Mock.

"Indeed. Then we ride through the mountains, and when we get to the other side, we're in our place."

Mock made room as Ben got up behind her. He gave Dusky a kick.

"Then show me the way."

Mock was surprisingly unobtrusive to ride double with. Ben kept expecting her to slip or topple out of the saddle during her constant fidgets, but her balance was impeccable. She didn't have a scent like a person or even a horse; she smelled like meadow, all grass and wide sky.

Dusky kept up her impossible speed, and within half an hour, Carson City gazed at them from the distance. Ben wondered how far ahead Jesse was, and whether he'd stopped for water and rest.

It didn't matter what Jesse had done, Ben thought bitterly. Their partnership had ended.

"You will see him again," Mock said. "Do you want to rest? You've been riding near a day straight."

Ben touched the side of Dusky's neck. The invincible mare's blue and silver coat was warm to the touch, but she didn't seem tired, though steam puffed from her nostrils as she regarded the distantly rising sun.

"If she can do it, then so can I. If we keep up like this, I'll have you across the border by the end of the day. I can rest then."

The way west of Carson City was steep and rocky. It was hard to tell how far the mountains went; as far as Ben could see, they might as well have been endless. He grimaced at the terrible stab of guilt and loneliness in his gut. Jesse would've known the settler's names for the mountains, and surely Mock knew the names given to them by the Native tribes. But Ben didn't know and didn't ask, and so they went nameless and infinite.

He didn't realize he'd been nodding off in the saddle until a waft of sweet, wet air woke him. Dusky's saddle changed pitch, and instead of climbing they were suddenly descending. The midmorning sun blazed in the sky.

All round them, the mountainside was overgrown with trees. Towering pines and firs, broken by yellow-leaved aspens, grew like hair on the back of a boar, climbing the west side of the mountains. The air was alive with the scent of vanilla and citrus. Birds sang on all sides, the underbrush dappled with their fluttering shadows. Deeper in the dense wood Ben thought he saw the silhouettes of deer.

"Where ..."

Dusky's path took them round a bend. The trees cleared on the slope and Ben's question died in his throat.

At the foot of the steep, lush mountain, a blue lake filled the valley. The sun set fire to its waters, cascading waves of brilliant indigo and cerulean. It had to be at least ten miles across east to west, and twice that in length. Every facet of its sapphire surface was deep, clear, and immeasurably beautiful.

All the breath in Ben's lungs rushed out, lost in the rich air. After all the time in the windy plains and then the silent, wise desert, he felt as if he'd died and come back to life. He wanted to run down to the water and dive in, feel the cool drops on his face and inhale every breath of the land until his chest burst. It was all he could do to hold on to Dusky's saddle as she began the descent, picking her way through trees and rocks and scurrying animals.

This was the land he'd dreamed of—not when he'd gone to the other place, but in his self-made fantasies. In those dreams, some waking and some asleep, he felled the towering redwoods and built a cabin with his bare hands, log by log. A porch out front overlooking the lake. Two whole bedrooms inside, one for him and one for Penny. Real beds. A stove and a window. A bottle-tree, and no one else for miles. That was the dream he'd had, for him and Penny.

But now, he saw signs of human life. Footpaths through the leaves and pine needles, the occasional knife-cut bark. Like the desert where Nelly lived, this land was said to be uninhabited, but that was a lie. Who lived here? And if he cut down the endless-seeming trees, even just enough to build a home for himself to live out the rest of his days—even if he made peace with his neighbors, who had known this land for thousands of years— what right did he have to live there, anyway?

Yet he didn't know where else to go. The tradition of taking and owning was all he'd ever known.

Dusky's path took them closer to the lake, until they walked along a ridge so close Ben could see the sand and the tops of gray rocks bobbing in and out from under the gentle waves. He couldn't take it any longer; he let Dusky stop to drink and yanked off his boots, wading across the gold sand into the water.

Mock watched solemnly from the saddle. She had said nothing since they'd come in view of the lake. In fact, Ben wasn't sure she'd said anything since the morning, on the east side of the mountains. It already felt so long ago.

"What's the name of this lake?" he asked. He cupped the blue water in his hands and let it run down his tired wrists.

"Some call it Dá'aw."

"Does that mean something?"

She grunted with a hint of annoyance. "It means *the lake*."

There was no joy in her voice. It all felt . . . wrong. They'd been driving toward California almost a week, endlessly and tirelessly. Ben had expected the usually excitable girl to show more enthusiasm for their imminent arrival. All she did instead was stare silently ahead, hands gripped on the pommel.

"Everything okay?" he asked, putting his boots back on.

Mock sighed and said, "No. Ben Foley, listen. Look. We are at the south end of the lake. It sits in the crown of the mountains where the desert meets the forest. Don't you know what that means?"

"No. I never had a map like Jesse."

"It means you have reached California."

Ben spun at the familiar, smiling voice.

Shrike stood on the rocks behind them, cloak frothing round his shoulders and spear resting casually in hand. Though he had returned to his thin, gray, humanlike form, Ben could not forget the shape of his other body. The wings wide as night and the black, hooked beak.

"California?" Ben asked. "Then . . ."

"Yes. I'm come to get what's been brought to me. Thank you, thank you."

Ben glanced at Mock, confused. "We were bringing her . . . to *you*? But why didn't you just take her when we saw you outside Cottington—or Fort Laramie?" He shook his head. It didn't make sense. There was something missing. "Why now? With the gates, you could have taken her any time . . ."

"Shh, shh, shh," Shrike hushed, waving his hand. "You misunderstand."

Little dry fingers slipped round Ben's wrist—Mock's, holding firm. When he tried to pull away by reflex, her grip was unbreakable. Like it had been before. Inhuman and immovable.

"Mock, let go. Let me go," he said. What was she doing? Why?

She didn't answer. His heart clamored, chiseling the answer into the inside of his ribs. Shrike's tongue brought the words to life, confirming what he feared.

"You did not bring Mock to me, foolish boy," he said. "*She* brought *you*."

Ben struggled against her enchanted grip, feeling a fool indeed for being unable to pull away from a tiny girl. His bootheels dug ruts in the wet sand, but he couldn't break free.

She had planned to do it all along.

"What's going on?" he asked. "Where—what are you going to do?"

"I'm going to show you what I've been working on," Shrike said, his smile like a moon at midnight. "My masterpiece!"

He thrust a hand toward Ben, his cloak billowing out round them like wings. His hand clamped on Ben's face, muffling a scream. The earth dropped away as Shrike's claws dug into his skin, squeezing, blackness consuming the light coming from above. The air grew paper thin, threatening to tear.

He tugged at Mock, trying to pull away from her. It was impossible, but he had to run—had to survive—had to *breathe* . . .

Shrike released him. Air filled his lungs again and he coughed, heaving, consciousness returning just before it vanished. He tasted grass, smelled flowers. Opened his eyes.

The misty mountains still gazed down at the pristine lake, the hillsides still rich with the same ancient pines, but they were *different.* As though he had always looked upon the land while it was sleeping, but now, it had opened its eyes and looked back. The waters were deep and dark, and when the waves lapped the sand it sounded like babies laughing. Lights danced in the distant shadows, and the sounds of creatures howling and chirping and singing echoed from the wood, and just beyond it, Ben thought he might hear music.

But none of it surprised him. He knew this place.

Shrike leapt forth, throwing his arms out and shouting into the sky like a rooster crowing at the sun. He shouted and sang, voice full of pride and exhilaration.

Mock didn't let go when Ben tried yet again to pull away from her. She stood beside him, looking down, grounded to the earth like always.

"Mock. What's going on?"

"He's given you the sight. To see the invisible."

Her little gray face was emotionless, black eyes without their sparkle. In one hand she held on to Ben's sleeve, but in the other she held a chain. A chain the color of the sun shining on gold, with links as big as stirrup irons. It was taut in her hand, its other end stretching back the direction they'd come—into the east, a trail of gleaming gold. Ben followed the straight line of it and gasped.

Jutting from the mountainside behind them, some miles off, was a *blade*.

That was the only word Ben could think of to describe it. Enormous, even from the distance, a double-edged blade sharp and straight like a shaft of light. From its knotwork-engraved pommel to the tip buried in the cliff, every inch was solid gold.

Behind it, the mountainside was split into a clean gorge. Though the mountains blocked his view, Ben knew, somehow, that the deep cut went far beyond what he could see. East, across the desert. Through Salt Lake Valley and the Rockies and the Great Plains.

He knew in his heart what it was, though he had never seen it before. Knew what it was doing. Understood that since the moment they'd left Cottington, she'd been dragging that terrible blade.

His hand fell to his side, no longer pulling against Mock, as he realized how thoroughly she'd betrayed them. It wasn't just now, with Shrike. It had been the entire time. Every time he'd tugged on her and felt her steadfastness—since the first night when Shrike had come to them and offered them gold.

"Mock," Ben gasped. "What have you done?"

"Ah, yes," Shrike said. His voice was hoarse from his crowing, a crafty smile painted on his face. He sighed and gazed at the blade, putting his hand over his breast. "I am pleased. Now you can finally see the product of my labor. My beautiful Faerie blade."

"What is it for?" Ben stammered. "What are you going to do?"

Shrike put his hand on Ben's shoulder and smiled.

"Come with me, Ben Foley. Come with me, and you shall see."

CHAPTER XXII
JESSE

Jesse considered jumping out the window. A two-story drop might not break any bones if she landed properly, and even if it did, maybe that'd be worth escaping the tavern room and what was happening inside it. She wondered how quickly she could get to the door and out it.

"Jessamine?" Edward said again. The name sounded wrong, like clothes that were too big. Or too tight. Or maybe that was just Jesse's undershirt, squeezing her breaths back into her chest. Edward rubbed his eyes and squinted, so hard a time he had seeing his daughter inside the person before him. "What're you . . ."

The end of the question was almost infinite. *What're you doing in Carson City? What're you wearing?*

What's wrong with you?

"Jessamine?" Daisy repeated. Why'd they have to keep saying it? "You're a girl?"

Jesse wanted to say no. *No, I'm not, and what business is it of yours?* But she felt trapped. Forever a daughter disappointing her father. A woman who'd betrayed another woman in the same way she'd been betrayed once by a man.

"Jess, what . . ." Edward tried again and finally got a question out: "What're you doing here?"

"Looking for you."

Jesse had practiced throwing those words like she'd practiced throwing punches, but now they hardly made a sound as they flopped onto the floor.

Edward opened his mouth and his hand, voice starting and catching and then dying in his throat. He cast an apologetic, guilty shrug at Daisy, who had taken to staring at Jesse. Still trying to figure out who she was, why she was dressed as a boy, and what business she had with Edward. Jesse's heart shriveled at Daisy's total confusion. She hadn't even known Edward had children. If she'd known he'd had a daughter barely older than she was, maybe she would've thought twice about taking him to bed.

"Alice," Jesse said, choking up the words she'd rehearsed. They were still coming out all wrong. "She's gonna have a baby. You're gonna be a grandpappy."

There was more, but she couldn't bring herself to say it. It wasn't how she'd imagined it. None of this was. She thought about what she'd promised Alice. She'd been strong then. Meant to be strong now. But instead all she was was Edward Murphy's unnatural daughter, ashamed. Her eyes started to sting, and she swore.

"Alice?" Edward whispered, his brow bending softly. He stepped forward, setting his shotgun down on the chest, reaching out with a big upturned palm. Jesse tried to ignore it—the hand that had waved casually as he'd left, like he was just going into Kansas City. "A baby? I'm gonna be a grandpappy?"

"Any day now, Aunt Mary says. So I . . . I promised I'd ride out here and find you. Wherever you were. And bring you back."

Edward pointed at the gold neckerchief. "So you dressed up like a boy and joined the Pony? Cut your pretty hair . . ." He sighed. "It'll grow back."

Jesse's cheeks burned. She wished to God that Daisy didn't have to be there watching it all. It was beyond mortifying. "So here's the part, Edward Murphy, where I tell you to pack your bags and saddle your horse. Tell Daisy goodbye and that she'll have to find some other place to dig for gold."

"Jessamine!"

"Don't you Jessamine me!" She fixed Daisy with a glare so she knew who Edward Murphy belonged to. His family, that was who. Not some saloon girl. "Is she why you never came home? Look at her! Hardly older than Alice."

Daisy leapt to her feet like she was going to hit Jesse, but Edward held her back. He strode over to Jesse, looming like a stormhead coming across Nebraska, his voice thunder rolling across the plain.

"Jessamine Murphy, you'll speak to your *sister* with respect."

Lightning.

Jesse worked her jaw. She looked between Edward and Daisy. Only now all she could see in Daisy's face was Alice. The dark hair, their father's freckles. The singing voice. The world went upside-down.

"But you—you—you *paid* her!"

"For the honest work I did in the kitchen and the wash!" Daisy cried. "I don't—not with my own father— how could you even *think* that?"

"So you're a whore after all?" Jesse cried. Then to Edward, "You whore your own daughter?"

"You watch your mouth!" he shouted.

Jesse remembered that temper. He had never struck her, nor Alice, but she'd always feared when he'd yelled that he might bring the roof down on their heads. On nights he'd screamed at their mother, Jesse's temples had been sore from Alice's hands pressed against her ears.

But this time, he calmed. Lowered his voice. Smoothed his wiry hair.

"Jessamine. Listen, it ain't honorable, but you might as well know. Before I met your mama, there was Sarah . . . They were expecting at the same time. It was fine, for a while. Even after Daisy and Alice came out. But then your grandpappy found out and said he'd shoot me dead if I didn't marry your mama. He made me pick one over the other. So when your mama died, bless her soul, I just . . . I had to find Sarah and Daisy to make sure they were taken care of. But Jessamine, that don't mean I never loved you and Alice."

There it was. Jesse didn't speak right away, breath hitching harder and faster.

"Why?" she asked. "If you loved us, why didn't you come back?"

Edward spread his hands, opened his mouth to give an answer, but all that came out was a little strangled sound in the back of his throat.

"Because . . ." He gave a miniscule shrug, as if settling into the shamefulness of his answer. The second time he tried, it was more assured. "I didn't want to."

He coughed and reached into his pocket. Out came the little pouch, jangling with coin. Jesse felt numb when she saw it, knowing what he was about to do. She was surprised neither Edward nor Daisy seemed to hear the deafening sound of her heart breaking in her chest. Tearing apart, flesh screaming out. But the other two—her father and her half sister, her God-be-damned *kin*—hardly blinked. They heard nothing, saw nothing, did nothing.

Edward held out the pouch, like he might offer to a beggar. When Jesse didn't move, he jangled it in his palm.

"Go on, take it. I know it ain't much, but it's what I got."

Coins flashed. They fell to the wide floor planks like rain. Like hope, falling between the boards, spinning and rolling like so many chips of worthless golden trash.

Jesse's palm stung where she'd struck the pouch from Edward's hand.

She ran.

Out of the room, through the creaking hall, nearly tumbling down the flight of stairs into the tavern. No one noticed as she crashed out the swinging doors, round the building to tear Morgan's reins from the hitch. By the time she escaped the main street, her cheeks had dried.

Morgan took her fast out of the city. The higher land that rose on the eastern border of Carson City had just given way to the hard, unforgiving desert when Jesse felt his stride hitch and waver. She slipped out of the saddle when he stumbled, panting hard.

"Your tonic! I'm sorry. I'll get it for you. Just wait a moment."

She sniffled, trying to hold all the snot in her head as she dug the vial from her vest. Morgan's sides were heaving, his head low and ears back, favoring one of his legs. She'd forgotten the limits of a normal horse. The tonic took effect almost immediately, and she leaned her forehead against his sturdy neck as he recovered.

"Didn't want to," she said, trying not to stammer. Why was she talking, anyway? It wasn't as though Morgan could understand. "What am I supposed to do now? God, what am I supposed to do?"

Morgan grumbled and shrugged his coat, turning to nuzzle the back of her head. Out in the wood that bordered Carson City, they were alone. Without Edward or Daisy Murphy. Without Mock or the awful Faeries that seemed to follow her every move.

Without Ben.

She wished for him before she fully remembered what he'd said and why he wasn't with her. The reason and the words lingered outside her memory, like the movement of an animal in the woods just out of sight. She tried to imagine he was there, waiting for them to hurry on to Sacramento. Telling her it was okay that she was the way she was, even if he didn't fully understand it. Telling her it was all right.

All you'd have to do is put on a goddamned dress.

Jesse pulled his head up, wiping his nose on the back of his hand. No, Ben didn't just partially misunderstand. He didn't understand at all, not if that was how he wanted to think about it. Jesse didn't need Ben. He didn't need anyone.

"I'll regroup. Go back to the tavern tomorrow. And bring him home."

Jesse felt Morgan's muscles tighten the same moment he felt the chill of winter air on the back of his neck. He squeezed his eyes tight, hoping he had just imagined it. That when he turned, there would be no antlered snow spirit staring at him. No blue spirit, and no other magical creature. Jesse didn't want to see another Faerie ever again.

"*Oathbreaker.*"

Jesse pressed his forehead against Morgan's neck. The horse started to fidget, and Jesse heard footsteps. The voice came again, clear and prim.

"Oathbreaker!"

Jesse spun, readying his fists. "Stop calling me that!"

Of course it was him. Snow, but this time he was not cloaked in blue light. Snow and frost spread out from his bare feet, but not like when his power had filled the valley of Devil's Gate. He was very close, closer than he ever had been before, his bow tucked against his back and his long white hair spun in braids and twists, parted only on his brow for his felted antlers.

"Here to try and kill me again, spirit?" Jesse snapped. "Try it, I dare you."

Snow did not draw his bow, nor did he reach for any arrows. He hardly moved, except to say, "Your friend is in danger."

"What?"

Did he mean Ben? Jesse didn't have other friends, he realized. He unclenched his fists, heart twisting from a snarl of confrontation into a different tangle.

Snow only repeated himself and added, "You must come with me."

"I don't trust you."

The spirit tilted his antlered head to the side, taking a little breath of hesitation. "If I . . . If I paid you in gold, would you?"

Jesse waved the blue spirit's hands away when he went to close them in a cup, to conjure the wicked yellow pebbles. "No! No, you can't buy my trust! Why don't you just explain, straightforward-like? Is it Ben who's in danger, and how?"

"Your human friend . . . Shrike is hunting him."

"Shrike protected us. From Randall, and from you."

"I tried to stop him, but he has grown too powerful. He means to kill your friend and to use his blood for a spell. You must believe me. You must come with me. Right now!"

He reached out to grab Jesse, but Jesse pulled away. He still smelled a trap, but the truth was that although Shrike had supposedly meant to protect them and not to harm them, after he'd consumed Randall he'd become a monster incapable of telling the difference. That Shrike would go after Ben . . . could Mock protect him if he did?

"Please," the antlered spirit said.

Jesse growled. "Mock told me that she was trying to save your world. And that you weren't. Whatever's going on with Ben has to do with that. I'm not going anywhere with you until you explain yourself."

He drew himself up, deerlike ears twisting back. If he'd had eyebrows they might have furled into his antlers. Any moment Jesse thought he might draw his bow or that silver sword of his. That was how he'd solved his problems in the past, wasn't it? Jesse chewed the thought up and spit it out:

"So tell me! What is going on?"

He let out a snort of frustration, like a horse. "Shrike and his flock have written a spell and found a source of terrible power to implement it."

"His flock?"

"His followers. The bird spirits; the omen-bringers. They have banded with him to complete this spell. To carve a rift across the land, to split the spirit world from the human one. To choose and mark an oathbreaker . . . And finally, to spill blood and initiate the spell. In the beginning, I tried to stop you, to stop them. But I failed. So now, I must ask you to help me instead."

The spirit's words brought a vision to life in Jesse's mind: a gash stretching across the continent, ripping it into two separate, lonely worlds. And when he said *oathbreaker* . . . Jesse shuddered under the phantom heat of Shrike's thumb pressed against his forehead.

"I do not know when they will act, but the flock are creatures of the dawn. It will be soon, now that they have reached the lake," the blue spirit added softly.

Mockingbird.

Their mission had been to bring Mock from the eastern edge of Nebraska Territory all the way to California —tracing one of the longest lines across the continent. The California Road. They had never been meant to deliver her; she'd been where she wanted to be the whole time.

And now Jesse had left Ben with her, while Shrike circled overhead.

She didn't know what to do. It was too much, too fast, even after deciding to believe in Faeries. She tried to remember Alice's silly songs, about heroes who had to deal with Faeries and magic spells. Tried to recall anything that might help her through this maze. Anything that might help her save Ben.

"Give me your name," Jesse said. The spirit drew back, affronted, but Jesse understood. Names were important to Faerie folk, and not something given lightly. She sucked in the last of her tears and snot, standing tall. "Or . . . trade me? Your name for mine, and I'll come with you and do whatever I can to help. But I want your word that I can trust you."

He paused, breath coming out in wintry, silver clouds. Jesse took his hand, which had fallen back to his side. His skin was cool and soft, warming with light when they touched.

"Please," she said. "I want to trust you . . . I want to believe in you."

The terrible things that had happened in Carson City fell away. Daisy's pretty mouth crinkled in fear. Edward's face contorted by surprise and disappointment. The gold he'd offered instead of love. None of that mattered right now.

"I am the First Snow of the Winter," the spirit said. "You may call me Snow."

Jesse nodded and squeezed his cold hand.

"Thank you, Snow. I'm Jesse." The distant edges of the sky fell away. Night was in full bloom. Jesse was ready. "Now take me to Ben and Shrike. Show me what I can do to help."

CHAPTER XXIII

BEN

Shrike and Mock moved silently as deer, leaving Ben to follow with less elegance. Dusky's hooves might have been more tender in the wood, but Shrike had not brought her, likely because it would have been easier for Ben to escape if he'd had a mount. He wondered what had become of the tireless horse. Was she a spirit, too? Or was she a mortal horse like Morgan, enchanted by some magic? Ben had no idea how such things worked. He only hoped she was free to enjoy her well-earned respite.

Mock held his wrist all the way. Her hand was so small, but Ben knew it was enough to hold him, for in the other she pulled the chain of the giant golden Faerie blade. Only yesterday, she had been his ward, or so he had thought. Now he was hers. The childlike energy was gone from her cheeks, extinguished like a candle. He didn't know this Mockingbird, who seemed just as tethered to the blade as he was to her.

They skirted the south end of the lake, the sky all amethyst and rose broken by the limbs of enormous, twisting trees. The world sang in this strange parallel place, an unending melody steeped in perpetual twilight. Sometimes, he saw double, trees existing in two places, like a fish split as light refracts across the surface of a pond. Lightning bugs—or whatever they were, those little lights—floated and blinked near and far, bobbing in the cool air like petals on gentle waves.

There were others, too. Shadows with bright eyes watched them from the nooks and crannies of the trees. But he didn't feel fear. The slithering shape in his breast was calm. It was not asleep, no—but it was at home here, in the other place. It rested, awake, flicking its tongue out now and then. Perceiving. Listening. Watching. Communing silently with the trees and the stones, with every drop of water and grain of soil. Beholding the spirits of this place as they beheld him. And he was one with them, and of them. It felt as though he'd been gasping for air his entire life, a sea creature forced to live on land.

Was this what it felt like to swim?

"This place. It's always been here," he said. It was half a question, half a realization. "I came here when I was little. When I wanted to run away . . . when I wanted to go somewhere safe."

"The worlds were closer together, then," Mock replied. "Even closer together still a hundred, two hundred, a thousand years ago. Once, I think, they were so close that they were one."

"What changed?"

Mock glanced back at the golden blade that towered behind them, then down at the chain she held wrapped in her fist.

"A lot changed, Ben Foley," she said, and pulled him along.

The way grew steep, and they picked their way over rocks and boulders, away from the lake and down into a forest valley. Mock hopped from rock to rock, guiding Ben as he lowered himself down, unbalanced with only one free hand to support himself. Shrike took the descent in effortless, weightless leaps.

Mock watched after him with something like sadness; not that, Ben realized, but fear. Fear and desperation. Emotions that felt wildly out of place here, like invaders from a far-off place.

"Are you doing this because he'll hurt you if you don't?" Ben whispered.

Mock squeezed his wrist in a flare of anger. "I'm doing it because otherwise, I will die," she said.

She yanked on him and he stumbled. In the valley below, a shining stream braided through gray boulders and red-barked pines. Over the chime-like song of the water, Ben heard other music. Birds and beating hands, singing voices. The wood was thick here, protected from the light of the sky, and through the trees he saw the dancing embers of firelight. As they slowed and came closer to the music, Ben realized the sound that he'd taken for his heart was actually the steady beat of drums. Thumping and pounding in an escalating call. Drums calling the forest to arms, Ben thought. Felt, more like. Drums of war.

The wood opened into a glade of flowers and moss-covered rocks. In the center of the clearing, a large red-wood had fallen and been halved lengthwise, so its smooth side faced up in a long, flat table. Berries and vegetables, nuts and roots were stacked in overflowing mounds or piled on leaves and in broken pottery, woven baskets, and tin cups. Ben stopped and stared. Not at the table nor the food and drink.

Seated on stumps and logs and rocks were little folk. Hundreds of them.

Eating, drinking, sparring in the loose dirt. Sharpening spears and fletching arrows. Some were tiny and winged, flitting through the air like dragonflies; others were the size of boars and buffalo, with animal ears and tails. Small ones zipped up trees or stared down at them with huge, unblinking eyes. A big one wallowed in the shadows and grumbled as it sharpened its long bear claws on an ancient tree.

The drumming ceased when Shrike strode into the clearing, smaller spirits scattering in his wake. But it wasn't until Mock led Ben out of the cover of the trees that the music stopped altogether. An impressive hush swept through the clearing as the evening light fell upon him, all the movement of the glade going still. From the way some of the spirits fidgeted and licked their lips and sharp little teeth, Ben felt like food on a tray. The main course of a highly anticipated meal.

"Cousins!" Shrike crowed, spreading his arm and spinning so that he could address every little creature in the clearing. "Cousins of the wind! Cousins of the fire! Cousins of the water and of the earth!"

"Shrike!" a little voice piped up. A creature the size of a blackbird leapt from a tree, gliding in a spiral toward Shrike and landing on one of his outstretched hands. It was black from head to toe, except for dashes of red and orange on its shoulders. "We have been waiting! Preparing for your return! Look, our feast!"

Shrike smiled brightly, hiding the shadows behind his teeth. "It is a veritable feast indeed, little Redwing. Much deserved of what is to come . . . Come, cousins. I have brought you a present. A guest of honor."

Ben knew Shrike must mean him. The spirit people murmured amongst themselves, some edging closer. Ben jerked his hand up when he felt the wet touch of a tongue on his fingers; a particularly bold one jumped back, mouth still open from stealing a taste.

"Salty!" it cried, biting its tongue.

"I want a taste! Do you think it speaks?"

"How shall we make him believe in us?"

"I'm so hungry!"

The sentiment echoed in growing numbers. Hunger.

One question, from a tiny creature that stood no taller than Ben's finger, chirped out above the rest: "How can he even *be* here?"

The other voices reduced to a low murmur of agreement.

The one who had spoken fluttered up onto a stump. It had feathered green and black hair, and the dappled wings of a starling instead of arms. Now that it had the attention of the others, and Shrike, it added, "You said humans aren't allowed in our new spirit world. They die!"

Shrike knelt before the little one and softly tapped it on the nose.

"That is the plan," he said. "But this place is not ours alone yet. This double-good is going to help us. Welcome him at our table, that he may taste the secret world he will soon grant us, once my Faerie blade completes its work."

The little bird-person inhaled at Ben in amazement.

"I want to taste double-good blood," it said with a tiny sigh.

"Maybe later," Shrike said with a fond chuckle. He took Ben by the shoulder, pulling him away from Mock. She let go without a protest, a thousand tons dropping away from Ben's shoulder as her little hand left his.

Shrike gestured to the head of the table. "Come, my honored guest." It was half a strange, alluring invitation. Half a deadly threat. "Sit at my table. Break bread with me and my people."

Ben took the seat that Shrike indicated. Without Mock holding on to him, he felt oddly sure that he could run. Disappear into the spirit world like he'd dreamed of doing as long as he could remember. It was a strange feeling, that confidence. He knew logically he had no right to feel that way, and this was Shrike's home. But all of his instincts told him that if he were to leap into the deep water of the other place, no one would ever be able to catch him.

"Why are you doing this?" he asked. "Am I a guest or a captive?"

"Look," Shrike said. "Understand. Use the sight I have granted you." He gestured grandly across the table of bounty, and Ben looked.

Then he *saw*.

The berries were shriveled, the vegetables molding. The nuts and roots were dried and cracked. With the double vision he'd been granted—blessed with, or cursed —he saw what had appeared to be sweet and plentiful, split apart, was in truth a blighted harvest, black and dying from starvation.

"You see?" Shrike said quietly in Ben's ear, leaning his cheek against Ben's temple. "The spirit world dies. But soon we will be alone, in a world of our own. Cut apart from the world that preys on us, protected by a veil. All this, thanks to you and your oathbreaker. Now sit, and eat."

The fare was bitter, overripe, fuzzy—each bite with its own special hint at not being quite right, but Ben ate without complaint. He hadn't had a real meal in days.

Mock sat beside him, silent as they ate. Though Shrike had chosen her to carry the blade, he seemed to have no interest in her beyond that. Now Ben noticed the little spirits ignored her, too. They flitted about, avoiding her with their eyes and words, some taking note only enough to spy with narrowed gazes and hisses.

"They don't like you much, do they?" he asked quietly.

She didn't answer him, brow twisted in a knot, shoving a wrinkled blueberry in her mouth.

"Do you want to know why?" Shrike asked. He feasted without complaint on the withering fare and picked his teeth with a twig. Spirit people sat on his shoulders and curled up in the cowl of his cloak.

Mock shot Shrike a glare.

"Do not," she warned, but Shrike ignored her. With his usual flair, he rose, stepping first onto the stump he'd been sitting on and then right onto the table, his bare foot knocking aside a mound of molding oranges. Everyone hushed to listen, gathering round.

"I will sing the song of the Mockingbird," Shrike crowed. His voice carried through the spirit wood, loud and clear and bold. "Believe in the days of old, Benjamin. In those days, your kind had no tongue. No language with which to speak. Yes, those were the days when you existed with the earth and land. Gave thanks to the gods of the sun and moon, the earthworm and the robin. The rattlesnake and the elk. Things were in balance then. Humans giving faeth, spirits making magic. The world was one."

Mock balled her hands in fists. The other spirits

hushed each other, wings flickering and fluttering as they listened. Shrike continued.

"But the humans of the land were sad. They could not sing nor speak. They could not explain to one another their simple, primal feelings. And so one morning, a god took pity on them. She flew in when the sun rose and bestowed upon them the gift of language. The gift of words." Shrike's eyes narrowed and his voice softened.

"For many years they thanked her for it. Thanked her, and the other bird-folk. The bringers and singers of song and omens. Words and prophecies. They thanked her for the gift with their *faeth*."

He moved, his cloak sweeping across the table until he stopped to stand over Mock. She sat with her face down, jaw set and hard. The little folk whispered and murmured.

"For many years the humans used the language she had given them to speak only truth. But humans are deceitful by nature. It was only a matter of time before they learned to lie. To one another. To the gods to whom they should be faithful. They invented new gods to worship: Property. Territory. Gold. Their fealty to these took precedence over all that came before. Over gods and traditions and beliefs, with laws and rules and lies. They stopped giving faeth. They stopped believing. And this land that we were meant to share began to die. Without the words she gave them, they could have done none of this."

The glade reverberated with the cries and boos and tears of the little folk, who wailed, banged on drums, and stomped their feet. Ben felt ill to see their distress. One of the spirits threw a shriveled berry that bounced off Mock's cheek, but she didn't move.

Shrike sighed and knelt in front of her. "So you see, Ben Foley, why few speak to her. Why she carried my Faerie blade without complaint. She opened the door for humankind to abandon us. Now that they have taken all we have, we have no choice but to shut that door. To cut our own world and our magic away, to a place that they cannot drain with their faethlessness. Our little Mockingbird is paying penance."

Something rippled through the wood as Shrike ended his parable, like a cold front before a storm. Mock stiffened, glancing first at Ben as if she wanted to tell him something, but then at Shrike when the other spirits in the glade shivered to whispers.

Wind gusted as a large creature alit on a nearby tree, hunkering with big, fluffy owl talons. Its back was bowed, its eyes huge and yellow.

"Snow has come. He is bringing them."

Shrike's smile faded. He tightened his grasp on his spear. "Goody."

The owl spirit nodded back, unnerving gaze landing on Ben for only a moment before it leapt back into the air on silent gray wings.

Mock stood, speaking despite the way all eyes turned away from her the moment she opened her mouth. She looked at the fist where she held the chain that dragged the Faerie blade, then up to her cousin who still stood on the table.

"Shrike. Something's wrong."

Ben felt it, too. Deep in his soul, as he gazed upon the chain and the terrible golden thing that loomed beyond the silhouettes of the trees. Was it dimmer than before?

"Something's happened to the blade," he whispered.

Shrike ignored the both of them. He stared into the depth of the woods, as if he could see whoever the owl had warned him about. Ben thought he could see a soft white-and-blue glow. Could almost hear the soft crunching of snow and ice breaking under cloven hooves.

"They come indeed," Shrike said grimly. "And they come to die."

CHAPTER XXIV

JESSE

Jesse stared down into the lake that shimmered like a gem under the indigo Faerie sky.

They stood on a steep slope, their view limited by the trunks of the firs and pines that grew like columns. It was still night, but everything glowed, like on nights when the moon was full but out of sight. When Snow had met him and opened the door to Faerie, they had been east of the basin, still on the other side of the Carson Mountains. Now they were right inside, in this weird, bright night, and the lake was unmistakable.

Jesse grimaced. This was not how he'd thought he would arrive in California.

"Come," Snow said. "There is something you must see."

He was already on the move down the slope, frosting flowers and tree bark as he went, and Jesse hurried after. The hike was difficult, and his lungs burned in the thin air; Snow had not brought Morgan with them to this world, though the way would likely have been too steep anyway. Jesse would have to keep up on his own.

Halfway down to the lake, Snow strode out onto a rocky ledge that jutted out beyond the tree cover and pointed. Jesse followed him, eyes instinctively on his feet, watching his step so he didn't fall to his death in the dizzying valley below.

"There," Snow said, unimpressed by the height.

Jesse looked, and wished he hadn't.

Some quarter of the way round the lake, a giant blade of molten gold jutted out of the mountain.

It blazed like a shaft of sunlight in the basin otherwise filled with night. Jesse tried not to flinch at the sight of it —and at the terrible familiarity he felt when he beheld it. It sang in a tone that resonated in his bones. It hummed and shook with barely restrained power, like lightning waiting for the right time to strike. And most sickeningly of all, it struck a chord in him so personal, so saturated with unnamed fear and guilt, that when he heard it calling he felt as if it were speaking only to him, from inside of him, in his own voice.

A thin thread of gold stretched from the pommel of the blade to a spot lost in the forest. Snow gazed upon the chain that shimmered under the fat moon, like a single strand of gossamer, though Jesse did not know what significance it held.

"Shrike's Faerie blade," Snow said, answering the question Jesse had forgotten to ask. "Forged from powerful Faerie gold, tempered with words that split and rend —by oaths made, and then broken."

Oathbreaker.

Jesse shuddered, though whether it was from what Snow said or the inescapable sight of the blade, or that horrible word, he didn't know. He had so many questions, but they were long and tangled. He tried to unravel them enough to speak them, but in the end they resolved to a word that was too small and encompassed too much.

"Why?" he asked.

Jesse almost didn't expect Snow to answer. He was surprised when the blue spirit tried, though he started moving again as he did, sweeping down the side of the mountain into the thick wood.

"Men from across the sea ravaged the land, enslaved their own kind, murdered the people that already lived in this place. They laid dominion on that which cannot be claimed and, in doing so, disrupted the communion between the land and the people. Many spirits grew weak as they were forgotten over the following decades. When he could bear it no longer, Shrike brought before us an idea. One he thought would save the spirits from the changing world."

Jesse imagined Shrike, industrious and shrewd. Snow spoke of division and dominion as if they were spirits themselves, with greedy, ravenous mouths. When Jesse brought them to life in his mind, they had eyes that were gleaming nuggets of gold. Teeth that tore apart the sinews of the world, then spat them out in pieces.

So that was why Shrike wanted to divide the worlds.

"He wants to split the spirits off from our world so they can't be harmed," he said softly.

Snow nodded, his antlers brushing against low-hanging boughs as they entered the forest. Night draped over Jesse's shoulders like a blanket, and the scent of blossoming trees and weeping cedar bark lingered like a perfume.

"But that is not the way. We are supposed to live in harmony. All things of the earth, spirits and humans, together. The greater spirits challenged Shrike for his troubled thinking. It was then that we discovered it was a Fae who had put the idea into Shrike's head. A powerful Fae from the isles across the sea, who had offered to forge the blade that could divide our worlds."

"A Fae," Jesse repeated. "Mock called herself a Faerie, when she first told us. But you're not Fae, are you? Not really."

Snow tilted his head.

"Fae is the name used by the spirits who came with the men from across the sea," he said. "When they came here with the colonists, they saw us and called us Fae. Folk of Faerie. As they call themselves. We use the term with you so you may understand us, but it is not the term we use for ourselves."

Like calling someone an *Indian*, Jesse thought. He wanted to know what name the spirit people used, but didn't ask. If Snow wasn't offering, then it was not his to know.

And what of this place? Jesse had heard Alice speak of Faerie more times than he could count, but the magic land of Alice and Aunt Mary's stories was always painted as the moors of the British Isles. Toadstools and ancient hawthorn, rolling misty countrysides and whispering woods. Completely separate from the human world, divided by a veil that could only be drawn back by powerful magic. Not like this place, so similar to the world Jesse knew. Here, surrounded by the squabbling calls of blue jays and the chirps of cardinals, wary any moment he might see a foraging bear.

"And this isn't Faerie?" he asked.

Snow looked up into the towering redwoods, flanked by distant mountains.

"In the beginning, there was no difference," he said. "Spirits and humans inhabited the earth together. We fed on faeth and returned that love to the land. But over time, rifts formed. In places, the worlds were forced apart . . . by other Faerie blades, no doubt."

"But if the worlds are divided, then won't you be safe?" Jesse asked.

Snow fixed him with a chilling, sad look.

"If the worlds are divided, we will not be seen anymore," he said. "And if humans stop seeing us, they will stop believing."

Jesse knew the end of that story. When humans stopped believing . . .

"You'll die," he whispered. "Doesn't Shrike know that? Why would he do this?"

"I don't know," Snow said.

This wasn't the world Jesse had expected to find when he left St. Joe's. He had expected glory and freedom. A world that was wild, needing to be tamed. Uninhabited, ready to be owned. He tried not to focus on how wrong he'd been.

"He planned this all along. We played right into his hand."

The solid ground littered with pine needles was giving way to peaty marsh, broken by lichen- and moss-covered rocks. Jesse's boots sank up to the ankle and he struggled to keep up with Snow, whose bare feet seemed to rest just on top of the soft earth.

"Perhaps not completely. The line of this division has been slowly carved for decades, if not centuries. Scored by hundreds of thousands of boots and wagon wheels. From the shores to the sacred hills to the lake, through the plains, the mountains, the desert. Your parents and their parents, and theirs. From east to west, as they overtake this land. Shrike did not conceive of this; your people have done it on their own. He merely took advantage of it, at the suggestion of his benefactor."

"With Mock's help," Jesse said, giving voice to the betrayal. It didn't help, and though he expected to feel angry about it, he only felt profoundly sad.

"Indeed. The final part of the spell was to bind an oathbreaker to the blade. Shrike had to use a world-walker. A double-good. Someone who steps in two worlds."

Jesse shivered. *Double-good.* He and Ben both walked in two worlds, in different ways. But why Jesse? Why had Shrike marked *him* as the oathbreaker? Was it something in particular, or was he just a more terrible person? He tried to think of the things he'd done and said. But when he searched what had happened that night before the fire, the answer was plain, simple, and ugly. Shrike had even said it out loud.

It is done.

"I reached for the gold first," Jesse said. He rubbed at his forehead, as if he could break the spell so easily. "Shrike chose me then, to be the oathbreaker."

Snow nodded. "He tied your power to the blade. Mock dragged it behind you, poured your broken promises into it. Now the line is laid. When Shrike spills blood as his final act, the spell will ignite. It will be over."

Like a fuse, unrolled across the continent. What would happen when it was lit?

Jesse could hardly comprehend the repercussions. Almost every one of Alice's tales spoke of the veil that hid Faerie and the Faerie folk from humans, but in the stories, it had always been that way. He had never wondered why Faerie was separated, or if it had ever been otherwise. Now he knew. Something *had* happened. Something terrible, and it was happening again. Here and now, and this time, it was his fault.

But it hadn't happened yet. Not completely.

"We're gonna stop him," he said. "I promise."

Jesse heard water before he saw it. The waterfall appeared like it had been conjured from magic. The rock cliff it poured out from stood three stories high, black and brown and glittering with mist and the echoing sound of the thundering falls. They stood at the bottom, where the water frothed in a perfectly round pool, its heavy white chaos disappearing into calm waters. Moonlight danced in them, and Jesse thought he saw lights coming from within the pool, silver and purple and blue, green and red and gold.

He stopped where the shining mist just barely kissed his cheeks. Snow, too, approached the edge of the pool, the frost from his body just crystallizing the water, the mist in the air turning to a beautiful flurry of snow before it melted again into rain.

As Jesse watched, the lights within the pool intensified. Three figures appeared across the pond. The first was no taller than he was, with lapis lazuli skin and the lower half of a frog, shining and spotted as the water parted. The spirit's long, mushroom-sprouting hair trailed wet and long, weaving in the back between six dragonfly's wings.

The second, whose huge steps shook the earth, came to sit on the rock at the crown of the falls. This spirit had thick black hair and a warm, brown face, butterflies of every color flocking on fragrant wild ginger flowers that sprouted from whorled buffalo's horns.

The third, stepping out of the wood to Jesse's left, had the weight and face of a fox, with long brown hair wrapped with ribbons and goose feathers and autumn leaves.

"You brought a human to this place?" asked the one who stared down at them from above, heavy voice echoing down along the falls, hot as July.

Jesse shuddered uncontrollably as the three spirits watched her. She realized she knew their names without needing to be told. The one that came from the lake—Spring Rain. The one who watched from above—Summer Sky. And the one who leaned on a tree, fox ears twitching—Autumn Wind.

"The oathbreaker, no less," Wind said.

Snow glanced back at Jesse, as if she were an offering that left much to be desired. She resented the sentiment but dared not say anything here in this place.

"I was unable to stop Shrike," Snow said. "So, now, he has made it to the lake and brought with him another human. The one whose heart was broken by this oathbreaker."

"The betrayed," Rain whispered, voice like a frog leaping into a pond. "Shrike will spill his blood. His spell will be invoked. We trusted you to stop Shrike's spell before it was begun. To destroy the oathbreaker. We did all this, and instead you bring *her* here?"

Snow was hesitant, though still noble.

"There is something, I think. A way we can stop Shrike's spell," he said.

Jesse's pulse quickened. This was it. The reason she'd come here. Snow's kin all turned to Jesse, Snow's words awakening some idea in them. When they'd first appeared, they'd been aloof, almost cold. Now their eyes sharpened, their nostrils flared, their ears swiveling forward.

Wind was the first to come closer, weaving effortlessly through the trees, not a twig snapping beneath clever, padded feet. Jesse held still as the spirit neared, smelling of juniper and cranberries.

"Do you have what it takes? Do you believe?" Wind asked, inhaling the scent of Jesse's hair. Jesse shivered. "Oathbreaker?"

Autumn had been Jesse's favorite season since she could remember. The first cold nights in late September, pumpkins and squash ripening on the vine. Roasted corn and apples over the fire. She always waited out the hot summer days, knowing soon autumn would come.

"I believe," she said.

Sky rose tall and shining, then leapt, descending the cliff of the falls as nimbly as a goat. Within moments Jesse felt small under the heat and zeal of midsummer, the cloud of butterflies.

"The blood of one who has been betrayed is what will power the spell's finishing blow," Sky said, gazing down at her. "The spell built on deceit and broken promises. The rift cleaved by disparaging words. Every oath you broke toughened the blade. Added barbs to its edge."

"I don't understand," Jesse said. "What does that have to do with killing Ben?"

It seemed to Jesse the four were all of one voice, somehow. This time it was Rain's turn to speak. "He was the one you wronged. Murder breaks the most sacred oath of life. That promise breaking, and a life ending, will send the blade back along the line it marked, cleaving our worlds apart."

Jesse imagined a logger's bow saw driving through wood. It always started tough, but once the blade bit, the cuts were long and deep. And now, there was only one more draw of the blade before the log fell apart.

Wind spoke next: "But Snow is right. There may be a way to reverse it."

It should have sounded like hope, but their faces were all grim. When Jesse looked to Snow, he would not meet her eyes.

"What?" she said. "What is it? I'll do it. I don't care."

"Blood of the oathbreaker, spilled in sacrifice." It was Rain who spoke, standing upright on amphibian legs. "To save the one that was betrayed. That would reverse Shrike's spell."

"Bind the rift that's been cut," Sky agreed.

"Banish that foul blade from this world and the next," Wind added.

Jesse's hope sank like the sun going down. The four spirits watched her understand what they were asking of her. She wanted to protest, to say she hadn't asked to be part of this. To be used by Shrike. But the truth was that it didn't matter. The heart that powered the blade beat in her chest. The wrongs she'd done were done, and they'd caused all this.

The worst was knowing she wasn't the hero. She wanted to be the savior, beating back an awful outside evil. Coming to the rescue of others beset by a villain. Jesse had wanted nothing more than to rise to the call when it came.

"How much blood will it take?" she asked, not because her decision depended on the answer, but because she wanted to know what she should be preparing for.

"All of it," Snow said. "Do you accept?"

So many others had been fighting this entire time. The call had not been a single horn, but a thousand cries that Jesse hadn't been able to hear. What had Ben said? Not to tell him it was noon when he'd been awake since dawn? And now it was nearly midnight. In the end, the most heroic thing she could do was try to undo the damage she'd done. Before it was too late.

Jesse nodded. *I'm sorry, Alice.*

The four nodded solemnly back. Perhaps it was just a trick of the light, but each of them seemed to grow brighter, more vivid.

"Then we have an accord," Sky said. "We will follow the chain of the blade to Mockingbird. Where we find her, we will find Shrike. We will push him to take us to the place he has prepared, and to invoke his spell before he is ready. That is when you will do what must be done. You must spill blood before he does."

Jesse nodded. She hadn't seen the glimmering golden chain since entering the forest, but she could almost feel its presence stretching across the spirit land like a tightrope. She and it were bound. Had been bound since Shrike had marked her that first night.

Three of them—spring, summer, and autumn—gathered round and made to leave. But they stopped when they saw winter was not with them.

Snow had gone to the water's edge, face to the sky and hands out, palms up. Silhouetted against the rushing of the falls, the shape of the nearly full moon cradled between his antlers, he was the image of a tree cloaked in the cold of winter.

"If you are there, mother, we go to stop our cousin. Our kin. It is not the way, but I do not know if there is another. If you are there, please give us a sign. Please, guide us."

His plea was almost drowned in the crashing of the water. If there was an answer, it was lost entirely. They waited, straining for a sign, but none came. Snow turned away in the end, downcast. They left without another word.

Sky sent butterflies above the trees as they traveled, listening to their silent voices as they fluttered down and whispered the way. Rain leapt from bough to bough, leaving wet and dew and lichens behind. Wind disappeared as soon as they entered the wood, though now and then Jesse thought she spied a flash of brown and gold sprinting between the shadows.

Snow remained beside her, steady and quiet as

always. As they headed deeper into the wood and the beats of drums came through the trees and the earth, Jesse asked a question she had been meaning to ask a long time.

"Can spirits die?"

"Yes," Snow said.

By the time the drumming grew loud enough to shake Jesse's bones, her palms were sweaty. As the world entered its darkest hour, she saw firelight through the trees. The drumming was slow and rhythmic, powerful and driving, like the heartbeat of an enormous beast waking. Rising, preparing for battle.

Sky stopped up ahead. Beyond the tree line, Jesse could see burning torches and figures dancing, zipping through the trees. Hooting and shouting and singing to the beat of the pounding drums.

"Wait here, human. They are many. You must save yourself until the time."

Then, without waiting for Jesse's answer, Sky let out an earth-shaking bellow and charged into the glade. A war cry from above came like thunder and lightning as Rain joined on humming wings, bringing a storm from the sky. Screams broke out from the enemy camp, the cries of birds and the bursting of dozens of spirit people taking flight. The battle had begun.

"I will return," Snow said.

He put a hand on her shoulder for a moment before drawing his bow and striding forward, a gale of freezing wind sweeping in from the north.

Jesse did not fancy herself a coward, but standing there, huddled behind a tree, her knees were weak and her pulse thready. She could only glimpse what havoc Spring and Summer wrought upon Shrike's flock, the flames from the torches arching high and filling the wood with black smoke as they fought against the freezing rain.

Metal gleamed. A winged creature cried out and fell from the sky, its pinions cut short. Wind stood where it landed, squirming and squealing in the dirt. Jesse saw the flash of a sickle, and then the autumn spirit was gone again.

Silhouettes of birds and other flying creatures darted in and out of the smoke and flame, the drums giving way to the shrieks and calls of warriors thirsting for battle. Jesse's hands felt wet against the bark of the tree she was clutching, and she realized she had cut her fingertips on its rough skin. She pulled them into her palms, determined to save the precious red stuff.

Until the time. Like Sky had said.

A terrible cry pierced the din, sending an ugly chill up Jesse's back. She knew that voice. That sound. A moment later, a gust of wind blew back the smoke. Lit by the flames that had caught in the brush, a tall, lean figure stood high on a rock, his charcoal skin splashed with white and gray.

Shrike.

In one hand he held his spear. In the other, he had caught a fox. Wind hissed and spit, bucking against his grip and slashing. But wherever the blade cut, it drew no blood.

Shrike drew back his spear, grin splitting his face with white. But before he could plunge it through Wind's heart, Sky's horns were there, crushing his side. The crunching of bones echoed and Shrike screamed, dropping his prey—who was suddenly his hunter, springing back upon him with sickle drawn. He fell back as the two challenged him together, letting out an anguished howl when Snow and Rain joined them.

The calls to battle contorted into wails of defeat. Jesse crept closer as the feathered shapes of Shrike's flock fled. She expected the ground to be littered with bodies, but the closer she got, the more she could see that Snow and his siblings had been careful. Only a few of the little folk had died, their silhouettes blasted on the ground or against trees in dust and ash. The rest—the hundred rest —were fleeing. Crying and screaming curses, spitting in fear, but fleeing alive.

Where was Ben?

An explosion erupted at the camp, and a hot wash of fire blew her hair back. She barely caught sight of Shrike's shadow leaping into the air, catching an updraft of the fiery miasma that had burst in the glade where Snow and the others had cornered him. A moment later he was lost in the sky, black on black. The only thing that proved he was still there was the piercing cry that tore through the night like a spearhead through flesh.

Light caught Jesse's eye. Escaping into the wood, hidden in shadows and smoke, something glittered yellow. Like lightning bugs, blinking on and off, shining and shimmering and chiming like gold.

Jesse held her breath when she saw the flickering again. Without waiting for Snow, she gave chase. Quickly and quietly, hoping to catch up before they spotted her. As she drew closer, she heard footsteps.

Two figures moved briskly through the wood, one tiny and the other taller, reluctant but seemingly unable to resist. It was Ben and Mock, endless chain of gold in hand, jangling like bells through the spirit wood.

CHAPTER XXV

BEN

The chaos and calamity of the battle that had come to Shrike's feasting table would have drowned out any plea for help that Ben could have made—and anyway, there was no one here in the spirit world to hear his cries. So he said nothing, following Mock without protest or struggle through the labyrinthine forest, hoping time might someday soften the fearsome memory of the four beasts that had come into the glade, bearing their awesome and awful power.

Ben stumbled to a halt. The wood opened, revealing a long oval bay, linked to the big lake by a slim mouth to the northeast. In the palm of the bay was a small island, connected to the shore by a narrow stone bridge.

Overhead, the golden chain wrapped round Mock's wrist stretched like a wire. Ben followed it from where they stood to the far-off blade, visible on the other side of the great lake, a shining golden pillar of light. As he looked at it, he thought he saw it flicker. But perhaps it was a trick of the air or light.

Shrike appeared beside them. His shoulders were heaving with effort, blood splashed on his cheek and dripping from dozens of wounds across his body. He stood beside them a minute, catching his rasping breath. The moon had vanished, and Ben could see the outline of trees against the blue-violet of the sky. The witching hour had passed, and they were headed toward morning.

"It is time," Shrike said. "Before they find us."

He walked out onto the stone bridge that led into the lake, striding across it as if he owned it. The water shivered with the impact of his footsteps, and from deep within the bay Ben thought he heard an eerie, singing voice.

Mock hesitated to follow.

"This is a sacred place," she said softly. "Where the night granted Slender Moon the magic of the gates."

"Why are we here?"

She tightened her grip on Ben's wrist and pulled him after Shrike. "Because the others will not follow. Do not enter the water—it would be desecration for a human to touch it."

It was further to the center of the lake than it looked. Far away from the meadow and forest. The waters were quiet and deep, and the stone walkway was only a few feet wide. Though Ben could swim, he dreaded to think how quickly he might drown if he should stumble off the path.

"Mock. You don't have to do this," he said. "We both know—we can both feel that something's changed with the blade. Maybe there's another way."

Her hand faltered on his. "I am sorry, Ben Foley," she whispered. "I will understand if you do not believe in me after you are gone."

He wished he knew what he could say to change her mind.

Where the bridge met the island, a pile of large stones formed a circular platform. The sky continued to brighten behind the ring of trees, clouds rose and lavender.

Shrike discarded his cloak and stood naked, armed only with his ever-present spear. His body, the color of the butcher bird with black and white and gray feathers sprouting from his joints and down his spine, was marred by gashes, bruises, and cuts.

"Come, come, human. Betrayed. Our long journey has reached its end." His voice was less extravagant than before, but he still had enthusiasm despite his wounds. For him, Ben reckoned, it was hope.

"And come, cousin Mock. Time to be absolved. Time to bring it to me for the spell."

"Mock . . ." Ben began.

Mock looked at him. He tried to move her heart with his. Without a word, just by meeting eyes. Just by seeing her. *You don't have to do this.*

She turned away, jangling the golden chain bunched in her fist. "Shrike, something is wrong. The blade. It was ready, when we came here. But something changed. It's grown weaker—"

"Impossible. Can promises be unbroken? No! So it cannot grow weaker. Now, bring it to me!"

"But—"

Shrike glowered at her, tiny black pupils just pinpricks in his livid yellow eyes.

"Call the Faerie blade," he growled. "*Now*."

Mock looked down, mouth pressed in a flat line. She gripped her fingers round the golden chain and pulled.

The earth trembled and the wind sang, glancing off the edge of the blade that came at her call, toppling trees as it cut through the wood. As the sun rose behind it, its edges threw off beams of light that rippled across the waters of the lake and the undulating quilt of flowers that wreathed it.

It was beautiful, in that moment, Ben thought. Beautiful and terrible.

Distant footsteps drew his attention. Someone had come running out of the wood. A human figure, illuminated by no ethereal glow. Thin and wiry with a shock of copper hair set off by the golden light that filled the clearing. Ben shuddered uncontrollably at the sight, remembered how to breathe.

"Ben!" Jesse Murphy hollered. "Ben, I'm coming!"

Ben nearly bolted then, ran down the stone bridge toward Jesse, leapt into the deadly waters and swam to shore. But Mock still held his wrist. Jesse reached the edge of the lake, and Ben's voice lurched into his throat.

"Jesse! Don't go in the water!"

Shrike watched Jesse stumble along the shore. The bird spirit's thin lips slanted, tilting back and forth between anger and revelry. "Oathbreaker. It is too late. They all know it, too."

Eyes burned out of the wood where Shrike was gesturing with his spear. Gold and red, green and blue. Snow emerged from the forest. Silently and weightlessly, like an elk treading through the grass and daisies. At his sides were the three who'd waded into battle with him. But as they reached the place where the lake's waters lapped at the land, they hesitated. All their magnificent power that had swiftly crushed Shrike's rebel spirits meant nothing. Like devils at the steps of a chapel, they dared not pass.

But someone else would.

Jesse had reached the stone bridge. He slowed to a hurried walk, hands out for balance to keep from tumbling into the waters that reflected the light of the awakening dawn.

Mock's grip tightened on Ben's wrist as they watched. It almost felt hopeful. Was this what Mock truly wanted? Ben thought he saw some brightness returning to the spirit's little body. She whispered up to Shrike, whose gaze would not break from Jesse's approach.

"If Jesse's come for him, then isn't his promise . . ."

"*NO!*" Shrike's voice crushed hers beneath it. "The damage is already done. He vowed not to abandon his friend, and then he did. He broke his word, like all humans do. The evidence is lying dusty in the red desert.

Screaming into the nothingness where the sand meets the mountains!"

Shrike turned away and plunged the point of his spear into the water, as if trying to agitate a sleeping serpent. Ben felt the shape in his own breast stir in response, waking and writhing.

"Mangled and proud on broken hooves!" Shrike cried. "Praying, somewhere, under an apple tree! Are you listening, cousin? Ah, now. Here comes the dawn."

The red that crept above the trees reminded Ben of blood. Shrike gazed upon it with a wild grin. He lifted his spear, knuckles whitening with his eager grip. His voice rose in a chant as the sun brightened the dizzy sky. The stones below them trembled, quivering. The lake moaned.

Shrike's voice boomed low and loud over the shivering surface of the lake.

"Blood of the betrayed, whet the blade of broken oaths."

Ben reached out and took Mock's shoulder. Tried to get her attention before that spear came for him. He could hear it hungering for his blood. Soon it would feed.

"Whatever is going on," he said. "Whatever you've done—we can fix it. I'll fix it, Mock. Just help me. Tell me how to stop this!"

She watched Shrike, lips pressed together as if holding words captive inside her teeth. "You heard Shrike. There is nothing we can do."

"You're wrong. There is something."

Jesse had reached the platform. As if in response, the golden Faerie blade hummed louder, singing in a tonal chorus. He was holding a knife.

"Jesse, what are you doing?" Ben choked on his words when Jesse raised the blade, pointing the end of it up toward his heart.

"Ben, I'm sorry—"

Shrike whirled, face ablaze with rabid delight. In a single motion he lashed out with a claw, snatched Jesse up by the collar. He shook him violently, like a dog worrying a duck, and Jesse went limp for a moment, dropping the knife. It bounced off the stone and into the lake.

"Jesse!"

Ben launched himself forward, but their fingers only brushed one another before Shrike hoisted Jesse overhead. Then the shaft of his spear crashed into Ben's face.

It felt like cast iron. Ben's world spun as he fell, holding his head where he'd been struck. He tried to get up, over and over, but he couldn't find his balance. He could barely see as Shrike held Jesse by the neck, over the lake. He heard Jesse swearing, kicking, struggling—

Then Shrike tossed Jesse into the endless waters.

Mock let out a cry of dismay, muffled by the deadly splash. They watched as Jesse sank like a stone, taking the last bit of hope in Ben's heart with him. Mock fell to her knees beside him, burying her tears in her hands.

Ben didn't try to move as Shrike stepped over him,

raising his spear. He didn't care anymore. He barely listened as Shrike uttered the last words of his incantation.

"Your path is marked with broken words, sharp as shattered glass and bones. Their edges cut and slice and rend. And now . . ."

Shrike stopped when the lake tremored.

Ripples spread forth, originating from the stone platform. Bubbles rose, huge and billowing, like the exhale from a monstrous creature. As the sun's brilliant light peeked over the line of trees, shattering off the metal of the Faerie blade, the lake split open.

Go, Ben.

The voice came from all around. From the sky and the lake. From inside him. It was the voice that sang the song he had listened to since he was a child, calling him out into the night.

Go to your friend.

Shrike's chest lurched in jolting, fearful, short breaths. He cast left and right, eyes wide, mouth hanging half open in fear. He, too, knew whose voice was speaking.

Despite the heartbreak that felt bottomless inside him, Ben found his feet. Rushing past Shrike, he caught only a glimpse of the shape rising from the waters of the lake, the green and white light shining from the figure ascending in a cascade of cerulean waves.

Jesse. I'm coming.

He reached the edge, held his breath, and leapt.

CHAPTER XXVI

JESSE

Don't you worry, girls. We'll be fine.

Jesse barely remembered his mother's broken voice. It seemed so long ago.

A bubble of air ballooned out of his lungs, disappearing into the lake. He watched the last remains of the memory shimmer along its surface, and then it was gone.

She'd cried. And when they'd buried her, Alice sang.

So meet me by moonlight alone . . .

Jesse struggled suddenly, as if waking, though everything round her felt sleepy. She tried to pull herself up, but the still water was thick as stone, tugging her down, down. The last bubbles escaped from her mouth, the only part of her that might eventually reach the surface, and she wondered if, when they popped above, they would whisper the words she had been screaming.

I'm sorry.

Then she sank, heavy with the regret that she had not been able to spill the blood necessary to undo the spell.

To save Ben. She had failed even to die properly, and now they were both lost.

Hands grabbed her from above. Coming out of the lake felt like being born, and she retched up lungfuls of water.

She realized she was holding on to someone, both of them soaked. Strong arms were wrapped round her, thumping her back so the last of the lake came tumbling out.

"Ben," she mumbled.

Ben stared past Jesse. She followed his gaze.

Shrike had his back to them, waving his spear, facing out into the lake. He was screaming. Not words. Just a chain of guttural, avian screams, exploding from his body one after the other.

Standing opposite him, bare feet flat against the surface of the lake, was a lithe creature in swirling robes of blue and black. What Jesse at first took to be a pale green cloak were wings, which spread wide and gazed down with white, opalescent, ever-seeing eyes. Then opened the second pair of eyes, deep blue in a round face the soft silver of the full moon.

"Slender Moon," Mock breathed from where she knelt nearby.

"You're alive," Ben said. His voice was soft and in pieces with worry. He held on to Jesse like he needed her more than she needed him. "What were you doing?"

Jesse shook her head. She couldn't remember. "Trying to save you," she said. She knew that much.

"*Shrike.*"

Slender Moon's voice came through blue lips that did not move. The name drifted through the air, soft and gentle, cold and pale. It silenced Shrike's screams, though his body was still hunched in an angry, crooked curve, hands gripped white round his spear and sides heaving with rage.

"You cannot stop me," he panted, voice hoarse. "I will cut this flesh from bone. I will rip out its heart and hold it safely in my hand. I will save us when you would not. You cannot stop me. No one can."

Slender Moon held out a hand, hovering closer without taking a single step. Shrike shuddered when a silver palm reached out to rest on his cheek.

"It is not the way," Slender Moon said.

Shrike bowed his head, trembling, clearly reluctant to be a mere beast tamed by the glowing spirit's gentle touch. All was still and quiet, and Jesse thought it might be over. But then Shrike's hand tightened again on his spear.

"It is the only way."

Slender Moon's lips parted as Shrike's spear found its mark, plunging into and through and finally out, where it stopped. The sky and the lake flashed green with fluttering wings, white with eyes wide in sadness, and a deep blue brimming with pain. Then both darkened in unison, bleeding into red.

Mock screamed, and Shrike repeated his incantation,

gold eyes trembling as he faced the watery spirit he held impaled upon his spear.

"Blood of the betrayed, whet the blade of broken oaths. Your path is marked with broken words, sharp as shattered glass and bones. Their edges cut and slice and rend."

Slender Moon smoothed a hand over Shrike's where he gripped the spear. Blood stained the spear wood, then Shrike's skin. It seemed for a moment there would be no end to it, that it might pour out and stain everything in the world. But then the moment passed and there was nothing left. Shrike lowered the point of the spear, and Slender Moon slid away into the red lake.

"And now," Shrike said, "they end."

A blot had formed in the sky where the moon had been. It deepened, black and red and sparkling with green lightning. Wind tore through the trees, frothing red peaks on the waters of Slender Moon's lake. Shrike stood still as a statue in the center of it all, waiting.

He hardly seemed to notice when Mock threw herself at him, beating her fists against his heaving chest.

"It isn't right! I told you it isn't right!" She screamed her voice ragged, face wet with tears. She struck at him until she had no strength left, falling to the ground at his feet. "What have you done? I wish he had killed you! I wish he had killed you back in Devil's Gate! *What have you done?*"

Shrike paid no attention to her, fixating expectantly on the Faerie blade and its electric hum, vibrating with power. The earth shook, readying for a quake, but none came. The blade did not move.

Shrike looked upon it, eyes reddening with impatience. Then confusion. Then rage.

"Why isn't it working? Why isn't it going back to the beginning of the line?"

Mock could barely speak.

"I told you," she said, broken. "I told you something was wrong."

Shrike whirled on Mock, rage palpable as the bloodied waters. Jesse leapt for her, but too late. Shrike snatched her up, hoisting her by the neck, splattering her face with the blood and spit that flew from the back of his throat when he screamed, *"Why isn't it working?"*

Jesse and Ben reached her at the same time, but Shrike knocked them away with his spear, nearly sending them flying back into the lake. He screamed at Mock, throat and mouth bulging and growing, contorting his voice beyond recognition.

"You betrayed me," Shrike growled, deep as the chasm that was growing between the worlds. "You did this. *You.*"

"I told you," Mock whispered.

Shrike ripped the chain from Mock's clenched fist. As Jesse sprang to his feet, rushing forward a second time, Shrike's jaw hinged wide. Mock met Jesse's eyes, full of tears and sorrow.

"I'm sorry," she said.

Before Jesse could reach her, Shrike's jaw crashed shut round Mock.

She was gone.

Shrike tilted his head back and let out a howl.

"*It is not over!*" he bellowed. "*I'll drag it back myself!*"

He bowed his head, hunching his back. Bones split the flesh of his shoulders, black and gray wings rupturing from his back. His howling did not cease as he leapt, taking to wing with the Faerie blade's chain tangled in his claws. Higher and higher he flew, his cries tearing through the fabric of the sky.

The blade rumbled and tilted. As the chain grew taut and Shrike flew east, with a great heaving groan, it turned and followed.

All round them, spirit wails rode on the wind like the leaves being ripped from their branches in the storm. Jesse felt rain falling from the heavens, but when it touched his lips he tasted salt.

"We have to get out of here!" Ben yelled. Jesse could barely hear him over the thunder and roaring wind.

They raced away from the island. Snow met them at the shore, gentle face ruined by tears. Shrike's silhouette was a black scar in the crimson sky.

"What's he doing?" Ben cried. "What's happened?"

"I don't know. But you must go from here. The realms are dividing. Once that happens, you cannot stay here. Even if you are double-good."

Snow's words shook Jesse, deep in his bones and blood and heart. The worlds were splitting. Mock had said Shrike's spell had gone wrong, but whatever had happened hadn't been enough. The horrible tearing and ripping in the sky and the earth were proof as Shrike dragged the blade back east.

Despite all they had done, they had failed.

"Go," Snow said. He reached to them with both hands, closing their eyes with palms soft as fresh snow.

The storm and the quaking faded away. Everything was distant, even the abyss of failure lingering in Jesse's gut. He tried not to let it devour him, tried not to become lost in the dark. But he started to. Started to fall. Started to feel everything, and then nothing. Would have been consumed by it if it were not for the touch of skin as Ben reached out and grasped Jesse's hand in his.

CHAPTER XXVII
BEN

They woke in a tangle and the first thing Ben tasted was dirt. His cheek pressed against an unending carpet of grass, and he breathed in the cool, wormy scent of the earth. In a shared daze, they sat up. There was warmth in his palm; Jesse's hand was still entwined in his. Jesse gave it a quick squeeze and pulled away, knuckling the red corners of his eyes.

They were at the top of a high hill, surrounded by a handful of evergreens. The sky was dawning violet, mottled with cottony clouds. There was no sign of the terrible red storm Shrike had set loose in the spirit world. No sign of the chaos they had left behind. The moon still hung in the sky, just above the horizon, as if nothing had changed. But Ben had seen what it had turned into in the spirit world. That shadowy hole. He had seen Slender Moon die. And as he looked at the pale thing now, he felt like he was looking into a coffin.

Even without the sight, Ben could tell. The worlds were moving further apart from each other. Split like a tree rent by lightning. He could feel it.

At the bottom of the hill, warm lights flickered. There was a settlement down there.

"Carson City," Jesse said. He must have recognized the landscape or some other feature Ben had missed. "There's a stable. I don't know how much time's passed, but if Morgan's found his way back there . . . or we can find other horses . . ."

"To do what with?" Ben asked, but Jesse didn't answer. The two of them rose and stumbled down the hill. Neither of them needed to say what they both were thinking: They had to hurry. They had no time to waste.

When they reached the packed dirt perimeter of the settlement, Jesse moved with a purpose. Ben would have liked to believe it was because he had a plan. A well-thought-out plan that would involve horses, that could fix their situation. That could stop Shrike from completing his spell when he already had such an enormous head start. But from the way Jesse's jaw was gritted and his hands shook when he pushed open the door of the stable beside a tavern, Ben could tell there was no plan beyond finding Morgan.

Two horses were tied down the center aisle, while others peered out of their stalls at the commotion as they entered. Jesse gasped with relief at the familiar chestnut face with the white blaze down his forehead. He wrestled the stable door open, and Ben looked across the other long, big-eyed faces.

"What's going on in here?"

A man with a red beard stood in the door behind them, holding a shotgun. Jesse clenched his fists like he was about to jump into a fight. Ben's hand flew to the gun at his belt. He'd forgotten it was there, when he'd been in the other place—guns didn't seem to do much to spirits. But now that they were back here, he remembered it quickly enough.

"You!" Jesse spat.

"Jessamine! Thank God you're all right . . ." The man's eyes flashed with lightning when he took a harder look at Ben. His freckled cheeks wrinkled as he squinted. "And who's this? You lay a hand on my daughter?"

Daughter. This was Jesse's pa? Ben felt like he'd swallowed a beetle whole.

"Hey! I said, you lay a hand on my daughter?"

"No, sir," Ben said through clenched teeth.

"Stop it! Goddammit, stop!" Jesse swore, striking his pa in the chest. It blew the steam out of the man, at least for now. "He's my friend. He's done nothing wrong."

The man gave Ben a last warning glance before turning away, letting out a big huff of air. "Jessamine. Listen, I've given it some thought. I've decided you and Alice will come to Carson City. She'll have the baby here. I'll make it work."

"What? She's eight months pregnant!"

Mr. Murphy balled his hand up in a fist, as if offended that his apparent change of heart was being disrespected.

"Jessamine Murphy, you are *my* daughter, and you'll do as I—"

"That baby ain't coming to Carson City, and neither is Alice," Jesse said. He finished leading Morgan out of the stable. "Now tell me which of these horses has your name on it. We need another mount."

"My horse? You'll do no such thing!" But his eyes gave him away, pointing to a palomino in a nearby stall. Jesse walked Morgan over and pulled the palamino's gate open, then brushed past his pa on his way out of the stable.

"I'm taking the horse either way, but the least you could do is give your blessing," Jesse said.

Mr. Murphy set his jaw, squaring his shoulders in affront. But then he looked down. Jesse thrust the palomino's reins at Ben. It was only because Ben was so close that he could see Jesse's hand was still shaking. He took the reins and mounted as Jesse took his spot in Morgan's saddle.

"Tell Daisy I'm sorry," Jesse said, voice cracking. Then he dug his heels into Morgan's side and rode out of the stable, turning his face away before Ben could make out what broken expression was on his cheeks.

"Jessamine!"

When Mr. Murphy stepped forward, Ben put himself in the way. He didn't have time to care what kind of person the man really was. He just hoped Jesse never had to look on his face again.

"It's *Jesse*," he said, and chased his partner into the night.

Jesse drove Morgan clear through Carson City and

east into the desert on the other side. Ben's horse paled in comparison to Dusky; he missed the spirit horse's speed and power. Within minutes they were out in the dirt, faced with the merciless desert and the blinding morning sun. He knew the Faerie blade cut through, right there, but it was invisible to them without the sight. No one knew about it but the two of them, and they seemed powerless to stop it.

Ben called Jesse's name, again and again, but Jesse didn't stop or look back until they reached some invisible landmark. Then he barely pulled the reins before leaping out of Morgan's saddle, running off into the dirt and rocks, and falling to his knees. Ben pulled on the reins and slid out, sprinting to where Jesse was desperately digging through the earth.

"Jesse!" Ben panted. "What—what're you doing?"

He tried to pull the boy up. He had already bloodied his hands and knuckles on the hard, sharp earth, but he yanked away from Ben and kept digging.

"The Bible." When Ben heard his voice, he realized Jesse was crying as he clawed through the endless dirt and rocks. "If I can find the Bible—"

"The Bible!" Ben exclaimed. This spot in the desert—was it where they'd fought, where Jesse had thrown the book at him? Ben grabbed Jesse's sleeve. "Jesse, stop it. You're bleeding."

"I have to! All this is happening because of me! The promises I broke—I have to make it right!"

"But how does this—"

Jesse yanked away, hitting at him with his other hand, but Ben didn't give up. They grappled, dust rising and rocks digging into the thin flesh of their knees. Jesse was like a wild animal, shoving and swearing, throwing himself back at the earth whenever he broke free of Ben's grip.

"Jesse. Please!"

Ben finally got a solid grip and did what he had wanted to do the moment he'd seen Jesse come for him in the spirit forest. He swallowed his embarrassment, wrapped his arms round the other boy, and squeezed.

Jesse stiffened at first, wiry and taut like an angry cat, but when Ben held on, he melted. His shoulders shuddered. Then the dam broke and he sobbed, face pressed against Ben's shoulder, soaking his shirt in tears and snot and hopeless, angry moans. Ben held on.

"I can't," Jesse moaned, voice muffled in Ben's shirt. "I can't fix it with my pa—I promised Alice—if I could just keep that promise, just that single one, then maybe—"

Ben put his hand on the back of Jesse's head, touching that strawberry hair for the first time. It was greasy and gritty with dirt and dust, but still soft.

"Jesse . . ."

After a while Jesse's tears dried up and he sat back. He was drained of everything, red-eyed and exhausted. He sighed big and stared at the wet spot on Ben's shirt. "It doesn't matter whether I'm Jessamine or Jesse, in the end I'm just going to ruin everything."

Ben might never really know what Jesse was going through, but in spite of what they'd said to one another last time they were here, he reckoned it was not too different after all. Destined to be part of two worlds . . . or balance on the line between them, with no one to catch them if they fell. No one but each other.

"I'm sorry about what I said before," Ben said. "When we were out here fighting."

"No!" Jesse made like he was going to punch Ben in the shoulder but struck his own thigh instead. "You've got nothing to be sorry for. I was so selfish. I can't imagine what you've been through. What so many people are going through. It's happening all around, right now, and I just pretended my whole life like it wasn't. People like me just look away. That's why the spell is working. You've got nothing to be sorry for. This is my fault."

The confession ended in a whisper. Ben didn't know what to say. He knew what he wanted but had no idea how to get there. Jesse drew himself up and wiped his face.

"I promised to protect you," Jesse said softly. "When you were asleep at Nelly's. I didn't even say it out loud. And I messed up. But maybe I can still make good on it."

Before Ben could resist, Jesse pulled him in. Wrapping him in a tear-damp embrace, the same as how Ben had held Jesse only moments ago. Ben closed his eyes.

"It ain't your job to always be so strong," Jesse whispered. His arms tightened, and Ben wanted to believe. "You're always trying to do that. Be strong for everyone else. But how can you help everyone when no one's helping you?"

Ben didn't have an answer for that, either.

They sat in a sad heap, listening to the wind rush through the sagebrush. Ben tried not to look at the dead moon in the morning sky. The creatures of the land were silent, all round them.

"Do you . . ." Jesse began.

"What is it?" Ben asked.

Jesse stared out into the desert, looking in the direction Shrike had dragged the blade. Ben could only imagine it, cutting its gash across the earth. Undulating like a curtain of light, streaming green and purple and blue out of a radiant wound.

Then he squinted, following Jesse's gaze. No, he realized. It wasn't his imagination.

Whether because of their time in Faerie or because he simply now knew how to see it, there really was something out there. The longer he looked, the more he saw. Starting from behind them in the west, a glowing flare of light rippled out of the earth. In the abyssal rift that was the path they'd cut, light and shadow tangled and pulled. The fibers of two worlds stretched and strained like fabric struggling against a tear. They were so close to being rent beyond repair, divided in two when they should have forever been one.

But something about it was different. When they'd seen it in the spirit wood it had been bright, blindingly so—but now, it was less searing. Less vibrant.

"It's slowing down," Jesse said, putting it into words. "I can . . . feel it."

Ben caught his breath before responding. When he did, his voice came out buoyed with awe and something else. Lightness, hope.

"It's working," he said. "Whatever you did, it's working."

CHAPTER XXVIII

JESSE

Jesse stared, wondering if what he was seeing could be real.

The bow saw was stuck in the log. Dull, dragging, unable to cut through that final bit. His heart leapt with hope. The tear was not complete. At least, not yet. If they could take the teeth out of the blade, one by one . . .

Ben finished the thought Jesse had started: "We might still be able to stop it."

The blade was a beacon on the horizon. Charging east, Shrike dragged it back through the earth like a plow. Jesse thought of the times he'd felt that weight attached to Mock's little body. How had she endured it, all the way to California? Seeing it every day and night, knowing what it would do. Believing it was the best thing she could do for her people.

And then she'd vanished, down Shrike's endless gullet. Just like that.

He couldn't just sit around, kicking rocks in the desert and feeling sorry for himself. The answer had to exist, somewhere. He had to find it. It was his responsibility.

He tried to think of what he'd done. Tried to remember what had happened. Mock had tried to warn Shrike that something was wrong. Jesse'd heard her little voice saying so.

Oathbreaker.

Jesse had been called by that word so many times now he'd almost forgotten what it meant.

"Alice," he said. Ben looked up and Jesse repeated it, firmly. "I promised Alice . . . Listen. The blade is bound to me, and my broken promises. I promised Declan I wouldn't abandon you, but then I did. I promised I would protect you, but then I didn't. But then . . . I came for you. I tried to save you." *I was prepared to sacrifice my life for you.* "I think that's why the spell didn't work like it was supposed to. I took some of its wind out by . . . by trying to make things right. By trying to fulfill a promise that I had broken."

"What does this have to do with your sister?" Ben asked.

"I didn't just promise Alice I'd settle with our pa. I promised her I'd be back to her before the baby was born. She was afraid I was leaving her like he did. I can't become my father. I just can't!"

"If you can return to Alice," Ben repeated. "Before you break your promise. Before the baby comes. But is it enough?"

It had to be. It was all Jesse had left.

He fumbled in his vest for Morgan's cooling tonic. The horse breathed heavily, eagerly lipping the vial as

Jesse got the stopper out. They still had nearly half a bottle—plenty to get them back.

"But the gates . . ." Ben trailed off, gesturing upward. Jesse already had his hand on Morgan's pommel and turned back.

"What?"

"Mock said the gates only opened because of Slender Moon's magic. And now . . ."

Jesse tried to stay calm. Tried not to curse or swear or scream. Every time he tried to get back in the saddle—even literally—something was always there waiting to bite him in the ass. His heart was growing tired of holding on to hope. It felt like treading water. But he couldn't give up.

"Then . . . then I'll just have to ride," he stammered. Locking his jaw, he got up in Morgan's saddle. "I'll just have to ride until I get back. I have the tonic. We'll be cutting it close, but if I ride hard, we can still do it."

"Jesse, wait!" Ben called.

"I don't have a choice!"

Ben grabbed Morgan's reins and held them against Jesse's tugging. He gestured with his chin at the horse he'd taken from Edward Murphy.

"I know. Give me the tonic for the palomino. We'll go together."

Hot and fast as the sun climbed in the sky, they raced east, following the cascading light that marked the path of the Faerie blade. The light, and the deep ravine filled with the tangled purgatory of half-divided realms.

By midday, Morgan's coat was slick with sweat, frothing white where the reins ran along his neck. Jesse couldn't place exactly where they were, and they hadn't time to stop at any stations to find out. His whole body ached, and he wasn't even the one doing the galloping. He couldn't imagine how Morgan must feel.

"Look at that!"

Ben pointed. On the horizon was the Faerie blade. It was just visible, a beam of gold at the head of the chasm it was cutting. And somewhere ahead of it, chain in his claws, was Shrike.

"It's right there," Jesse said. "We're catching up to it?"

Ben looked grim. "He's still got a hundred miles on us, and without the gates ..."

Jesse wished he could fly. Watching it from so far away tore him apart.

"Maybe," Jesse shouted desperately. "If we push the horses ..."

I promise. I'll take care of you, old boy. You can trust me.

Jesse went straight in the saddle. The memory was so vivid she felt as if she'd been knocked back into the person she'd been when she said those words. It stung worse than being punched in the face.

Promise.

She reached out and put a hand on Morgan's shoulder.

He ran and ran, without a complaint. But when she pressed her palm against his muscles, she gasped and pulled away.

Something was not right. Not right at all.

Clenching her teeth, Jesse pressed her hand against Morgan's coat again. The writhing, pumping muscles below his smooth chestnut fur were wrong. Pulpy-feeling, like an overripe fruit. Destroyed, kept moving only by . . .

By what?

Jesse pulled on the reins and fell out of the saddle before Morgan had stopped moving. Behind them, she heard Ben shout at his horse to slow. Jesse yanked down on Morgan's reins to still him. He shied away from her, grumbling and huffing. Turning away as if he knew she'd suddenly realized what she'd done and wanted to hide it from her. As if he knew what she'd find when he finally stopped resisting.

No, no, no . . .

He finally bowed his head, giving in. When Jesse pressed her hands against his hot, fidgeting legs, her heart burst, flooding her with grief.

Beneath Morgan's skin, hidden by his coat and his exuberance, every bone was shattered. Every muscle in shreds, every ligament torn. It was only the magic cooling tonic that kept him appearing as he did: healthy, energetic, fresh.

Alive.

Morgan nuzzled Jesse's vest where she kept the tonic.

She pulled away, her whole body flinching with guilt. She took out the vial, wishing she'd never laid eyes on it. Ben had finally calmed his horse and was striding over, but when he saw what Jesse had in her hand, ready to smash it, he stopped.

"Jesse?" he asked, because he didn't know what she knew.

"This awful potion kept him on his feet and running," she said. "But he's been in agony, and for how long?"

Ben approached carefully. "But then . . . if you destroy that, there's no way . . . We're in the desert."

They were. Surrounded on all sides by sand and rock. Salt Lake Valley was still at least a day's ride by horse—by Morgan. Jesse tried to keep breathing. Morgan waited, ears forward, quivering in anticipation of the drug.

"I know. I'm sorry." She heard her voice breaking in terrible, ugly heaves, speaking now to Morgan and not to Ben. "I'm so sorry. I'm so sorry."

She threw the vial. The glass shattered, the tonic inside evaporating almost instantly. A breeze took the last of it and Jesse clenched her hands in fists. Waiting.

At first, nothing happened. Morgan nosed her again. For more tonic, or water. A favorite apple treat. Jesse watched his big brown eyes. She wanted to touch him, to pet and hug him, but she didn't. She didn't deserve to. He winced and let out an irritated nicker, shaking his head and nosing her vest again. Still seeking the tonic. She pushed him away.

"I'm sorry," she repeated. She tried to say more, but her voice wouldn't work. Apologies didn't matter. Not to a horse that had no idea what was happening or why. And it was Jesse's fault.

Morgan whinnied, now with an edge of pain. He leaned down and sniffed the place where the vial had broken. He pawed at the gravel and dirt, lifting one hoof and leaning on the other. Nothing gave him relief. Every one of his legs was destroyed.

He nosed Jesse again. She held on to his muzzle when he whinnied again, then followed him down when he knelt. He lay on his side, his heavy head crashing to earth. Eyes rolling back, spittle curdling round his mouth. His coat frothed, smelling of death.

Jesse whimpered at a new rush of tears. Would they ever stop? Ben called her name, but she barely heard him. She pulled Morgan's face down and pressed her forehead against his, hugging her arms round his muzzle.

"Jesse, stand back."

Ben stood over them. He had the gun in his hand.

She shuddered and did as he said. He released the safety.

"Wait," she said, voice raw. "I have to do it."

The gun was heavy and cold. Jesse wiped the tears away enough to be able to see clearly. Morgan gazed at her with milky, bloodshot eyes. She wondered at first if he recognized her, but in the way that he looked at her now, she knew he did. She could only hope that he didn't hate her.

"I'm so sorry," she said again. It could never be enough. She lifted the gun. *Both eyes open.* Her thumb was so weak against the hammer she had to use her left hand just to cock it in place. More words were tumbling out, but they made no sense, impossible words that were both an apology and a goodbye. And then she fired.

When it was done, Ben took the gun from her limp hand.

"It was the right thing to do," he said.

"It was too late."

"When it comes to doing the right thing, it's never too late."

Jesse wasn't sure she believed that. She wanted to, but she was so exhausted from hoping and being let down, and letting everyone else down, over and over. But she couldn't bear to give up in front of Ben, who stood silently at her side.

"Can you see the blade?" she asked numbly. With her heart too heavy to feel for it, she tried to look for it instead, but either the curve of the land was hiding it or Shrike had already dragged it out of view, speeding along while they had stopped for her to say goodbye to Morgan.

Ben said nothing. Apparently he couldn't see it, either.

A desert breeze brushed against them, dry and papery. At first it felt like any other wind, like a curtain being drawn against the skin, but at the fringe of it Jesse shivered at the cool touch of winter. Next came the blue and white glow, and then Snow stood beside them, eyes wide.

"What are you doing?" the spirit asked, with a bright intensity Jesse hadn't seen him express before. "What did you do?"

She opened her mouth to answer, but the silhouette of bird wings rippled over them. Jesse stiffened, every aching muscle tensing for a fight. A cloaked figure—or was the swirling, feathered shape his wings?—alit some thirty yards away, spear in hand. His dark form, seemingly half transformed from his monster shape, split the rose and gold of the desert like a hole into a world of black.

"I was going to let the two of you be, in gratitude," Shrike said. "But now you have interfered."

"The blade has stopped," Snow exclaimed, finishing what he'd begun to say before. "It's not sharp enough to cleave any longer!"

"*For now!*" Shrike screamed. Jesse could practically hear the blood in his throat.

He leveled his spear at them, casting off his cloak. Snow drew his bow and Ben raised his gun. Jesse had no weapon, but if this were her opportunity to take her revenge on Shrike, for Mock—for all of them—she would do it with her bare fists if she had to.

"Come, then," Shrike growled. "Show me what fools you mortals be."

CHAPTER XXIX

BEN

Ben knew nothing about fighting spirits.

But he felt sure shooting would not touch the war-thirsty monster that roared before them, more ravenous and terrifying than ever before. He had followed them all the way from the east. Devoured Randall and chased them to Devil's Gate. Swallowed Mock whole. What could a puny mortal gun to do to this furious bird-god?

Snow stepped forth, nocking an arrow. At least that was something that had thwarted Shrike in the past, if only for a moment.

"Admit your faults and step aside," Snow said. It sounded noble and right and hopelessly small. "They know how to drain your Faerie blade of power and will do it. Step aside, and no ill will befall you."

"The spell cannot be reversed," Shrike declared. "It was made with bonds. Once a promise is broken, it cannot be mended. That is the way of the *oath*."

"Yet here you are trying to stop us," Jesse said. His voice sounded empty, but there was a calm in it, as if he had nothing left to feel in that moment—not even fear. Unlike Ben, who felt his entire body shaking. It took everything he had just to keep the useless gun held upright.

Shrike's yellow eyes shook in their sockets as if he wanted to eat all three of them. Ben wondered how many more bodies would fit in his stomach.

"Oaths cannot be mended once broken," he reiterated.

It was a threat, but it gave Ben hope. It meant they'd been right.

"Let him be wrong and die," Jesse said.

Snow strode forward, his hair and cloak streaming behind him, and loosed his arrow. It flew true, would've sunk into Shrike's heart had he not moved his spear to intercept it at the last moment.

"Snow . . ." Ben began. He remembered the other times Shrike and Snow had met in battle. The things Shrike had said and shown in the spirit world as he'd prepared for his conquest of the human one. "He ate Mock —killed Slender Moon! Are you sure you can . . ."

"Do you believe in me?"

It was a common-sounding question, but there was a profound sorrow in it. When they had first seen Snow, he had been barely an apparition; now, as he fought by their side, the details of his lovely face were handsome and clear. But was he strong enough to defeat Shrike, when he'd never been able to best him before? Ben thought of the first snow. The taste of the air when it changed, signaling that autumn was over. The knowing that winter, and the long nights, had arrived, and that every creature would soon be at its mercy.

"I believe in you," he said.

Jesse nodded a little nod, then a bigger one. "Me too."

The cool, wintry light round Snow glowed brighter, the fine hairs of his eyelashes coming into more pristine focus. Ben could see the flecks of alabaster and silver in his gentle eyes.

"Thank you."

Snow turned toward Shrike, nocking two arrows and raising his bow.

The arrows flew as soon as they were level. Even Shrike could not evade them both. He deflected one, but the other sank to the fletching in his shoulder.

He screamed and tore at it, but another was already flying. Shrike fell back, screaming and thrashing. Snow loosed arrow after arrow from his bottomless quiver until Shrike's body was struck with them, undulating like stiff grass as he shrieked and clawed at them. He fell to his hands and knees, back and body pinned in shafts of glowing white.

"Can he really do it?" Jesse gasped.

Shrike's back heaved with fury as Snow approached him, nocking a final arrow.

"You'll die today," Shrike growled. He laughed, red bubbling up from his throat like mud out of the Platte. He sucked in a shuddering breath, spat blood across Snow's bare feet. "When he comes. A last oath will break. One so strong the blade may even move on its own once again. If it means our people will finally be free, I'll rip that pretty antler crown from your head and impale you on it."

With the speed of a wolf, he lunged on all fours at Ben's horse. The palomino bolted too late, falling under Shrike's claws, blood painting its blond coat. Shrike grew as he fed, until he was large enough that the remains of the poor horse disappeared down his gullet, hooves, bones and all. He howled, neither man nor beast, saliva and blood spraying across the sky.

Then he began his horrible change.

Bones snapped and cracked. Flesh tore as he outgrew it, stitched together again in sheets and tendons and sinew. A terrible *crrrraacckkkk* ripped from Shrike's skull as it broke apart and came together again to form the face of a monster.

Shrike cracked his wicked beak. Let out a low, raspy breath heavy with the stench of the horse in his belly. Snow released his arrow, but it was devoured by the flesh on Shrike's neck. Shrike bellowed, but not in pain. In challenge.

"Ben!"

Ben's legs locked as Shrike's enormous claw shot toward him. Jesse had shouted his name, but it was Snow who was suddenly there. Between them, all white and blue, blowing Ben out of the way with a gust of cold wind. Cutting Shrike's splayed talons with the string of his bow. Blood flew and Shrike screamed, flinching. Then, in a single swipe, he scooped the blue spirit into his claw and *squeezed*.

Bones cracked and Snow screamed.

"That is the pain you owe me!" Shrike bellowed. He squeezed again, claws constricting round him like an enormous snake of talons and razor pinions. Snow had no more screams to give, and Shrike smiled in victory.

"And now," Shrike said, "*you die*."

"No!" Ben cried. He fired, five times, emptying the chambers.

The bullets did nothing. Shrike clenched his giant fist and bashed Snow against the earth, snapping one of his antlers from his head. When Shrike raised his fist again, Snow was limp and still.

Ben's head spun, reeled with despair. Snow should have won. They had believed in him. He was strong—but not strong enough.

Shrike tilted his head back and laughed, then lifted Snow over his gaping beak. In a moment, Snow would join Mock and Randall and the palomino in his monster belly.

If he could not stop Shrike, then who could?

In case of emergency.

Something in Ben's pocket burned cold. He dropped his gun and took out one of the bottles of medicine Nelly had given him.

"What is that?" Jesse shouted.

"A blue bottle," he said.

Shrike opened his beak and Ben threw the bottle. It sparkled like a drop of heavenly spring rain, then vanished into Shrike's gullet like a stone down a hellish well.

Shrike's bloated body shuddered. He retched, and then he screamed, tilting his head back. He threw Snow to the side, plunging his claws down his own throat.

Ben scrambled to Snow as Shrike tore out his own insides, trying to get at the bottle buried in his rapidly deteriorating body. Gouts of blood and black bile poured from his beak as he threw his head forward, entire awful body convulsing in his attempt to eject the tiny glass bottle.

"You'll never!" Shrike screeched in Jesse's direction. His skin was not shrinking as quickly as his body, blubbering round him and glistening like tar. "You'll never make it back to your sister in time! My—he—*he'll* make sure you don't. Without Slender Moon—without the gates—"

Ben caught his breath in the unintelligible sounds that followed, words and shrieks that dissolved into moans and howls, like bellows cascading out of the mountains, until finally the cries stopped altogether. A gust of desert wind scattered the remaining feathers like cold black ashes.

"Look," Jesse whispered. Something glistened in the remains. He ran in, boots kicking up black slop, while Ben gathered Snow in his arms. The blue spirit chuckled despite the pain it caused him.

"Double-good after all," he said.

Jesse came back. In one hand he held a blue medicine bottle full of dissolving black muck. In his other arm he cradled two birds. One dark gray with white stripes in its wings. The other the color of ash, with a white belly and a black mask. A mockingbird and a shrike.

He took off his neckerchief and folded it into a hammock, placing the sleeping birds inside and tying it at his belt. Then he stooped next to Ben to take in Snow's damage.

"Is he . . ." He didn't finish. Instead he said, "What now?"

Shrike was defeated, but their troubles weren't over. They looked out along the wound carved by the Faerie blade, brightened by sun overhead. Far off, Ben could see the light of the blade. It was still there, half-finished cleaving their world apart, even if its bearer rested at Jesse's hip.

"We can't just leave it there," Jesse said. "Still stuffed full of my broken promises. If I don't make it back to Alice . . . I don't know how much time we have. And without the gates . . ."

"And Snow's in no condition to travel," Ben said. "If we don't get him help, I don't think he's going to make it. And without the horses, how are we going to get out of the desert, much less all the way back to St. Joe's?"

They looked down at the spirit creature in Ben's arms. Snow had hardly any weight to him—like Mock, when she wasn't bound to the blade—but from how he slumped Ben could tell he had no strength. His broken antler was splintered and jagged, a bruise forming on his temple where it was rooted. His eyes were closed, his blue lips slightly parted round shallow breaths.

"The lake," Snow said. "The lake can heal me. And there, I can ask for the power of the gates."

"But Slender Moon . . ."

"There is someone else. The one who granted Slender Moon that power. I do not know if she will answer, but I can ask."

"Who? Who will you ask?"

Snow's murmurings faded. Ben listened. To the blue spirit, and to the shape inside him that whispered to him that no matter how many times Snow asked, she—whoever *she* was—would not answer him.

But she may answer another.

"Jesse, I think—"

His gut lurched, as if there had been an earthquake. But it was not the earth below his knees that moved. Something powerful was headed their way, through the other place. Through the tear between the worlds.

"Someone's coming," Ben said.

"Shrike's benefactor," Snow said. "He comes to finish the spell."

Shrike's benefactor. Jesse had told him what he'd learned from Snow about a Fae from across the sea, who'd promised to solve the spirits' problems with the Faerie blade. If Shrike had been powerful enough to do what he'd done to Snow, Ben didn't want to imagine what kind of force was wielded by the one who'd offered the blade to begin with.

"I think I know who it is," Jesse said.

A chill zipped up Ben's spine. He tightened his hold on Snow, and Jesse backed up, standing protectively over the two of them.

"What? Who—"

"Go to the other place. Bring Snow to the lake. If he thinks he can figure out how to reopen the gates, then do that. If you can't, at least you'll be safe."

"Jesse, no—"

Jesse fixed Ben with a determined gaze. "If you can come back to me, I'll be glad to see you . . . but I promised to protect you. This is my fault, and I will see it through."

Ben bit back tears. "I'll come back," he said.

Snow reached up, and Ben surrendered to the feeling of the doorway opening to the other place. As he and Snow faded from the mortal realm, through the veil that was falling across the land, the earth split before Jesse and a figure emerged.

The last thing Ben saw was the man's shadow towering over Jesse, every inch of his enormous height soaked with a dread power, from his gold waistcoat buttons to the top of his stovepipe hat.

CHAPTER XXX

JESSE

"Hello again, Mr. Murphy."

Stationmaster Declan reached into his coat, withdrawing his pipe. He took his time lighting it, tossing the spent match and grinding it against the desert road with his buckled shoe. The high noon sun beat down on him, his hat casting his face in shadow.

Jesse was too exhausted to be surprised by the pieces she had assembled at the last possible moment. Instead, she tried to savor the relief that Ben and Snow had gotten away. Pride that they had defeated Shrike and rescued Mock. Loss over Morgan's death and bitterness at her own failure to do better by him. Hope that she might still make it to Alice in time. Her heart and mind had many rooms, but every one was full. The only thing left to do was acknowledge that the stationmaster who had hired them was the one who stood before her in this final-seeming place.

"You're a Fae," she said. "The Fae that made the blade for Shrike."

"Yes. Though I think of myself not as a Fae, but as a businessman. An investor, here to protect my investment."

It all made sense. Declan was a Fae, but he was also a man. The man whose partnership with Alexander Majors had allowed him to organize and deploy the Nightland Express, the route along which he'd send his carefully selected boys—boys who were willing to bend the rules to win the job. And the route that would guide them east to west, laying the line for a rift that would divide their worlds forever.

"What did he promise you?" she asked.

Declan laughed. "You have to ask?"

"Passage."

The tiny voice came from inside the necktie hammock, and Jesse peered inside. Mock was barely awake, her dark eyes the same whether she was in the form of a bird or a girl. She moved her wing and Jesse took her out of the neckerchief, holding her gently in two hands. She weighed nothing, body light and fragile and soft. It seemed impossible that the little bird was her friend, though after all they'd been through together, impossible seemed merely a matter of course. She spread her wings to keep her balance, flashing the stripes of white.

"He promised passage," she whispered again, voice like a song. "When the worlds were split, there would still be certain places where spirits could pass through. Like doorways . . . but it would cost us faeth to use them."

Jesse's blood boiled.

"You were going to *charge* them to cross the veil?" she cried.

Declan smoked and chuckled. He gestured with his pipe, like a kindly uncle telling a tale. "You didn't think I was going to let them starve in the other place, did you? Oh, it was a goodly deal. One I earned, methinks. I did all the work, after all! It wasn't easy finding double-goods to take my job. Oh, but Jesse. I'm glad you were the one. I liked you best of all, my fine Irish lad. So eager for gold. So eager to take this job and make me rich."

He puffed on his pipe and leveled his gaze at Jesse. Then he leaned down as if telling a secret, and Jesse could smell the tobacco clinging to his breath and beard.

"Jesse. Let me see the Faerie blade through to its end, and I will give you all the riches you desire. Perhaps I'll even entertain a negotiation. A cut of what they pay me to visit this world . . . I'll even waive the fee to convert their faeth to gold. For you, as an early investor in my enterprise."

Jesse held Mock. She felt as though she should fear the stationmaster. After all, he was powerful enough to create the blade. And yet Declan had come here, all the way to the desert, to stand between them and St. Joe's. She thought of the first and last time she had seen the Faerie blade up close—it had been brilliant yellow.

Gold.

Gold was power. To some. The wind blew, and Jesse yearned to hear a familiar voice in it. Alice's voice, singing of clever heroes, of little folk and Faerie. She yearned for home and the sweet smell of the Missouri cornfields, autumn blowing through the apple trees. The home she'd left for the wrong reasons. She hadn't listened to Alice when she'd asked Jesse not to go. She hadn't listened when Alice had said all she needed was her sister.

Now all those things she had and hadn't done were come for her. Now she knew though she'd always said she'd left for Alice, the truth was he'd left for himself. For Jessamine—for Jesse. There was nothing wrong with that, so long as she admitted it. So long as she came home to Alice changed into a person her sister could believe in. A person who believed in her sister. Silly fairy tales and all.

I will come home to you. I swear it.

"If I said yes, would you give me another advance?" Jesse asked. "Like you did when I signed on to the Express?"

"No," Declan said. "You'd be paid after you prove yourself to me. After the blade is taken back to St. Joe's and finishes its job."

Jesse crossed her arms. "Then will you at least *show* me the gold you'll pay me? Surely you can do that much, can't you?"

Declan didn't budge a wink, his heavy stare keeping Jesse from looking up past his red nose and black mustache. She had noticed before, when he'd hired her, that it was hard to look him in the eye—but she had been nervous, afraid he would see her for what she was. Whatever that was.

But now she knew that wasn't the reason.

"No," Declan said again.

"Because you can't."

Jesse's knees ached as she stood. She tucked Shrike away, holding Mock close as she rose against the stationmaster. She remembered the night Shrike had pressed his ash-stained thumb into her forehead, the night Snow had called her oathbreaker. Remembered the blade itself, rippling yellow and gold.

"Your power's all locked up in that blade, isn't it? Without Shrike, and without me, it's stuck out there, going nowhere. I'm the only thing that can move it now."

Shadows pooled in the creases of Declan's face as he tilted his head forward, the brim of his hat hiding his bunching brows.

"I can release the blade by undoing the bond," he said slowly. Dangerously. "All I need to do that is kill you."

"If it were that easy, shouldn't you have done it by now?" she asked.

It was a gamble to incense him more. If he decided to come at her to kill, she wasn't sure what she'd do. Even with his power bound in the Faerie blade, he was a big man. He could crush her skull in the palm of his hand, magic or no.

"With all your power locked away in that blade," she went on, "I reckon you don't have much left to work with, do you?"

Declan growled.

"I saved enough to do away with you, little man," he said.

Little man.

Jesse looked past Declan's impressive mustache and straight into the shadows. She planted her feet and stared him dead in his black, inhuman eyes.

"Darcy Declan, Darcy Declan, Darcy Declan."

At first he didn't move, and she thought she'd made a terrible mistake. It was like looking into the face of a nightmare, standing still on iron tracks as an engine headed straight toward her. But she stayed fast, pulled the words out of her stomach one by one like drawing buckets of water out of a well.

"Tell me where you stashed your lucky gold."

Declan's glare caught fire, as if his eyes were two windows to hell. She almost looked away, almost took Mock and ran, but her bones were all locked, her muscles all turned to stone. To look away would mean death, now that she'd challenged him. But would it work?

Then he moved his hand. Without looking away, Jesse waited as he raised his finger, vibrating with rage. When it stopped, in her peripheral Jesse could see he was pointing to the golden button at the top of his vest.

"I will destroy you, Jesse Murphy," he said.

Mock leapt from Jesse's hands, fluttering out and landing on Declan's vest. She grabbed the shining button in her feet and yanked, breaking the threads with her beak and springing away. Jesse held out her hand and Mock pressed the warm, soft metal into her palm, collapsing in a shivering pile of feathers again.

The moment the gold touched Jesse's hand, Declan began to shrink. He couldn't move so long as Jesse kept her eyes on him. Couldn't do anything but glare, face getting red as he grew smaller and smaller.

"You're still going to break that last promise," he growled through clenched teeth. "You'll break it. Mark my words. You'll break it and that blade will be so strong with the stench of your human oathbreaking that it will fly to St. Joe's. Fly! And the Fae will be locked away in Faerie, with no choice but to pay me to visit this world they love! Oh, I will be richer than ever! And I will ruin you, Jesse Murphy—*ruin you.*"

Jesse calmed her breathing, staring down the little man who stood before her. He was as tall as her waist, a miniature replica of the Darcy Declan that had looked down on her only moments ago.

"Not if I ruin you first," she said.

But Declan smiled. She hated it when he smiled.

"Oh, I see," he said. "You think that if you defeat me, you'll have time to make it back to your sister. You think you'll have time if your friend can reopen the moonlight gates."

Jesse's confidence faltered, though still she didn't look away. She had hoped that Declan didn't know what Ben and Snow were doing. But maybe it had been foolish to think they could get away with it.

Damn.

When he saw the doubt, Declan's smile darkened, eclipsed by the terrible hate in his eyes. He blew a ring of smoke from his tiny pipe.

"Know this, Jesse Murphy," he said. "I've sent Fae to your little house every night. Opening all the cupboards and drawers, untying every knot. Casting spells. It is easy for us folk to bend such an insignificant thing as a week or two. Sister Alice is in labor. The baby will be here by tomorrow's dawn. Then your promise will be broken and there will be nothing you can do about it."

Tomorrow morning. They'd never make it across the continent before then. Not without horses and magic tonic. Not even if Ben and Snow somehow reopened the moonlight gates.

Declan watched with dour amusement as Jesse's every limb went cold. But she still couldn't turn away from him, not yet, not even after the terrible news. How could this happen?

She steeled herself. She would figure things out. She and Ben would, when he came back. She believed that they could fix it, somehow. She had to.

"No," Jesse said. "No, I'll find a way. Ben and I will find a way. And in the meantime, I reckon I'm through dealing with you, Darcy Declan."

"Oh? You can't stare me down forever!"

Jesse held up the gold coin in her hand.

"You've put all your faeth in the Faerie blade, bonded to me. I hold the last ounce of your power in my hand . . . and in my heart. But not for long. I think I've decided I don't believe in you anymore. And if I don't believe, then you've got nothing left, and you'll disappear. Isn't that right?"

Declan's eyes went wide.

"No," he said. But his little face grew redder. "You look away and I'll disappear. I'll disappear, but when your sister delivers, oh—oh, Jesse, I shall steal away the babe to raise as my own. In the new world I have created! Do you believe that, Jesse Murphy? *Do you?*"

"Goodbye, Darcy Declan," Jesse said. "I have more important things to put my faith in."

Then she turned away from him and did not look back.

CHAPTER XXXI

BEN

The desert vanished, taking Jesse and Stationmaster Declan with it. Ben felt a storm of emotions rush through him. He wanted to go back, wanted to stay with Jesse. But he also had to trust his friend.

"I'm sorry," Snow said faintly. He shuddered, willowy and fragile, leaning against Ben's arm. Now that he was back in the other place, he seemed less disoriented than when he had been ailing in Ben's arms. "But Jesse is strong. Believe in them."

Ben forced himself to agree. He had to. He had no other choice. They would have to work together, but apart.

"Which way is the lake?" he asked. "Is it far?"

"All lakes are the lake," Snow said. When Ben hesitated, he elaborated: "We do not need to return to the lake where Shrike killed Slender Moon. To ask for what we ask, any lake will do."

Ben finally looked around, trying to let go of his fear for Jesse. He had to do what *he* could do, and that was heal Snow and find a way to get Jesse back to his sister. They were in the desert, of course, but the spirit half of it, the other just out of reach.

"And about the gates," Ben said. "Can that power be granted to anyone?"

"Many have asked and been denied. I do not know what else we can do but ask again. That way. I can smell water."

Ben lifted his head and went in the direction Snow indicated. When he sniffed the air, he, too, could smell something. A familiar scent, like minerals and steam. His heart leapt, then sank.

"Won't it . . . melt you?"

Snow chuckled.

"I am called Snow, but I am not made of it," he said.

Ben tried not to move too roughly. With Snow's arm slung over his shoulder, Ben's fit easily round his slender waist. He'd expected that being so close to the spirit of winter would be unbearably cold, but as he grew used to the cool, fragile breath on his neck, he found it strangely comforting. Like waking to find the first blanket of white across the fields.

Would that stop if Shrike's—if Declan's spell were successful? Maybe it didn't even need to be completed. It had begun years ago, before Ben and Jesse had been born. It had already done immeasurable damage.

"Even if we stop Declan, things will never be the same, will they?" he asked.

"Things have never been the same," Snow replied. "Every day is different from the last. I used to believe that if I waited long enough, things would return to the way they were. But every new day brings me further from the place I knew. I do not think that we spirits can wait for the old ways to return anymore."

Ben remembered what Nelly had said: that humans changed, while the spirits did not.

"Do you think there could be another way?" he asked.

"The unchanged me would have said no. But if I am to survive, I think I must wake up in this new day and see it for what it is. If I can do that, then perhaps others can, too. But I don't know if we will be able to find that other way alone. Without humans, if the golden blade reaches its destination and completes what it has begun."

The scent of water struck them in full as they rounded a mound of black soil crowned with flowers and stones. Pooled in the gentle crescent of the hill was a green spring. Grass and flowers grew in the little oasis, and several spirit folk crouched at the water's edge. They flitted about and whispered and cried at Snow's sad state as Ben approached the spring and carefully lowered him into its waters.

The blue spirit let out a wince and a sigh as he sank in to his shoulders. To Ben's relief, he did not melt. Ben stooped beside him, watching. Hoping that maybe the healing would be instant, and that they could return to Jesse right away.

"Now what?" he asked.

Snow pressed his dark lips into a flat line. Ben followed his gaze into the deep, impenetrable water of the spring. It was impossible to know how deep it was, though reflecting the sky the way it did, Ben imagined it was just as infinite.

"Now I will go below and ask," Snow said.

Ben asked, even though he already knew the answer, "Is there anything I can do to help?"

"Have faith."

Then Snow closed his eyes and slid down the mossy, sloped bank to rest just beneath the surface of the water.

Ben sat beside Snow in the deep silence. Some of the other spirits settled next to him or watched him cautiously from the other side of the pool. The water had a gentle ripple to it, though there was hardly any wind.

He tried not to be impatient. He didn't know what Snow had to ask and couldn't begin to guess how long it might take. The water was too dark to show color, but Ben could only imagine that it was tinted with Snow's blood.

He looked up. The sky was that crimson-blue, if that was a color—twilight and dawn and day and night, rippling with a painful red as the fabric of the worlds tore apart. The vast expanse of rocky land and soft-topped mountains was pulsing with dim light. Every bush and twig and rock huddled into itself, hoping that soon it would all be over.

But with which resolution? If the worlds were split, impassable by mortals and spirits alike—as it was in other parts of the world—was that good? Or bad? For those little spirits who were starving for faeth, perhaps it was good. Perhaps this way, they could survive being forgotten by humans.

He jumped when Snow gasped, his eyes flying open as his chest heaved with new breath.

"Are you all right?" Ben asked. "Did it work?"

Snow caught his breath and struggled to pull himself out of the water. Though his movement was still less than graceful, he seemed to have renewed strength. He hoisted himself onto the lip of the pool, and as the waters drained off his torso Ben could see that his wounds had been healed, replaced with faintly glowing scars. The glow dimmed as the water slipped back into the pool.

"I was revived. But my request went unfulfilled. She did not answer."

Snow put his hand on his chest, then his arm. He reached up and touched the jagged end of his antler, where it was still broken. Ben looked into the pool, as if this time he might see something new.

"What if . . . *I* were to ask?"

The question startled Snow, as if it hadn't even occurred to him. A thousand words seemed to cross his lips: protests, explanations, doubts. Hopes, dreams, and wishes. In the end all he said was, "I do not know."

Ben leaned back. He hadn't even noticed that he had gone to a crouch, coiled, ready to dive. His entire body was preparing. The creature—that writhing, anxious, shape that had grown within him—was ready. So ready it had almost acted without him.

"How deep is it?" he asked.

Snow stood beside him and replied, "Endless. Ben, I must warn you. You are human. Even if you are double-good. If you ask, and your wish is granted . . . I do not know what will happen."

"But if I could open the gates, we could get Jesse back to his sister and take the power out of the spell. Maybe we could find a way to bring the worlds back together again. Undo the damage."

Ben didn't know how likely that really was. He realized, as the shape inside him buzzed eagerly in his fingers, his shoulders, his knees, his toes, that he wanted to dive not only because it might mean a chance to fix the problem at hand, but because something was calling to him from the water. Something down there was reaching for him, and the slithering shape at his core was reaching back. It reminded him of the night, and it was calling him by name.

Snow must have noticed it. He bowed his head.

"I will not stop you," he said. "I just want you to be sure, before you go."

Ben looked to the west where, on the other side of the spirit veil, California still existed. That place he'd been trying to reach in the hopes that he would finally find where he belonged. After looking in houses and fields, in meadows and mountains, after a lifetime of being told the world was not for him. But he knew now that Sacramento wasn't the answer to the question he had been asking his entire life.

"I didn't know what else to do, when Penny told me to go. I didn't know how to stand up to Randall. I didn't know how to protect Penny. I didn't know where to call home. I kept running, trying to find some magical place where I could finally be myself. Where I wouldn't be alone."

Ben took a big breath in and held it. Let it out. Spoke the truth.

"But I got it backwards. My place is wherever I am myself. And that means my place is anywhere. This world, that world. Day or night. It doesn't matter. As long as I can fight for and protect the people I love—I am home. If this is something I can do, then I want to do it. For me. For Penny and for Jesse . . . for everyone."

"But you're crying?" Snow asked with an affectionate smile. "Your kind is so strange."

Ben touched his cheek, surprised to find it wet. Snow reached out, his hand bringing with it the smell of cedar and juniper, soulful eyes earnest and indigo. Ben fell into those eyes and shivered when Snow gently brushed his cheek dry.

"Strange . . . and wonderful," the spirit added.

"Will you believe in me, this time?" Ben asked.

Snow bowed. Glittering snow carried on the air as he breathed, filling Ben with life. With faeth. From this powerful, beautiful blue spirit who now gazed at him with gentle, fierce eyes.

"Of course," Snow replied. "No matter what happens, I will be here when you wake."

It had been a long time since Ben last heard words like that. He hadn't known Snow very long, but it was easy to believe his reassuring promise. Ben took in a breath, filling his lungs as deeply as he dared, and dove.

The water was not as warm as he had expected from the steam rising off its surface. It was clear, and supernaturally dense, like a blanket. He sank without much effort, encountering no bottom. Though there was no light, he still felt as though he could see—not with his eyes, but with the rest of his senses. Murmurs bouncing off the rocky vertical tunnel. Waves rippling against his skin.

Hello?

He didn't know who he was speaking to. Slender Moon was dead. But could spirits really die? Or did they just go away for a time, and resurface when enough faeth in them had been restored?

Is anyone there?

But no one answered.

Ben's lungs pulsed with an ache. He would not be able to stay below forever, not even in the spirit world. His heart beat quickly, suddenly, the creature in his breast fluttering with anxiety. Was his time already up? It had only been a minute. Seconds, even.

He tried to calm the slithering shape. The more it quivered, the faster he would reach the limit of his human body. He had to keep going. They had to keep going. He pressed his hand against his chest, hushing the creature. The creature that wanted desperately for him to dive. Wanted desperately to go home.

Be calm, you and I, he said. *We will do this together.*

The world above had all but faded, and Ben drifted downward into a shadow as expansive as the sky. The muffled echoes of the walls became distant, and Ben wondered if there was a cavern at the bottom of the spring—or if it was merely his mind fading under the pressure of the depths. He felt as if a film had been drawn over his eyes, clouding all his senses. Coalescing round his body, slowing his movements. He remained as still as he could, holding on to the shape inside him, his only companion. Letting the current and his weight take them down, down, down . . .

Please, he thought, making it his only effort as his lungs began to ache. *I'm here. I'm asking. I'm done running. Let me help. I can do it. I'm ready . . .*

Benjamin.

He felt pressure against his cheek. Slowly and gently, he landed against something soft. The voice in his ear was familiar, as if she had always been there, whispering to him. Enfolding him in her lap and arms, brushing her hand over his forehead and hair. He buried his face in her inky skirts. Through the gauze that enveloped him, he could see hazy spots of light.

You're here, he said. Thought. Hoped.

I have always been here, she said. *I have always been with you.*

He no longer needed to breathe, wrapped in her midnight embrace, surrounded by the echoes of stars within her endless body. He could not move, could not see. Could only hear the distant vibration of a song, coming from her thousand voices.

I'm ready, he said.

For what? she asked.

He didn't know the words for it. He only knew the feeling. Everything within him hummed, but his skin had grown tight round him. He wanted desperately to sing.

I want to become, he said. *I want to be.*

Then be.

She touched his forehead, drew a deft line down the bridge of his nose and lips. Fresh water seeped in, and as he felt it calling, a surge of understanding coursed through him. His skin itched from his nose to his fingertips.

The creature that filled his body shivered with excitement. It was time.

Through the opening she had made, he pushed, nose first. He felt the old skin peel away, across his cheeks and neck, down his shoulders and back. It fell away in a single pale sheet, papery and weblike, a perfect image of him in reverse. He watched it drift away into the endless water, then turned to see the one who'd held him.

With his new eyes, he saw her face as clearly as he had as a child, when Penny had taken him by the hand and they'd run through the fields. She was infinite, deep blue, speckled with stars and moons and comets. She hummed with the voices of a thousand creatures, that soothing, unending melody of the night.

"I know you," he said. His lips and voice were free again, and it took everything he had not to burst into song. Song or tears, or both.

And I you, my child, she replied.

"Was it you, this whole time?" he asked. He searched within himself for the creature, that dark, serpentine creature that had been within him for so long. It was still there, but it was no longer buried. No longer small or afraid.

It was me. But it was also you. That creature which loves you the most. It waxes and wanes. It never stops growing. It sheds its skin and becomes brilliant once again. That is you, Benjamin. That is me. It is all of us.

"Thank you," he said. He looked up. Or down, he wasn't sure anymore. It didn't really matter. "I have to go. But I'll be back . . . I want to know everything."

We have all of time, she said.

Ben nodded. He peered into the place where his old skin had disappeared, whispered a solemn thanks. Then he closed his eyes and recalled the place from which he'd come. He had work to do.

CHAPTER XXXII

JESSE

"I wish I could help him!"

Jesse let out a loud cry of frustration, but on the flat desert there wasn't even anything to echo it back to her.

"Shush," Mock said. She huddled in Jesse's hands. "If you really want to help Benjamin, then believe in him. Don't make this about you."

"Mmph." Jesse couldn't juggle her anger and worry, dropping everything—including herself—in a confused, anxious pile. But Mock was right. The most important thing right now was trusting in Ben. Believing in him. She tried to take it one moment at a time. She ignored the sun, which had passed its peak and was now on its way west.

"Even if he's able to heal Snow, it won't help me get back to Alice." Jesse sighed. "But even if it's over . . . even if we failed, and the worlds are split apart . . . I just want Ben to be all right."

Mock's head popped up with a start. She stood in Jesse's palm, hopping one direction, then the other.

"Not like that, Jesse!" she chirped. "Believe harder. Harder!"

"I don't understand!" Jesse exclaimed. "I'm believing in him as best I can! I just want—"

"It's not about what *you* want," Mock insisted. "What you want is based on what you know, and what you need. Your Ben. Friend, companion, partner. But to truly give him your faeth, you need to believe in him for who he *is*, not who he is *to you*. You need to give him what he needs for him, not what you want to give for you."

It made sense, but Jesse struggled. It was easy to believe that the Ben Foley she'd met in St. Joe's—the one who'd ridden beside her across the plains and mountains and desert—accepted her for who she was. But that was what Ben meant to Jesse. Not who he was.

So who was Benjamin Foley? And what did he need?

The desert seemed like it stretched to the ends of the earth. Though she could see for miles, Jesse had never felt so trapped. She wanted to leave the terrible site that smelled of death. She didn't want to see the black spot where Shrike had been defeated. But she didn't want to leave, in case this was where Ben came back. Even if it meant waiting days. Days she didn't have.

At least she could give Morgan a proper goodbye. She stowed Mock in her vest pocket and, covering her face with a hand to mask the stench, went through Morgan's mochila for the matches. She labored all afternoon, gathering as many sticks and as much dead brush as she could. Then, as the sun set, she and Mock watched the flames consume him, transforming him into a pillar of black smoke. Sending him to the big meadow in the sky, she hoped.

"What about Shrike?" Jesse asked. Though the other spirit's breast quivered with breath, he had not awakened. Mock, however, was regaining strength. Enough to perch on Jesse's shoulder, under her lapel for warmth.

"He will sleep, for now. When he wakes, I do not know."

The day dragged on into night. Jesse sipped out of her water sack as infrequently as she could bear, but it would be empty soon. It was cold now, and soon it would be colder. She had used up all the brush in the area for Morgan's pyre.

"Is time the same in the two worlds?" she asked as the last rays of sun winked over the horizon. Mock leaned against her, light and warm, but she didn't answer except for a miniature shrug.

Jesse watched the sun set. She yearned to see the moon rise above the hazy line where the earth became the sky, but it did not come. Even the stars were sad and quiet, like memorial candles lit in the entryway of a church.

Jesse wanted to believe. She believed as hard as she could. But she couldn't shake the nagging worry that Ben had failed. By now it would have been one or the other, wouldn't it? No. She couldn't think that way.

But what if?

Jesse closed her eyes against the empty-mooned sky. She pushed her hands into the cooling sand. Tried to count the grains. Tried to do anything to focus. To believe that when she opened her eyes, he would be standing there. Safe. He was counting on her. As she was counting on him.

She took in a breath. Held it, filled it with her hope. That she would see him again. Gentle, strong, compassionate. Like a navigator in a storm, focused on finding the way through. For himself, for Jesse. For everyone. When he led, she would follow. When he was hurt, she would protect him. No matter what. When it came down to it, Jesse realized it was easy, in the end: She would see him for who he was, even if that was something she might never fully understand. That was her faeth to him. Faeth like a promise.

When she let the breath out, it came with words. A melody; the song Alice used to sing. The song Daisy had sung, in her pretty voice. A voice like Alice's . . . a voice like Jesse's.

"Meet me by moonlight alone . . ."

It was a wish.

A prayer.

Oh, meet me by moonlight alone.

A breeze blew and Jesse smiled, letting it dry her cheeks. She didn't look, not yet. She didn't need to. She could feel the sky brightening. The stillness of the land coming to life. The night finding its voice again.

She heard it and believed. She believed and it grew louder.

Jesse opened her eyes.

He was standing there, as she knew he would be. Radiant in a cloak of deep blue and black, overflowing with feathers and flowers and fur. His skin was the color of glittering night, his hazel eyes bright and full. A silver disc blazed from his forehead, shining with the light that poured down from the full moon in the sky above.

Beside him was a great, glowing, wintry stag with thick blue fur and a single broken antler. He bowed in greeting. Together, the two were brightness and darkness, the moon shining on fresh snow in winter.

Ben hesitated, unsure.

"Jesse," he said. His voice was the same. "I—"

Jesse bolted to him and threw her arms round him. He held her tighter than he ever had before, and she tried to capture the moment in her heart. He was shaking under his cloak, leaning into her, and she held him. As she had promised to.

"We have to go," he said. "I'll open the gates."

"But how will we . . ." Jesse began.

Snow stepped toward her in reply. In spite of his weariness, he was majestic, larger than even Declan's monstrous Shire horse and easily big enough for both Jesse's and Ben's slim figures. He lowered his head so Jesse could take hold of his broken antler and lifted her to his back. Next came Ben, behind her. Snow wore no halter, saddle, nor reins, so

Jesse grabbed handfuls of his thick mane, gripped him with her thighs and knees. It wouldn't be easy, but she'd never expected it would be. Mock left Jesse's shoulder, flying up to perch in Snow's antler crown.

The great blue beast wasted no time. Before they had a chance to settle, he was moving, in fleet, powerful strides. His cloven hooves barely skirted the earth, his monstrous glowing form weightless. It was more like flying than riding.

Jesse clung to his mane as the air whipped by. Ben grabbed handfuls of the fur rippling from Snow's shoulders, in front of Jesse's thighs. Without a saddle, stirrups, or anything, Jesse exhausted every muscle to keep from falling. As the land flew beneath them at impossible speeds, all she had to do was hold on. Hold on, and believe they could make it in time.

The desert dissolved below them like sand on a beach giving way to the ocean as they followed the glowing ravine of the Faerie blade's path. Trees and rocks grew round them, rising on either side as Snow brought them past the Salt Lake Valley.

Mock gave a whoop and a holler, like she had the first time they'd ridden with her. Her song was loud and joyful, and all the night creatures replied.

Jesse searched the dark expanse for the house where Nelly lived, but it was hidden in the blur of the countryside. But she was there, and always would be. In the house of stone or not. Jesse vowed never to forget.

Ben tugged on Snow's fur, guiding him to the left. Jesse felt a shiver as he moved, following Ben's lead. The familiar wash of mist blew past them like a cloud—

Then they were riding through the Wyoming mountains near Devil's Gate. Glowing spirit eyes twinkled from the sagebrush. Snow's hooves glanced off the rock and they were suddenly airborne, high above the swooping valley of mountain and black trees. The wound in the earth burned below, dark and gold. Jesse's heart was in her teeth and she let go of Snow's fur, tasting the air between her fingers—

Another flash of mist and they landed, cold droplets of water splashing against her cheeks as Snow burst through the river and onto the cold mud of the Platte, his glowing form shining off the wet shore, his fur speckled by the earth mixed with water.

Gate by gate blew by them. Jesse was struck with the familiar scents of grass and wildflowers, autumn blowing through apple trees and juniper. The plains. Nebraska Territory. The Faerie blade was huge before them, a thing of gold and power. Its edge was buried in the ground, cleaving the earth and the fabric between this place and the next so wide Jesse could see the tendrils and trees and monsters waiting on the other side.

"Snow!" Mock cried. "Snow, you can do it! You can!"

Snow closed in on the blade, hooves driving through the soft prairie. As they came alongside it, Jesse saw her reflection in the gleaming golden surface. Warped and rippled along its edge, like two of the same person, super-imposed upon one another. But her nonetheless.

Him.

Them.

Jesse felt the ringing of its power. The vibration that shook worlds, the burning edge that they would be forever trying to keep dull. For the rest of their life, knowing it was made of them, bound to their heart. A fault that would forever be on the brink of divide.

Then Snow overtook it, leaving it behind as he closed the distance between them and St. Joseph. Jesse looked away. Looked ahead, to where the sky was brightening.

"Last gate," Ben said.

Jesse closed her eyes and felt them pass through. When she opened them, she knew the land. The hills, the thickets and trees. The little barn nestled off the road.

Snow stumbled to a canter, then a walk. His sides heaved, his head drooped, steam pouring from his flared nostrils. They dismounted, and he transformed as the sun's first rays peeked over the horizon. Ben held him.

"Go," he said. "To Alice. Quickly!"

Jesse faltered. She took the neckerchief from her belt and handed it to Ben. He looked at the sleeping bird inside, then folded it into his cloak of night.

"Will you be here when I come back?"

She felt everything building up in her chest like a river against a dam. Searched Ben's new face, finding his same eyes.

"Go," he repeated.

"I'll see you again," she said. "I promise."

Then she turned away, using the flooding feeling in her chest to propel her feet forward, one after the other until she burst through the thicket. The little farmhouse near the wood was the same as she'd left it, lights on and warm inside. A young man was squatted on the stoop, smoking a pipe. He recognized Jesse and stood as she ran up, doffing his hat.

"Jess!"

"Oscar?" she cried. "Oscar Montero, what the—"

His brown cheeks were splotched with worry, eyes glassy and anxious, wide like he thought she might knock his teeth out right there.

"Jess, I can explain. My father, when he found out about Alice . . . He sent me away, told me I couldn't— I wanted to be here— Please don't send me away!"

Jesse shoved him to the side. She thought of a great many things in that moment, of a man in Carson City and his daughter with the voice of a nightingale. But she didn't say anything to Oscar. Just tossed him a half a nod —generous, she thought. He caught it and nearly dropped it, stupefied. Then Jesse shouldered through the front door to the sound of Alice's wailing.

Aunt Mary turned round from where she crouched at Alice's bed. A blanket was draped over Alice's knees, a basin of steaming water on the floor. Alice's pained face broke into more tears and a smile.

"Jess," she said. "I knew you would make it. The baby waited for you."

Then she let out a moan that rose into a scream that could've woken a giant. The baby was coming. Jesse ran to the bedside and grabbed her sister's hand, holding on tight and kissing the back of her freckled knuckles.

CHAPTER XXXIII
BEN

"Did we do it? Is the blade . . ."

Snow looked up so the white orb in the sky glimmered in his eyes. "Know for yourself, Benjamin Moon."

Ben stared into the place where Jesse had gone. Though the trees hid the little cabin from view, cloistered in their twilight shroud, he could still see it. Feel it. The cry of a newborn came to his ears. Joining the mother's exhausted, heaving breath. Jesse, soothing his sister. Encouraging her. Where the moonlight reached inside the little house, Ben had eyes and ears.

And elsewhere. Across all the land. Everything the moonlight touched was in his mind, under his tongue. Like a silk sheet resting atop the world. He could feel the gentle hills of the plains and the steady rise of the mountains. The silent, endless desert.

The golden blade, at a standstill. Its edge no longer a beam of light, merely a flicker like the glow of a lightning bug. Shrinking smaller and smaller, until it fell into the earth and disappeared altogether.

They'd done it. They'd stopped the blade.

But not until the last minute. As he beheld the landscape, all the world under the watch of the night, his mind reeled. The worlds dangled nearby one another, adjacent. Not separate, not completely divided, but so close. Like lovers holding on to one another with desperate fingertips. It would not take much to pull them apart forever.

He closed his eyes against it. For the moment, it was too much.

"It will become easier."

He opened his eyes. Snow watched him from where he rested against an old birch. His form was losing articulation, like a snow dune blowing into glittering pieces a little at a time. He held up a blue hand, watching the detail of his fingers soften.

Mock sang from her perch on the blue spirit's antler. "He's weak. With the worlds like this, we cannot live here without faeth for very long. Snow needs to go to the spirit side. And soon, so will I . . ."

She trailed off. Ben still heard the rest of her words.

"I want to stay just a little longer," he said.

Mock opened her beak and whistled. A distant whinny came in response, then the gentle padding of hooves on grass and leaf. Mock flew down, alighting on Ben's shoulder and brushing his cheek with her wing.

"We'll take Snow and Shrike back," Mock said. "We'll wait for you."

A blue and silver figure moved within the light wood. At first Ben recognized the sound of Dusky's hooves, but the willowy spirit that emerged had taken on a different form. Her true form, he realized, with dusk-colored skin and long black hair that he'd felt against his hands countless times as they rode together toward California.

She smiled at him when he recognized her. Together, he and Mock helped Snow to his feet and put him in Dusky's arms. She held him effortlessly, as she had carried them all before. Finally, Ben gently removed Shrike from Jesse's neckerchief. Dusky took the little bird, but Ben kept the tie for himself.

"I await you in the other place as well, my friend," Dusky said. She kissed Ben's cheek. Then she took Snow, Mockingbird, and Shrike away. Through the new veil that crept across the land like a partially drawn curtain.

Once they were gone, he stood in the cold, but the freezing air sent no shivers across his skin. He fell to his knees, pushed his fingers into the soil. He could feel every grain of dirt, but it was changed. Went deeper than touch. He could see deep into the ground, hear the earthworms moving. Feel all the way to the rock and water running below it, the lifeblood of the planet. Even with the worlds in such a state, he could still see the glow of spirit nectar—of faeth. In mountains and towns, in churches and the Great Plains. It came from the hearts of humans, sweet and powerful and rare. He was not alone. And he never would be again.

He felt a waning and looked at his hands. The glittering was fading, his skin wavering as he'd seen Snow's do. He felt weak. In the sky, the sun was rising, the moon setting—no, that wasn't right. The sun and moon were not the only things that moved. The world itself was also turning.

"Ben?"

Jesse came out from between the trees. When he saw Ben kneeling, he ran to him, kicking up dried leaves and cold earth. He held Ben at the shoulders, hands warming his skin and electric eyes steady and firm. The earnest attention felt like life, and Ben inhaled as much of it as he could.

"Ben, I can't believe it. I mean, actually, I can. I do. But it's all so . . . Why don't you come in? Meet Alice and Oscar and the baby? We can have dinner and . . ."

Jesse trailed off and Ben let a silence fall between them. Like a veil. Though they could see through it, eye to eye, they could not deny it was there.

"Jesse," Ben began. "The blade has stopped, but so much damage has already been done. I can feel it. There's work to do. What I mean is . . . I have to go."

Jesse's eyes filled with tears. They were sweet. Another kind of faeth.

"Oh," he said. He knuckled his eye. "Of course."

"I'm sorry, Jesse. This is something I have to do."

Ben's heart hurt to tell Jesse the truth, but leaving his friend was part of the commitment he'd made. To Snow and the spirits. To Night, who had unlocked the power within him. To Penny, who had raised him to believe it was there all along.

"I understand," Jesse mumbled. "And I believe in you. I'll believe in you until the end of time."

It seemed stupid, but in that instant the only thing Ben could think of was the necktie. He took it out from his cloak, though he desperately wanted to keep it for himself. He wanted something of Jesse to take with him. Something to remind him, but it wasn't his to take.

"Your necktie—"

"Now it's *yours*," Jesse insisted. "Wear it, and I'll know you're thinking of me. While you fight in the other place and I fight here. Even if we're apart, we don't have to be alone."

Ben nodded, and the spirit world pulled. Pulled him back, toward the vast lake, where Mock and Snow and the others waited for him. Depended on him for guidance. To learn how to change. How to stay upright in a turning world.

How to change as humans did.

How to change and live.

"I have to go," he said again.

Tears ran down Jesse's face, and Ben felt the same reflecting on his own cheeks. He put his hands on Jesse's and squeezed. He had never wanted it to end, but now it had. They both knew it. This was goodbye, for now. But not forever.

"Will I ever see you again?" Jesse asked.

"Every night," he said.

Then the world escaped him, rushing out from between his fingers.

ONE YEAR LATER

Jesse took care not to wake the sleeping parents or the baby where they rested in the bed near the fire and warm iron cookstove. They slept so soundly it wasn't hard to sneak out the front door and skip the squeaky step. Trot out into the wood behind the house at the crack of dawn.

An apple tree stump crowned by a candle waited, survived by a circle of old oaks with blue glass dangling from their limbs. Jesse stopped and struggled to wrestle a flattened box of candy out of pale blue pockets.

"Hi."

A silence followed in reply, but Jesse was used to it. It had taken months to learn to leave time. To fill the quiet with the memory and the feeling of the ones who were invisible. Believing they were listening. Believing he was there.

"I report for service tomorrow, anyway. Maybe you know that . . . I don't know how much you can see." Jesse coughed and ran a hand against the close shave Alice had made with Oscar's razor. "Anyway, it might be a while before I come back. So I'm leaving a little extra."

Jesse lit the candle and set three black molasses sticks beside it. Stood back, eyes closed, and took a deep breath of the September air that smelled of winter. Let out the breath at the creak of the door and Alice's bare feet on that squeaky step. Maybe one day it'd be fixed.

"Jesse?" Alice called. "You out there?"

Jesse gave the night a moment more.

Listened. Believed.

Then hurried back as the full moon rose, tinged gold, over the trees.